Where do you go from the end of the line? This is the question facing Kathy Woodbridge as she steps off the bus in the port city of San Pedro, California. Nineteen years old from Louisiana, she is running away from her past. There's a lot to run away from.

What do you do when there's no one to do for? That's what Lacey Greer wants to know, with her only child off at college. When Kathy gets a job at the office where Lacey works, she can tell that Kathy's in trouble. Lacey's husband advises her to stay out of it—but what's she supposed to do, buy a rocking chair?

Set in San Pedro, Baton Rouge, and New Orleans in the early seventies, *Pacific Avenue* explores themes of love, belonging, helpfulness, hope, reconciliation, interracial marriage, and healing from the trauma of war. At the end of the line, will Kathy find a way to return home?

Also by Anne L. Watson

Skeeter: A Cat Tale

ANNE L. WATSON

Pacific Avenue

Shepard & Piper
Olympia, Washington
2008

Cover illustration from "Common Blue Bird," by John James
Audubon

ISBN 978-0-938497-52-3

Library of Congress Control Number: 2007932234
Library of Congress subject headings:
Race relations—Fiction
Interracial marriage—Fiction
Sudden infant death syndrome—Fiction
Vietnam War, 1961-1975—Veterans—Fiction
Veterans—Family relationships—Fiction
Post-traumatic stress disorder—Fiction
New Orleans (La.)—Fiction
Baton Rouge (La.)—Fiction
San Pedro (Los Angeles, Calif.)—Fiction
Puppets—Fiction

1.2 (First Edition)

For Liz

Pacific Avenue

Part 1

❧ 1 ❧
December 1974, Interstate 10, Westbound
Kathy

I CHOSE A WINDOW SEAT on the Greyhound, but I didn't look out. For almost the whole trip, I stared at the rough tan upholstery of the seat in front of me. It had a rip on one side and three dark stains.

A woman settled into the aisle seat. She raised her footrest, but it clunked back down. When I glanced her way, she caught my eye and smiled.

"How do you make these things stay put?" she asked.

I meant to answer—the words were lined up in my mind. But before I could say them, they slipped apart like beads when the string breaks. I gave up and studied the seat cover again. Still tan, still ripped, still stained. The next time I looked, the woman was gone.

Evening came, but I didn't use my reading light. Late at night, awake in the breathing dark, I imagined running my fingers over the seat back, erasing the stains, mending the seam. In the morning, I almost believed I could fix it. So, I took care not to touch it, not to find out for sure.

In the afternoon, the bus left the freeway and crept through downtown traffic. I turned then, and peered through the mud-spattered window. As far as I could see, Los Angeles was a city of warehouses. I sank back into my seat.

When we reached the station, I claimed my suitcase and dragged it through the waiting room to the street. Outside I found blank walls and empty sidewalks. No direction and no one to ask.

Well, I ran away from college, then from New Orleans, and then Baton Rouge. Is it too soon to run away from here?

The traffic light at the end of the block turned green, and cars passed me by. When a city bus stopped and opened its doors, I climbed on. I couldn't think what else to do.

I paid the fare and took a seat near the front. Even though I pulled my suitcase aside, it poked out into the aisle. More people piled on at every stop, and all of them had to squeeze past it. I expected everyone to glare, but nobody gave me a second glance.

The bus started, stopped, started again. We passed through neighborhoods with trees and shops. The crowd thinned as passengers got off, going home. *Should I get off too? No, not here. Where? Next stop, no, the one after. No, not that one.* Every stop would be a whole different life, a different second chance.

Choose, choose. I couldn't. I rode till the bus pulled over and parked.

"Seventh and Pacific, San Pedro, Port of Los Angeles," called the bus driver. He turned to me and added, "End of the line, Miss."

I waited till the other passengers got out, hoping the driver would help me with the suitcase. He watched blank-faced as I wrestled it down the steps. Setting it on the sidewalk, I looked around.

I'd reached the end of the line, all right. Pacific Avenue was like a street in some Third World country. The candy-colored buildings were old and grimy. Christmas tinsel sparkled around the windows, but the sidewalk glitter was broken glass and gobs of spit. The crosswalk lights cycled green and red, green and red. Their afterimage flashed inside my head when I closed my eyes: *Walk, Don't Walk. Choose, choose.*

I couldn't decide which way to go. The bus pulled away in a cloud of exhaust. A man ran past me, shouting, "Hey, stop, hey! Son of a bitch!" A few steps behind him, a woman jerked a crying child along by the arm. Gusts of wind sent sidewalk trash skittering after them like rats.

Seventh Street looked quieter, so I tried it first. But after the first block, the buildings thinned out and the street plunged downhill toward a gleam of water. Silhouettes of tall cranes made black Xs against the evening sky. Like scissors, waiting to cut it into strips. Nothing but the port down there. Nothing there for me.

So, it had to be Pacific Avenue. Night was coming, and I dreaded wandering the streets after dark with no place to stay. I backtracked quickly, then began to search for motels, rooming houses—anything halfway decent.

All I saw was stores. I passed the Thrif-T-Mart, with its displays of sun-bleached plastic housewares. The Angel Bakery— a wedding cake behind plate glass, a ventilator spewing the scent of sugar and grease. Next door, a boarded-up entryway added a reek of stale pee. A pigeon flapped past my face. Flinging up my hands to ward it off, I dropped the suitcase on my foot. My eyes filled with tears, but I didn't have time for them. I grabbed the suitcase handle and kept going.

I scanned the signs, but some of them meant nothing to me—Baile, Mariscos, Menudo Hoy. For all I knew, any of those might have meant Rooms. I hesitated a couple of times, but the places didn't look like boarding houses, so I walked on by.

ANNE L. WATSON

I passed Antiques, in a window with a black velvet painting of Elvis and a tangle of pole lamps. The next block offered Ten Minute Oil Change, Auto Upholstery, and Radiator. Everything for cars, nothing for people.

In the block after that, I rested beside a storefront—Salvation Army, used Christmases for sale. The dinged-up manger scene in the window was nothing like my family—the mother, the father, and the baby were all there. I laid my hand, then my forehead, against the cool glass. *Oh, God, let me find a place to sleep tonight.*

When I turned back to the street, I thought I saw a sign advertising Room and Board. I hurried toward it, suitcase bumping my legs. Two motorcycles roared from behind me and pulled over to the curb a few yards ahead. One of the riders looked back, and the low evening sun flashed from his blank helmet. Faceless, dangerous.

I bolted across the street, hardly checking for traffic, and scrambled back the way I'd come. Didn't even look over my shoulder for half a block, but when I did, no one was following. Shaking, I set the suitcase down and leaned against a wall. Right beside me hung another sign, Madame Sofia—The Mystic Eye—Botanica.

The dusty store window displayed roots, stones, and cards, like the voodoo shops in New Orleans. A sign propped against a plaster pyramid said Apartment for Rent. I went in.

A woman sat behind the counter of the dim shop, spotlighted by a small lamp. A black-and-white cat sat beside her.

She didn't smile as I came toward her. Her eyes were almost opaque, like pale blue marbles. Her face seemed young, but her hair was white as a piece of paper and nearly as straight.

Dime-sized mirrors glittered on her embroidered dress as she reached for a tarot pack at her elbow.

"Tell you the future, five dollars."

I would have paid more than that not to know.

"I came about the apartment," I said.

"Apartment?" She sounded so confused, I wondered if I'd come to the wrong place.

"The sign in the window," I prompted.

"Oh, the *apartment*. Two hundred a month, utilities included. You want to see it?"

"Yes, please."

She led me out the way I'd come and around the corner to a side door. Instead of unlocking it, she turned back to me.

"What's your name?"

"Kathy Woodbridge."

"Where you from, Kathy?"

"Illinois." My voice sounded squeaky and forced, but she didn't seem to notice. She let me into a narrow hallway that might have been white the last time it was painted.

A fluorescent tube flickered on the ceiling. The mustard-yellow carpet was a felted material that trapped twigs and cockleburs. The only way to get rid of them would have been to pick them out by hand, but it looked like no one ever did.

I followed her up a dark red stair at the far end of the hall. At the top were three doors.

"This used to be offices," she said, "but I decided to remodel them into apartments. There'll be two, but only one is ready." Judging by that faded For Rent sign, she was taking her time about it.

"What's the third door?" I asked.

"Stairs to the roof."

She unlocked the apartment door, jiggling the key to make it work.

I could tell the apartment had been patched together from offices. The rooms were all misfits—a living room with tin cabinets in one corner to make a sort-of kitchen, then a too-small bedroom and a too-big bathroom.

At least it was clean. Rips in the linoleum floor were mended with parallel lines of tacks. Everything else, even the light switches and doorknobs, had a fresh coat of paint.

I tried to raise one of the living room windows, but it stuck. Giving up, I stood and looked down at Pacific Avenue, its shabby buildings all but erased by the dusk. If I didn't take this place, I'd have to go out there and find another one.

I turned and considered the room again, wondering if I could stand to live in it. Madame Sofia watched me take it all in.

"The walls are white to go with your curtains and rugs," she pointed out.

Pictures swirled through my mind, almost like a movie. *I open my suitcase and pull out my curtains and rugs. A bookcase, a table, all my old stuff. My suitcase is bottomless. I pull out books, dishes, my paints and woodcarving tools, marionettes, our bed. Last of all, Richard steps out, with Jamie toddling beside him.*

Tears stung behind my nose, but I pulled myself together. Madame Sofia hovered expectantly. *Well, if she sees the future, guess she knew all along I'd go for it.* I didn't have two hundred in cash, but I still had my old checkbook. I fished it out of my purse and began to write.

"Make it to Marilu Collins," she said.

I had already written "Madame Sofia," so I started over with a new check. No reason to save them—two hundred dollars about cleaned out the account. As I handed her the check,

I realized my old address was on it and stifled an impulse to grab it back. But she didn't even glance at it, only tucked it into her pocket and gave me the key. I said good night and closed the door—*my* door—as she went downstairs.

A box of crackers and a bag of raisins from my suitcase would do for dinner. As I ate, the room went dark except for streetlights fanned across the ceiling. I spread my coat on the floor to sleep on and wadded up clothes for a pillow.

That was my first night on Pacific Avenue. Nobody knew my name but the woman dressed in mirrors. And no one at all knew where I came from, or why.

❧ 2 ❧
December 1974, San Pedro
Lacey

SECRETARIES DON'T GET RICH, that's for sure. I worked for Mr. Giannini at the concrete company in San Pedro. I didn't expect to make what he did—he owned the company. But the men in the yard didn't have the skills I had, and they made almost twice my salary. The company couldn't pay me less for being black, but they could pay me next to nothing for being a woman.

Just the same, I had too much pride to goof off. I did a good job—except when I did something for George, Mr. Giannini's son. He'd "joined the firm," as they'd worded their announcement, back in July. I couldn't stand him. He was such a jerk, he couldn't have worked for anyone *but* his dad, so I figured on being stuck with him forever. I did his stuff when I was good and ready, if at all.

In December, Mr. Giannini called me into his office about it. "Lacey, why didn't you do George's letters last week?"

"He gave me the roughs on Thursday. That was the day I had to type the change order requests for the UCLA job. You weren't here, and you did tell me projects under construction get priority."

"Why didn't you do them Friday?"

"Friday was the deadline to finish the bid for the port job."

He frowned. "Can you do them today?"

"Only if they take priority over your meeting reports from last week. And your own letters."

He sat back in his chair and thought a minute.

"I guess we'll have to get him his own secretary," he said. "Maybe a trainee? I'll rough out a want ad for the *News-Pilot*."

He brought it to me that afternoon. "George will interview the candidates," he said. "Then he'll give you the résumés and you can check references for him. I'm going to be out in the field for a couple of days, so I told George to decide which one to hire."

I could have told Mr. Giannini they weren't going to line up in the street for what he was paying. I didn't bother. He wasn't so bad, as bosses go, but talking to him about money was wasting my breath.

"Go ahead and put up the Christmas tree this afternoon," he said. "Make the office nice for the applicants."

I stifled a laugh. Partly surprise—I hadn't decorated my own house that year, and I'd sort of forgotten about Christmas. My daughter Angela had left in the fall for graduate school at Berkeley, and I'd decided not to fuss for just my husband and me. I was busy redecorating Angie's old room anyway, to use as a sewing room. So, I wasn't exactly tuned in to Christmas, the way I usually was. Besides, the office wasn't likely to be any cheerier with a dingy fake tree set up.

But I pulled it out, like I did every year, and decorated it with our garage-sale ornaments and a garland of paper clips. No lights or presents—nothing festive about it at all. In fact, that piece of green plastic junk was about enough to make you cry.

The only girl who came in for the ad looked like she might do that very thing. Probably not on account of the tree—she looked sad when she came in. Her blonde hair hung as limp as her thrift-shop dress. George talked to her awhile in his office. Then he turned and pranced out like Mr. Big Man. Through his window, I saw her hesitate for a second, watching him. With a fast flick of her hands, she tucked a sheet of paper into her purse. She scurried to catch up as he swaggered to my desk.

"Lacey, this is Kathy. She's going to be my secretary. Get her set up, would you?" George didn't give a last name for either one of us. Maybe he didn't know we had them. Since he always acted that way, I'd had a plastic sign made for my desk: Lacey Greer.

He went back to his office. The girl and I looked each other over. She peeked at my sign.

"I'm pleased to meet you, Mrs. Greer," she said. "Kathy Woodbridge."

Southern accent. Not that I thought southerners were necessarily any more prejudiced than California whites. But I didn't want to work with any redneck either. She seemed okay, though—not all closed in. I thought she'd be fine.

"Happy to have you. George needs someone. I can't do all his work. Did you ever work for a contractor before?" I smiled at her, hoping to encourage her a little.

She didn't look especially encouraged. "Not really," she said.

I didn't press it. I figured she was about twenty. Most likely she hadn't worked much of anywhere. George hadn't given me any references to check, just flat-out hired her. I hoped she could type, at least.

"When do you start?" I asked, remembering I still had to clean up the mess on the extra desk.

"Monday."

"I'll have the desk ready for you. Construction paperwork isn't too hard. I'll show you."

"Thanks. I'll see you Monday." She held out her hand for me to shake. It was small, cold, and soft. She frowned at the Christmas tree and went out the door. I wouldn't have been one bit surprised if she never came back.

☙

SHE CAME ON MONDAY, though, right on time. Her dress was another Goodwill special, and her shoes had the shape of someone else's feet. But she'd tried to make herself presentable. Her hair was fixed in a braid down her back, and she'd put on lipstick. It was mostly chewed off, but at least she'd made the effort.

"Here's your Social Security forms. Go ahead and fill them out on the typewriter." I motioned toward the other desk. A form's about the hardest thing to type, and I wanted to see if she'd do a decent job. She did it perfectly, and fast, too. I tried not to show my surprise.

When she was done, I showed her around the office. "Supplies are in this closet. This door is the copy room. The break room is over there. We keep a pot of coffee on for Mr. Giannini all the time. Did you bring your lunch? There's no good place to eat around here."

"No, I didn't know I could."

"Oh, yes. I do, nearly every day. But today I'm going to drive to a coffee shop over on Gaffey. Let me treat you." It stuck out all over that she was broke. I had a sack lunch in the refrigerator, but it would keep. If Mr. Giannini minded us both being gone at once, he could put up with it for one day.

She did filing all morning. When lunchtime came, I drove us. She didn't have a car.

"Where do you live?" I asked as I pulled out of the lot, dodging one of the mixer trucks. I was hoping her place wasn't too far away. Buses in L.A. were unreliable. I didn't want to get stuck with someone who was late every day.

"Down the street."

"On Pacific Avenue?"

"Pacific and Eighth. I just moved in. I found an apartment above The Mystic Eye."

That floored me. Pacific Avenue was not a good neighborhood, especially for a little white girl. Now, I knew the woman who owned The Mystic Eye. I wasn't a customer—no way I'd ever fall for her hoodoo. But I knew her well enough to speak to. Her real name was Marilu Collins, but she called herself Madame Sofia. "Knows all, sees all, tells all." Well, the "tells all" part was true.

But Pacific Avenue—I glanced sideways at Kathy. I was sure she didn't know what she was getting into. For such a small place, San Pedro definitely had its neighborhoods, and she'd picked the tough one.

The street wasn't bad on the north end, the industrial section where Giannini's was. South of us were thrift shops and discount, shabby but safe. At Pacific and Sixth, my husband and some other men had put together a little automotive mall. The next few blocks were probably not too bad—in the daytime, anyway.

But beyond there, the neighborhood got rough. Rough and smutty, and not all the girls standing on corners were waiting for the bus. Winos hung around outside the bars and spare-changed everyone who walked by. As if anybody would be stupid enough to give them a cent.

On the south, Pacific Avenue dead-ended at the ocean—no beach, only a chain-link fence with reflectors and warning signs.

No one but bums and gangs went past that fence. A long time ago, that end of the street was a nice neighborhood, but then there was a landslide. Most of the homes got pulled back and moved to other lots, but the paving and the building footings stayed, broken and scattered down a steep slope. They called it the Sunken City.

Kathy didn't look like the kind of girl who belonged on Pacific Avenue at all.

When we got to the coffee shop, the waiter gave us a table at the back. Kathy ordered the cheapest item on the menu, a cheese sandwich. I didn't know if she was in the habit of eating cheap, or if she was being considerate because I was treating. I ordered a burger and a big side of fries for us to split. She was too thin. And she was nearly the same age as my daughter.

As we ate lunch, I tried to find out a little more about her. "Where are you from?" I asked.

"Evanston, Illinois."

This caught my attention—she sure sounded like a southerner to me. A lot like my mother's family. No Illinois there at all.

"But you have a southern accent?"

"My parents are from the South."

I played along. "What took them to Illinois?"

"My dad teaches at Northwestern University."

I bought the "university" part, at least. It made sense she was a professor's kid. Shy, kind of correct, not sure of herself. Teacher, yes. Evanston, no. Not my business, I thought. But I wondered why she'd bother lying to me.

"What brought you to California?"

"The climate, I guess. I'd always heard about it."

She ate a piece of pie I'd ordered for her and gazed out the window. If weather was what she'd come for, she was getting her money's worth. Even in December, it was about seventy-five degrees and the sky was almost the color of a bachelor button. Matched her eyes. She would have been a pretty little thing if she'd fixed herself up some.

When we got back to the office, I set her to copying a big stack of contracts. While she was busy in the copy room, I pulled her employment application, trying to see where she was from. But she'd put Marilu Collins as who to notify in case of emergency, and the education and experience sections weren't filled out. She'd written "Attached" across the spaces where those things were supposed to be, but nothing was attached. I went into George's office and searched through the papers on his desk. All I found there was specifications for concrete.

As far as our records were concerned, Kathy Woodbridge had no past at all.

❧ 3 ❧
December 1974, San Pedro
Kathy

I LIKED BEING ALONE in the building at Eighth and Pacific after the shop closed. When I lived with Richard, there were always people around us, and unless they were friends of ours, I had to worry about what they might do.

When we first moved to New Orleans, we lived in a rooming house, a sagging wood building at the far end of Bourbon Street. It was a dump, but we were lucky to have it. The first two places we'd tried, the landlords said they'd just accepted someone else. We were sure they were lying, but what could we do? I'd gone alone to apply for this room, and the manager had rented it to me. But now he'd seen Richard, and we were afraid he'd kick us out on the smallest pretext.

One night we got home so late, we started tiptoeing when we were two houses away. Shushing each other, bumping through the unlit hallway like clumsy burglars, we crept upstairs to our room. Even after the door was shut behind us, we tried to be quiet. We didn't dare turn on the lamp—the manager might see light coming through the transom and get mad about it.

Richard was silent, invisible in the dark. I guessed where he must be and reached out for him, but my guess was wrong—my hands plunged into empty air. For a moment, I felt a familiar stab of aloneness. Then his hands grasped mine, and spread them open, and he kissed my palms, brushing them with his lips. My fingers read his face like a love letter in braille—the downturned eyelids, the short eyelashes with their tight sudden curl, the softness of his mouth. We made love stealthily, the way you do in your parents' house. Because somehow, everyone was our parents.

Everyone and no one. I'd lost my parents because of Richard. When I told them I was moving to New Orleans with him, I knew how Mom would act. But Dad surprised me.

"You're making a mistake, honey," he said. "Please don't do this. It can't possibly work out."

"Baton Rouge is nothing but rednecks," I said. "Teenage kids who sound like George Wallace, almost like Adolf Hitler, if you really want to know. It'll never change. New Orleans is different. We can live there—no one will mind."

"Maybe someday," he'd said, "but not now. Not even in New Orleans. No one should give a damn what color Richard is. But they will."

"'A person's skin is an eighth-inch thick, and we're all the same underneath it,'" I reminded him. That's what he'd always told us when we were kids, when everyone was fighting about where people could go, or sit, or which drinking fountain they were allowed to use.

"That eighth inch is going to be your whole life." He didn't sound as sure of himself as he had when he'd said everyone was the same.

"Someone has to change it."

"You want to be first?"

"You mean, 'Not my daughter.'"

"I'm not even sure the two of you can love each other in the middle of all this."

"You know all about not being able to love." I slammed the door as I left.

That was the end of one conversation. But it wasn't when I lost him, and it wasn't why.

Once I got to San Pedro, the past closed behind me like water behind a swimmer. I wasn't sure there was a future, but if there was, it had a name: five years. Richard's sentence.

It was my sentence, too. A different kind of "someday, but not now." This time, I didn't have a choice.

I did my best. I didn't feel like getting up most mornings, but I did. Got up and went to work at Giannini Concrete. After a few days, I didn't even hear the stutter and whine of the dim fluorescent lights, or the rumble of the mixer trucks in the yard. Didn't notice the dingy gray concrete everywhere. I belonged there. I was dim and dingy too.

Not like Lacey, Mr. Giannini's secretary. Lacey Greer was anything but drab. She even laughed about the building. "Here we are in a concrete box—concrete walls, concrete floor, concrete *ceiling*. You'd think we'd have better sense than to keep making more."

She could laugh. The dreary room only made her stand out more. Madame Sofia was fake exotic, but Lacey was the real thing. She looked like she was even trying to tone it down, in her tailored suits like a lawyer's secretary and her hair pulled back in a tight chignon. But there was no way she could be anything *but* exotic. She was nearly six feet tall, for one thing. With her light-brown skin, high cheekbones, hooked nose, and big eyes, she might have been Puerto Rican, or maybe Indian. I couldn't guess.

The second week I worked at Giannini's, a man came in and talked to Lacey in a foreign language.

"I don't speak Spanish, I'm sorry," she said.

He stomped out, yelling, "You damn snob, won't even talk to your own people!"

She shrugged. "Happens all the time. A lot of people mistake me for Hispanic."

"What are you, then?" I felt rude and nosy, blurting it out, but I wanted to know.

She ticked it off on her fingers. "Martiniquean, Greek, and Cherokee."

"How did they ever get together?"

"My father's family is from all over the South, Tennessee originally. That's where the Cherokees come from."

"What about the others?" I wasn't sure what a Martiniquean was.

"Well, there's more kinds of people in the Deep South than you might think. New Orleans is one of the biggest ports in the world—lots of people from foreign countries settle there. I grew up on the Gulf Coast. Moved to California when I was about your age. You ever been to the South? You must have, if your parents are from there. Ever been to New Orleans?"

I hadn't counted on having to fool another southerner. I played dumb.

"No, my family's all in Illinois. What's New Orleans like? I want to go to Mardi Gras someday," I said.

Lacey snorted. "Mardi Gras. Willis—that's my husband—he sometimes drags me down there for Carnival. He loves it. I see all those poor tourists in their resort clothes, shivering like Jell-O. They buy coats after they get there. Scarves. Umbrellas. The stores double their prices—they make a fortune."

"I want to see the parades."

"Beer bottles up to your ankles, barf in the gutters, and pickpockets on every corner. Stay home, girl."

She knows her way around New Orleans, all right. Hope she doesn't keep up with the newspapers from there. "Oh, I think it would be fun," I said. "Maybe I'll go someday." I turned back to my typewriter.

New Orleans. Pale cobblestones and painted doorways. The smell of the Quarter: roasting coffee, bus fumes, and river clay. The reek of the Jax Brewery, like an old drunk's breath. Sitting on iron chairs under the awning of the Café Du Monde, trying to talk to Richard. Loud babble all around, and the traffic on Chartres Street a few feet away.

Richard had powdered sugar on his chin. He stared at me, making me wonder if I had some on mine, too. "You don't have to keep it," he said.

I refused to listen. I thought I could make him change his mind. I bit into a beignet, greasy sugar wrapped around thin air. Sweet and hollow.

I'd felt sick then, and I felt sick now. *Everything is my fault because I didn't know what to do that day, because I never know what to do. I want that afternoon back. Maybe if I had another try, I'd get it right.*

"You okay?" asked Lacey.

"Yes," I said. *I'll never be okay till I forget Jamie. Which is never.*

Jamie. She isn't eleven months and five days old anymore. Maybe she isn't any age at all. Or she may be growing like the rest of us, in some other life I can't see yet. Like the way she grew inside me—it was invisible, but it was real. Somewhere now, she's growing into a little girl. Somewhere, we're looking forward to the future.

My imaginary future, the one that matches the imaginary past where I did things right.

"We gotta finish these meeting reports," said Lacey. That's what we did for the rest of the morning.

Roll another sheet into the typewriter. Get it nice and straight. Don't think about Richard in his jeans and the faded plaid shirt he wore that last day at the zoo. Richard, with Jamie straddled on his hip.

He might come back someday, come up the dark red stairs to my apartment. But if he ever does, there won't be any Jamie with him. Jamie's gone.

❧ 4 ❧
December 1974, San Pedro
Lacey

WHY DIDN'T I GO to Mr. Giannini, or at least to George, and ask where Kathy's résumé was? Why did I just file her papers as if nothing was wrong? I turned it over in my mind a lot for the next few days. What was the point of stealing a résumé? What was the point of lying about where she came from?

I pictured it again, the glimpse I'd had, Kathy palming those papers like a magician—or a shoplifter. That worried me a lot. Lord knows we didn't have much cash lying around, but we handled checks for hundreds of thousands of dollars. If Mr. Giannini found out Kathy had swiped her résumé back, he'd let her go, no hesitation.

He'd probably forgotten he'd told me to follow up on her references—but if a big check went missing along with our new assistant, he'd remember in a hurry. If I had the brains God gave a goose, I'd tell Mr. Giannini right away that George had hired Kathy on the spot, and that I hadn't been able to call her references because they'd disappeared.

On the other hand, Kathy was just a kid. What would she know about the kind of money in heavy construction? Probably she was running away from a bad marriage or a mean stepfather. I felt sorry for her, and I'd feel terrible if she lost her job because of something I said.

I *could* try to find out what her problem was. Most likely, it was only a family misunderstanding, something like that. I might get Kathy to confide in me. If that didn't work, there was always Marilu Collins. She didn't have a lot of sense, but she must have gotten *some* background information before she rented to Kathy. The more I thought that idea over, the more I liked it.

Of course, there were about a dozen ways the whole thing could blow up in my face. I was starting to wonder if I was getting a little nutty, the way my husband had been hinting ever since our daughter moved out. But Willis was imagining things—and anyway, it wasn't nutty to help a kid. Anyone would do it.

So, I started trying to get Kathy to open up. I baked cookies and brought them in, and I told her little things about Willis and Angela. She ate the cookies and she listened politely enough to the stories, but she didn't tell me anything about herself. Of course, that made me wonder even more.

It was easy to see she was unhappy. She came in red-eyed a few mornings, and I heard her crying in the restroom once. When I asked her if anything was wrong, she said no. I shut right up. Better not scare her off the way I had Angela, asking questions and giving advice.

But my first impression that Kathy was a good kid held up, too. She was obviously well brought up. Not society or anything, but she was always polite. I asked her right off to call me Lacey instead of Mrs. Greer, but I appreciated her showing me respect. She was funny when she asked about how dingy the office was, way too tactful to come straight out with it.

"Did the company just move here?" she asked, looking around.

I knew what she meant. We didn't have anything extra, no carpet or good furniture. But most of the people who walked in were likely to have concrete on their boots, so there was no way to fancy the place up. It was an industrial building with mixer trucks parked in back and the office stuck in like an afterthought.

"No, we've been here awhile. Mr. Giannini built this building five or six years ago."

"You've worked here *six years?*"

"Nearly eight—since my daughter Angela was in high school. She's starting graduate school this year."

Kathy looked astonished. Was she surprised that a black woman's daughter would go to college?

"I thought . . . ."

I waited. She stuttered, looking around like a cornered cat. Finally she said, "I thought you were about thirty."

"No, I'm in my forties."

"I'm sorry." She looked out the window, like something interesting had turned up out there all of a sudden. Her mouth was trembling—she was close to tears. This did not make sense.

"Don't be sorry. Nothing wrong with looking thirty. I wish I did!" I kept my tone light and pretended I didn't notice anything was the matter.

I could see why she might think she put her foot in her mouth. If I were white, it would be a compliment for her to think I was younger. Not being able to guess my age would be different—too much like what the rednecks used to say: "They all look alike." A nice girl like her would have been embarrassed to say anything that sounded like that. But I couldn't figure out why she would be so upset.

To change the subject, I gave her a whole bunch of stuff to type. I spread papers all over my desk and faked being busy. She turned to her typewriter and got started.

I remembered to rustle my papers once in a while as if I was working. But I didn't see them. My mind kept picking at me about who she was and what was going on, the way you pick at a ragged cuticle till it looks like hell.

❧ 5 ❧
December 1974, San Pedro
Kathy

THE ENTRY HALL had two black metal mailboxes with holes cut out in front to show when a letter was inside. White showed through mine. I opened the box.

Two letters. One envelope was addressed in my sister's writing. The other was in Richard's.

I plodded up the stairs, feeling like the five minutes before a math test. When I got to my door, I dropped the key twice before I got in. I stood in the living room and tore Richard's envelope open. Might as well get it over with.

> Dear Kathy,
>   I love you.
>   Richard

I dropped his letter on the floor and opened my sister's.

> Dear Kathy,
>
>   I was really worried when you took off like that. Are you all right?
>   I wish you hadn't left my car at the cemetery. The last thing I needed was go back there. Anyway,

thanks for sending the card with your address. Please
don't move again without telling me.

Love,
Sharon

Well, it could have been worse. I'd been afraid she wouldn't
even answer my card. I wasn't sure she'd still be speaking to
me. Mom wasn't. I didn't think she ever would again. When
the emergency room nurse came to tell us Dad hadn't made it,
Mom turned on me.

"Was your little pickaninny worth killing your father for?"
And she walked off behind the nurse without looking back.

Sharon put her hand out to stop me from following. "Let
it go. She's upset."

But I wasn't following. I couldn't have. "I didn't make him
have a heart attack," I said. "It's not my fault."

"Look, Kathy. I'm not saying Mom's right. You know I'm
on your side."

"But it's not my fault. And that was a horrible thing she said
about Jamie." I didn't even try to wipe away the tears running
down my face.

Sharon pulled a package of tissues from her purse and passed
one to me. She wiped her own eyes and nose with another one.
"I know," she said. "Mom's pretty out of it. I don't think the
two of you should even be talking right now. How long are you
staying in Baton Rouge?"

"I hadn't thought. I mean I didn't think—"

"Stay at my place. I'll be over at Mom's most of the time anyway. She'll need me to help with the arrangements." She sighed.
"Everything's so awful—do me a favor? Please? Keep out of sight
at the funeral. We don't need anything more. Please, Kathy."

"But it's not fair."

"I know. But don't let her see you anyway."

On the morning of the funeral, she took a taxi over to Mom's. Sharon was riding in the limo, so she gave me her car keys.

It was easy to keep Mom from seeing me at the church, because it was filled with Dad's friends. I stayed in a back pew, hoping no one would notice. If they did, they'd push me up front with the family. I kept my head down.

When the funeral procession left for the cemetery, I waited until last in the queue. The police escort rode behind me on their motorcycles. At the grave, I couldn't hear the priest—the wind took his words away. In the church he'd said, "We brought nothing into this world, and it is certain we can carry nothing out." I kept thinking of that, over and over. Dad had so much—his friends, the house, his garden, his work.

His daughters.

His granddaughter.

I sat on a cold iron bench a long time after the last of the crowd was gone. Just stared at the patchy grass, at the leaves giving up and letting go of the trees. Finally, I stood up, chilled and stiff. I didn't go to the grave. I didn't want to see it. Or Jamie's, right next to it.

When I got back to the car, it wouldn't start. I'd forgotten to turn off the lights, the funeral procession lights. The battery was dead. Dead—the word hit me like it hadn't done before, and my teeth started to chatter. *I always thought that was only an expression.* I clenched my jaw. *Don't think about it.*

I called a cab from the cemetery office and went back to Sharon's place, trying not to shake in front of the cabbie. I left a note about the car and got all my stuff, which wasn't much. I took another cab to the Greyhound station. The next bus that didn't go somewhere in Louisiana was an express for Los Angeles. It didn't leave for two hours, and I spent the whole time sitting on one of the station's hard plastic chairs, looking at the terrazzo floor between my feet. The dirty globs of gum trampled into it were just like me.

❧ 6 ❧
December 1974, San Pedro
Lacey

WHEN ANGELA CAME to stay for the holidays, I wasn't done painting the sewing room. In fact, I hadn't exactly started. I was putting masking tape around the wood trim so the paint job would come out neat. Angie pulled up short in the doorway, suitcase in hand.

"Where's my room?" she yelped.

"I needed a sewing room," I said.

"What do you mean, you needed a sewing room? You don't even sew."

"I might, if I had a sewing room."

"You didn't even let my bed cool down good before you got rid of it!"

"I didn't get rid of it yet—it's out in the garage." I finished taping the baseboard and started on the windows.

"I'm supposed to sleep in the garage?"

"Don't be silly. I'll move the bed back in when I'm through painting. Or else I'll buy a daybed."

"Where do I sleep tonight? In a motel?"

"On the couch. Maybe I'll finish tomorrow. You could help."

"Well, if that's what it takes. Where do I put my stuff?" she asked.

I couldn't figure out why she was staring at me like something was wrong. All I was doing was painting the front bedroom.

"I cleared out a space in the laundry room."

"Man, is there no room at this inn!" Angela flopped down on the floor beside her suitcase.

"You did move out, Angela," I said. "I meant to have it finished. I've been busy at work. Don't sit on that sack. It's got my putty knife in it." I set the tape down and reached for her to pass the sack to me.

Angela pulled it out from under her and handed it over. "Why are you so busy at work all of a sudden? Big project or something?" We both glanced up as Willis came into the room.

"Mr. Giannini got me an assistant," I told her. "It's more trouble training a new person than it would be to do the work myself."

"Who did they hire, someone who never had a job before?" Angela asked.

I pulled my knife out of the sack and held it up to inspect it. The blade looked a little bent from being sat on. Angela didn't much look like she cared.

"To tell you the truth, I don't know if she's had one or not," I said. "Her résumé disappeared."

Angela shrugged. "Can't you tell her to give you another copy?"

I shook my head. "I decided not to. I'm pretty sure she snitched it back." I sighted down the blade to check if it was bent. It wasn't.

Angela and Willis peered at me like a couple of owls. "What do you mean, snitched it back?" Willis asked.

"It wasn't with her application. I think I saw her slip it into her purse after George interviewed her."

They broke off staring at me and looked at each other. Willis swiveled back to me. "Well, didn't anyone else notice the résumé's gone?" he asked.

"Guess not. Mr. Giannini is far too important to touch a file cabinet," I said. "And I'm not sure George has learned to read. Very few jackasses have."

I picked up my masking tape and unrolled a length with a little zipping sound. As far as I was concerned, they could drop this now. My office wasn't any business of theirs.

But Angela wasn't about to let go. "Mama, how do you know this woman isn't some criminal on the run?"

That one took the cake. Angela was getting her master's in criminal justice, so she suspected everyone.

"I wouldn't go so far as to call her a woman," I said, pressing the tape carefully against the window frame. "She's younger than you. Way too young to be much of a criminal—and besides, she isn't the type."

"There *is* no 'type.' Don't you know that? There's no age, either. What about those people who kidnapped Patty Hearst? Barely old enough to vote, some of them. Maybe she robbed a bank, same as they did. Hell, she could be *one* of them. They could be anywhere by now."

I tried to picture Kathy robbing a bank. She'd drop her gun on the guard's foot and say, "Oh, excuse me." No way Kathy could rob a bank.

"I doubt it," I said.

"What about the Mansons? How do you know she's not one of *them?*"

I patted my tape work carefully into place. If I didn't get all the wrinkles out, the paint would leak underneath it. "They're all in jail," I said.

"How do you know? Maybe she's one who got away—now she's trying to live a normal life. Waiting for them to get out. *Mama, will you stop with the damned tape for a minute?*"

I set it aside. "If she's waiting for Charlie Manson, she'd better be prepared for a long wait. He'll get out of prison one day after hell freezes over. You ought to go to work for the studios, Angela—this stuff would be about right for *Columbo*."

Willis chimed in. "It's not that far-fetched, honey. She sounds guilty as hell to me. Better lock up the petty cash."

I laughed. "Any petty cash at Giannini's is so petty, no one would be interested."

"No lie," said Angela. "That dude is a serious miser. The first time I saw the office Christmas tree, I started looking around for Bob Cratchit. I was sure Mr. Giannini had him in there someplace."

Willis snickered. "You got his number, all right."

"Anyone can get his number," Angela told him. "It's the one the Arabs invented. Zero."

Willis turned back to me. "Why don't you make the old fool fix the place up? He's making enough money."

"I already decided to talk to him. I guess I've gotten used to it, but Kathy asked if we'd moved in recently. Made me notice."

"Oh, right—Kathy!" said Angela, veering back to her single-minded track. "She's up to something, Mama. If you won't find out what's going on, I will."

"How?" I wasn't exactly paying attention. I was checking out the walls to see how many holes I had to fill before I painted. I hoped I wouldn't have to go out for more spackle. Angela had put up a lot of pictures over the years.

"The library at school has newspapers from everywhere," she said.

"You won't find anything there." I made a mental note of a water stain on the plaster under the window. Maybe we had some sealer in the garage. Angela was frowning, so I tried to pay a little more attention. "Look, honey, most likely Kathy had a bad husband. Those don't make the paper—they're not news."

"I don't see why she'd take her résumé back if it was her marriage," she said. "Mr. Giannini should get the police to do a background check. Want me to tell him how to request one, next time I'm in there?" She had a real edge to her voice.

I snapped back, "Angela, you've been telling me for a year or more to get a life of my own. So, I did. You live yours and I'll live mine. Don't butt in, you mind?"

I picked up the tape again, but she glared at me, and I put it down. I pushed my annoyance down, too. "Let it be, really," I said. You'll stir up trouble for nothing."

Angela gave a theatrical sigh, the way she used to do when she was a teenager. "If you're right about her being so innocent," she said, "there's no trouble to stir up."

"It's not your concern, Angela. You leave it alone—completely alone, you hear me? I'll find out for myself."

She got up from the floor and stood over me with her arms folded. "I don't see where it's your concern either," she said.

"You were just telling me it was. Wasn't it you, one minute ago, saying she was probably a criminal in disguise?"

Another theatrical sigh. "Mama, it's your concern to get it looked into. But last time I checked, the job description for 'secretary' didn't include detective work. It's your job to point out that something's going on—but whatever her problem is, it's none of your business."

Willis stepped into his peacemaker role. He was getting good at it.

"Well, maybe it is and maybe it isn't, honey, but how could you find anything out anyway?" he asked me.

"I have my ways."

Willis snorted. Angela shrugged and left the room, dragging her suitcase. I hoped she was just taking it to the laundry room, not back to Berkeley.

"Let's have some coffee in the living room, honey," Willis said. He put out a hand to help me up.

I was happy to drop the whole subject. But I hoped Willis and Angela didn't expect any Christmas cookies to go with their coffee. If they did, let one of them make a batch.

For the next few days, I was busy getting the painting done and hanging new curtains. Willis and Angela helped, and they didn't say a single word about Kathy. We finished the room and moved the bed back in. Angela went to the market and bought some holiday goodies, and she opened all the cards and stood them on the mantel. No one brought the decorations down from the attic, but at least it was a little like Christmas.

Saturday was the day of the annual Holiday Craft Faire at the Point Fermin lighthouse. I walked over in the late afternoon, just to get out of the house. As I inspected a hand-knit sweater to see if it was the right size for Angela, I caught sight of Kathy. She seemed so forlorn, walking along with her arms drawn in and her head down. Color and music and fun all around her, and she never looked up once. At work, she seemed down most of the time, but she still got carried along by the busyness. Watching her on her own now, I got the idea that whatever was wrong might be more serious than I'd thought.

She wandered to the last table in the Faire and kept going, walking straight as a chalk line now, right to the edge of the cliff behind the lighthouse. I pushed money into the vendor's hand

and didn't wait for a bag or even a receipt. Wadding the sweater up, I followed Kathy at a little distance.

Don't be melodramatic, I told myself. *She's looking at the ocean. Everyone does it when they first get here.*

She stood there way too long for a sightseer, staring out to sea. She'd have been peering into some window in Japan if she could have seen five thousand miles. And she almost looked like she could.

I kept an eye on her, worrying and trying to talk myself out of it, first one and then the other. Behind us, the haggle and laughter of the Faire petered out. By the time she turned back, there was almost no one left in the park. I had to dodge into the restroom to make sure she didn't see me. I tried to laugh at myself for letting my imagination run away with me, but it didn't work.

When I got home, Angela saw me come in, still clutching the sweater. I went upstairs to gift wrap it, but it was the wrong size after all. Completely wrong—too big for her, too small for me. I stuffed the sweater in a drawer. It would do for someone.

I could hear every scratchy tick of my old alarm clock in the quiet room. Once in a while, there was a swish as a car drove by, or maybe what I heard was waves breaking—sometimes the wind would bring their sound in close.

I shut my eyes, picturing Kathy standing on the cliff at Point Fermin. I'd started trying to find out about her because I was curious, and to cover my hindside in case Mr. Giannini made a fuss about her references. I'd hoped she had some easy problem, like in a television show—something that could be solved in thirty minutes, not counting commercials. Now I suspected she really needed help. I didn't know what I could do, but I decided I'd better do something. It didn't look like she had anyone else.

Deciding was one thing, figuring out where to go from there was something else. I wasn't exactly experienced in checking up on people. For the past couple of years, Angela had been pretending I was some kind of master spy, but that was ridiculous. She had no idea how helpless I felt. Being a mother was like watching a sleepwalker—I worried about Angela every minute, but I didn't dare say one word about it. And that was my own daughter, who I'd raised. How in the world could I find out about someone I hardly knew?

Part 2

⚡ 7 ⚡
September 1972, Baton Rouge
Kathy

ON FRIDAY AFTERNOONS, the Student Union was packed. I hated crowds, but I'd left my lunch at home, and there was nowhere else to eat. Just inside the door to the cafeteria, I stopped short. Loud chatter ricocheted off the glass walls and bounced around the room. Voices rose, competed, fell again. Smells competed too—cabbage, fried fish, a sharp tang of onions—nothing I wanted.

A bunch of girls charged in, laughing shrilly. They jostled me, and I stepped aside to let them pass. They scanned the room and headed toward a group at a corner table, waving to more friends as they threaded their way through the mob. It looked easy when *they* did it.

But it wasn't easy for me. It was only a few weeks into the term, but the dorm students had already become a sort of tribe, and I wasn't a member. A townie and a freshman besides, I hardly knew anyone. So, I wasn't looking for friends to join, I was looking for an empty table to claim. There weren't any, but I spotted someone I recognized, at least—Phil from English class, sitting with some other guys. He leaned back, feet on a chair.

They all watched me approach, but Phil didn't say hi. He didn't offer me the chair his feet were on, either. I stood and waited.

"Car!" he bellowed to a boy who wasn't more than six feet away from him.

"Aston Martin!"

"Not you. You wouldn't be an Aston Martin, ever. You're a 1966 blue Volkswagen van with a low tire."

"Mustang," hollered someone else.

"Yeah, cool, a Mustang. With a dent in the driver's door. What kind of animal?"

"Lion."

"Racehorse."

"Cat."

"Cat, my ass. Polecat is more like it."

They were playing "What kind of"—what kind of car would you be if you were a car, what kind of animal.

"Town!" yelled Phil.

"Paris," someone said.

"Yeah, the sewers of Paris. That's you. The sewers of Paris." Phil finally turned around to face me, waiting for me to say what town I'd be.

I'd be the Nevada desert, the stone building facades standing up with nothing behind them, the mountains looking out through the windows. "Rhyolite," I tried.

"Where's that?"

"Nevada."

"What's there?"

"I don't know. Desert. It's a ghost town."

"Rye-oh-LITE!" shouted Phil. Much louder than before— people were looking. "The capital of Nerdland!"

Someone snickered. A narrow smile flickered on Phil's lips.

"I'm getting out of here," he said. "I don't want the nerds to catch up with me. Whole hordes of them are on their way from Rhyolite, even as we speak."

He pushed back his chair and walked away. The others flocked behind him, laughing. I opened my mouth to say good-bye, see you later, in a flip, offhand way, but nothing came out. *He was only kidding, the way he teased his friends. No he wasn't.*

This is high school all over again. College was supposed to be different. Do we ever start being grown-ups?

Right in the middle of my misery, I imagined a business lunch. *Bankers or lawyers or something, all in suits, getting into a food fight like little kids. One banker gets hit between the eyes with a glob of mashed potatoes. As they plop down onto his pin-striped vest, I see he looks a lot like Phil.*

I stifled a laugh—if I let it start, I'd end up crying. I pulled myself together and looked around. Curious faces turned hastily away. *Well, that was one way to get an empty table. Too bad I'm not hungry anymore.*

I went on to my next class. Psychology 101 was a survey—a one-size-fits-nobody kind of course. I was an art major, but the university made all the freshmen take a social science class, and this was the one I'd picked. I was already wondering why I'd thought it might interest me. A graduate assistant gave the lectures in a big hall, almost an auditorium. After the first day, I always sat in the back, trying to take notes but mostly doodling. I usually slipped in as class started, or even late. That day, I was early.

The lecture room was empty when I got there, but another student came in almost on my heels. I'd noticed him before, mostly because he was the only black guy in the class. He sat across the aisle from me and read a book, looking up a couple of times. Smiles, here, gone, private. Here again. I imagined thoughts tumbling around his mind like a rock polisher.

I sketched his face in my Psych notebook, but the expression wasn't right. I tried again—closer. *He's so alive. He's different—not just because he's black. Except why do we say "black?" He's some shade of brown. Sienna, maybe? Just not "café au lait" or some polite little phrase like a lot of people use. Rude-polite—a person isn't a piece of food. I'm the color of cheap bread, but no one ever says so.*

The room had filled up while I was drawing. The teacher came in and opened her notes on the lectern. The class quieted obediently, and she started the lecture, droning away like she always did. "In 1937, Lorenz established the pioneering research on imprinting in young animals," she said. "Imprinting is the process by which animals learn their species identity. By substituting himself for the animals' mother during the critical period, Lorenz induced them to imprint on him."

The guy I'd noticed before class raised his hand. The teacher stopped, with a slightly put-upon air. "Yes, Richard?"

He stood, holding up a book for the class to see. "Here's a picture of Konrad Lorenz and his geese," he said. "He hatched these goslings in an incubator, and the first thing they saw was him. They thought they were junior Konrad Lorenzes. They followed him everywhere."

Suddenly the idea was interesting. How could a goose think it was a man? How did he ever get rid of them?

Here's Konrad Lorenz, trying to give the geese the slip so he can get together with his girlfriend. Here's Richard, a jack-in-the-box with a pile of helpful books, one for every subject the teacher talks about. Boooiiiinnnng! "Funny you should mention the psychodynamics of Martians, I happen to have a book here."

My fantasies unreeled like old black-and-white slapstick movies. I stifled a laugh. Richard caught my eye and smiled.

It wasn't quite a real smile, but it was better than one of those smiles you have to do. Maybe he could see the movie too.

After class, I hurried down the hall until I caught up with him.

"Hi, I'm Kathy," I said. "That was neat, what you said in class. How did you know all that stuff about the geese?"

He shrugged. "It's interesting, how we learn what we are. Normally, the first thing goslings see is their mother. That first look tells them they're geese. Maybe people do something similar—probably over a longer period of time. But when a baby learns what he is, he also learns what he's *not*—and then, maybe all his life, he'd see it as a threat."

"You make it a lot more interesting than Miss Sharpe does."

"I'm probably more interested in the subject than Miss Sharpe is."

We fell into step, headed for the Student Union. The sidewalks were thronged—almost everyone was either going to the Union or leaving it. A few people smiled at us, and some frowned. Everyone seemed to feel entitled to a political opinion about a black guy and a white girl walking together. But I wasn't political—I was just interested in Richard.

He waved to a few people as we walked through the Union, but when we reached the cafeteria, no one signaled us to join them. We bought coffee and took it to a small table of our own, abandoned near the edge of a loud group. There weren't any chairs. I stood by the table to claim it while Richard scrounged a couple of chairs.

"So, how did you know Miss Sharpe would talk about imprinting?" I asked, as he dragged the second one back.

"I had a similar course in high school. The subject came up then."

We both sat down. "You had Psych in *high school*? Where did you go to school?"

"All over. I'm an army brat. My father's family is from here, but he joined the military to get off the farm, then he stayed in. I grew up on army posts—Texas, Missouri, Virginia, and Oklahoma. Even Germany for a while. Some of them had good schools." He gave me a quick look, then a longer one.

"Your father's family had a farm near here?" I asked.

"Right in town." He laughed. An embarrassed laugh, awkward. "My grandfather is one of the local characters. He still farms his land, right on the edge of that business park near the airport. Behind a pair of mules."

"Oh, *him*. *He's* your grandfather?" I'd seen the old man for years, every time I went to the airport. I always wondered what he was thinking about, walking behind those mules, ignoring the traffic a few yards away. "I think he's kind of cool. People must have offered him a fortune for his land."

"They have. He's stubborn. Like his son. And his grandson."

I wondered what it would be like to live on army bases. I didn't think I'd like it. On the other hand, you'd live in different towns, even in foreign countries, instead of in the same house year after year. Would you get to start all over again every time you moved? Be someone different, try something new?

"What's it like, living on an army base?" I asked.

He grimaced. "You don't want to know."

"Does your dad want you to join the military, too?" I asked.

"I already did. He didn't like it much."

"Why not?"

"I enlisted right out of high school. He wanted me to wait and get an engineering degree—go in as an officer. Maybe in the air force." Richard fiddled with the sugar packets, looking uncomfortable. "Now I'm starting college, five years later than he wanted, but I am majoring in engineering. Maybe he thinks his dream is back on track. I don't know—we haven't discussed it."

"Are you planning to go back after you graduate?"

"In the military? No, thanks. I don't think so." He shook his head sharply. "What about you? Where did you grow up?"

"Right here. I was born in Illinois, but we moved when I was three. My dad teaches here."

"What does he teach?"

"Philosophy. Mostly graduate students."

The coffee was nearly gone, and Richard began to gather his things. *He's about to leave now. He won't ask if we can get together again, I know he won't. He's not supposed to ask a white girl. Girls can't ask boys, either. But why not?*

"I was wondering, I mean . . . ." I felt like a fool, but I made myself go on. "My sister was supposed to go to a movie with me tonight, and she backed out. Would you go with me?"

His hands stopped moving. He didn't look at me, or at anything. "Do you live at home?"

"Yes, why?"

"What will your parents think when I show up to take you to a movie?"

"Nothing."

"You really think—nothing?"

"Yes, I do. They're not like that. I'm not like that. Please go to the movie with me." I wished he didn't look so sad about being invited to a movie.

"What time should I pick you up?" he asked.

☙

TELLING MY PARENTS at dinner that night about my date with Richard, I felt awkward, and ashamed of being awkward.

"Sharon had to cancel for the movie tonight, but I'm going with a guy from school," I said.

"Oh, how nice," Mom said. "Now that you're in college, maybe you'll be dating more. What's his name?"

"Richard Johnson."

"Johnsson?" she asked. "Is he from around here? He's not related to Erik Johnsson, I suppose?" Erik Johnsson was one of Dad's colleagues, a math professor whose classes I had managed to avoid.

"No," I said. "He's from around here, but I doubt he's related to Erik Johnsson. He's black." *Better let them know right away. But it's weird that I have to prepare them so they won't look surprised when they see him. Like we were bigots or something. Are we? I've never come home and said, "Oh, by the way, I'm going to a movie tonight with so-and-so. He's white."*

Dad glanced at Mom, then turned to me.

"What's his major?" he asked casually.

"Engineering."

"Ah. What year is he in?"

"He's a freshman. He's a few years older than me, though. He was in the army."

"Well," said Dad, "we'll look forward to meeting him. Are you planning to be out late?"

I had no idea what they thought. We finished dinner without saying much more and then sat in the living room, lined up one, two, three on the couch. Backs straight, feet together, already on our good behavior, we waited for Richard to ring the doorbell.

⁓

IN THE WEEKS that followed, Richard and I kept going out. But he didn't come to the house. I'd meet him somewhere or pick him up, since he didn't have a car—he'd borrowed one for our movie date. I loved setting out on autumn afternoons to go to dinner or a movie with him, driving my Volkswagen off by myself instead of waiting passively for my date to take me from my parents.

One Saturday in early November, as Dad and I cleaned up the garden for the year, he said, "Haven't seen Richard in a while. How's he doing?"

"He's fine." I struggled to pull up a tomato stake that was taller than me.

Dad gave me a hand. "He never comes to the house," he said.

"Magnolia Woods isn't too convenient. It's better for us to meet near campus." I pulled out the next stake without help.

"Are you sure he feels welcome?" Dad sounded anxious.

"Sure," I said. "That's not the problem. He just doesn't have transportation." *Or is that an excuse? Guess who's not coming to dinner.*

"Why don't you pick him up one evening and bring him over?" Dad asked. "He seems like a nice young man. We'd like to get to know him better."

I noticed some crabgrass had sneaked in where the tomato vines had been particularly lush. I pulled at one of the clumps, but it came off in my hand the way crabgrass always does, leaving its roots behind to spread.

"One evening or a particular evening?" I asked. As soon as the words were out of my mouth, I wished I hadn't asked.

"Next Saturday," Dad said. "Ask him over for dinner next Saturday."

So, Richard came to dinner. Over roast lamb and Potatoes Anna, he and Dad debated the war. Dad was a pacifist. Richard agreed the war was wrong, but he thought most of the soldiers were only trying to stay alive.

"I didn't meet any monsters in the army," he said. "Everyone I knew did what they had to and that's all."

"What about Lieutenant Calley?" asked my father. The scandal had been going on for years—the My Lai massacre and then William Calley's court martial.

"It wasn't all like that. The war is no good. We shouldn't be there. But not one man in a thousand is like Calley."

"'An isolated incident'?"

"Not isolated enough. But most of us weren't anything like that. And things like My Lai will go on happening as long as there's war. It's no good to blame each and every soldier."

At first I was happy at how well Richard and Dad were getting along. After a while, that wore thin. Neither of them seemed to know how to bring the bull session to an end and talk about something else. Mom would ordinarily have diverted a runaway conversation at a dinner party, but this time she didn't. She sat stiff and wordless, with a vacant look in her eyes. Except for her fixed hostess smile, she might as well have been at the dentist's.

They're not even talking to me. Mom's never liked me, and Sharon's moved out, and I haven't even been able to talk to Dad for a while, not the way we used to. And Richard—when I asked him about the army, I could see he didn't want to talk about it, but here he is yakking with Dad like they were at a VFW meeting. Damn it, I was afraid they wouldn't accept him, but it's me they don't accept.

The next day at school, I ran into Richard in the library. First words out of my mouth, I tried to pick a fight with him.

"You seem to have more in common with my dad than I do."

Richard laughed. "Well, at least we don't have the opposite problem—your parents refusing to let me in the door."

"What about the other way around? Maybe the two of you won't let *me* in the door."

He shrugged.

"Don't take it personally, Kathy. Your dad is way to the left, for Baton Rouge. He probably can't say stuff like that to his friends. He likes to talk politics, and I happen to be someone he can talk to."

"Well, I happen to be someone he has nothing to say to anymore."

"Join the club. I don't talk to my father at all."

That made me feel less alone. "Why? Because of the army?"

"It's a long story. The army was the last straw."

"I have time for a long story."

A librarian frowned at us and put a finger to her lips. Richard gestured toward the door. "Let's go somewhere else, and I'll tell you."

We went out onto the long main quadrangle. The prettiest buildings on campus were here—tan, tile-roofed, connected with arched breezeways. Small oak trees spotted the inner court with patches of shade.

We sat on an out-of-the-way bench. Richard stared at an azalea bush like he'd never seen such a thing before. He didn't look my way at all.

"My father has a real thing about the army. He enlisted one week after I was born. My mother hated that—a new baby, and her husband decides to go fight in Korea."

"Wouldn't he have been drafted anyway?"

"Probably. He made it a crusade, though. Most of the officers were white, and some of them said right out that black soldiers were cowards."

"Why?" I pushed my books off my lap and stacked them on the bench, fingering the edges carefully, lining them up. Anything to keep from looking right at Richard. *I've never talked with a black person about prejudice. I didn't know you could.*

"Partly racism. There was also a scandal about a mostly black regiment that ran. He set out to prove single-handed the racists were wrong. Sometimes when Dad talked about it, I wondered who the enemy was—the Communists, the white officers, or the black soldiers who fell short of his ideals."

"Why did he stay in the army after the war?"

"It was a good place for an ambitious black man in the fifties. The army cared more about rank than race. He ended up a master sergeant in a transportation company." Richard kept staring into the azalea bush, like he was reporting a story shown there on a little TV screen.

"What's a master sergeant?" *Dumb question, just to keep him talking. The way girls are supposed to do. All the magazines say that—though, most likely this kind of conversation isn't what they have in mind.*

"It's an NCO, non-commissioned officer. Dad should have been a general—he's perfect for the military—neat, pressed, polished, the whole nine yards. I used to be proud to be his kid. All the same, it was hard on me."

"What do you mean?" I reached out to touch his arm, but as my fingers brushed his shirt, he glanced at me, startled. I jerked my hand back. At least I'd gotten his attention away from the azalea.

"He expected me to be perfect too. Even when I was knee-high. Anything I did reflected on his career, and on all blacks in the army—on all blacks, period. Like I was an ambassador to another planet. Some ambassador." His voice was hoarse, like he was about to cry.

"Were you that bad, or just a kid?"

"I was just a kid. I made good grades, but they were never good enough. Sometimes I wished I could quit trying, wished I could cut loose and give him a taste of 'bad son.' I never did. Over the years, I quit talking to him instead."

"Is it still like that?"

He frowned, hesitated. He seemed less open when he went on, almost dismissive. "I've only seen him once since I got back from 'Nam. I still wasn't an officer and he was still mad about it." He laughed, but he didn't sound amused. "And if I had been, I doubt he would have liked that either. He didn't exactly roll out the welcome mat. He said he didn't like my Afro, and that was about it."

"Maybe that was all he could say."

"I guess so." Richard stood up, balanced his books in the crook of one elbow, and held out his other hand. Before I could take it, he pulled it back. *He's pretending he didn't offer.* I gathered my books, holding them close with my hands locked together. *Now I'm pretending I didn't notice.*

"Want to get a cup of coffee?" I asked.

"I guess so."

We headed toward the Union. Once again, I thought everyone was looking. *Do people always pay attention to people walking the other way? I never thought about it. Everyone has eyes. What do they usually look at?*

For once, the cafeteria was nearly empty. We sat down with our trays. *He thinks I didn't want to touch his hand. Maybe he saw the way people were staring too. Talk about something else.*

Nothing came to mind. I looked around, waiting for something to occur to me. At the far end of the room, a middle-aged man in a suit gathered his briefcase and tray to leave. As he walked toward the counter, he stumbled over a chair and dropped the tray onto the terrazzo floor. The dishes smashed, coffee and food slopped all over. He grabbed some napkins from a table to clean his clothes. A light-brown woman in a green uniform hurried to pick up the shards of his dishes. The man scrubbed at his shirt and walked off without looking back. The maid fetched a mop and bucket and cleaned the floor.

Richard watched them. After a moment, I said, "Could I see your apartment?"

He turned to me, his face surprised and open. "It's not much, Kathy. Even the landlord calls the place 'the Ghetto.'"

"I want to see it."

We didn't talk as we walked past the campanile and the drama building, past the edge of the campus to East Chimes Street. Next door to a greasy-smelling diner was a long gray apartment building. This was where the hippies had lived, such hippies as were left in Baton Rouge after the serious ones hitchhiked to San Francisco.

Richard had the first-floor place at the back. It was a one-room apartment, clean but dingy just the same. Stains on the ceiling showed where the plumbing upstairs had overflowed. He didn't have much furniture—a flimsy table with scratched paint, a couple of straight chairs that didn't match, and a mattress on the floor, made up taut and perfect with a paisley bedspread. And a board-and-cement-block shelf stuffed with books.

His windows looked out onto a huge fig tree. As I glanced out, I saw a rat eating a fig. Richard must have seen it too. I heard a sharp intake of breath.

I hadn't felt so ashamed since the time Sharon caught me stealing a pack of gum in the A&P when I was nine. *I'm pushing myself on him, and he probably thinks I want him for a boyfriend until the next white guy comes along. Or even that I want to get involved with him in some sick way.*

Here I am, invading his privacy—who asked me? He'll think I'm so patronizing, insisting on seeing his water-stained paint and his cheap furniture and his rat.

"I'm sorry." *Oh, great, now I'm going to cry in front of him.* But I couldn't help it.

He offered his upturned white palms to me for comfort. *Does he think he can only touch me in the places where his skin matches mine? I don't want it to be that way anymore.*

I pulled him close and laid my face against his. I had never gone to bed with a man before, never even wanted to. I almost laughed, there in his arms. *How could anyone think we're different in any way that matters?*

℃

ON THANKSGIVING DAY, I woke to a splash of rain blown against my window. The banked-in sky told me that it wasn't going to let up, but I didn't mind. Rain was the best we could do in the South to mimic the crisp-weather holiday coziness that we'd learned from children's books. Years when it was hot and sunny, it didn't seem like Thanksgiving at all.

In the kitchen, Mom was already fussing. She had the classical radio station on, playing Charles Ives. Cranberries seethed in a copper pot, exploding one at a time with soft pops. A bowl of chopped onions filled the air with tears. I got a cup of coffee and made room for it on the table between a bunch of celery and a stack of old *Gourmet* magazines.

It looked like Thanksgiving dinner was going to be an even bigger production than usual. I sat at the kitchen table for a few minutes, but Mom worked around me, first on one side and then the other. She didn't make conversation or even ask for help with the preparations, so I took my coffee back to my room, planning to study. But I couldn't concentrate. I kept imagining the dinner that evening.

Sharon would be bringing her boyfriend Sam Quinn, who none of us had met. All we knew about him was that he was a doctor at the hospital where she worked. Uncle Joseph and Aunt Ruth were coming—they had Thanksgiving dinner with us every year. And I'd invited Richard.

Impressions of his face came between me and the books. I smiled as I pictured him, gentle and serious. I thought of him trying to please his father and never making it, like me with Mom. Now that we were grown up, didn't that mean we got to start over with someone else, start over and please each other? I was sure I'd never hold back from Richard—I could give him what he needed.

I hummed a little of a favorite tune, "Song for the Asking." That was what I felt, that I'd been waiting all my life for someone like Richard. I'd always offered people love, but he was the only one who would put out his hand and take it. So simple, but he was the only one.

Mom's voice broke into my thoughts.

"Kathy," she called.

I got up and went to the kitchen. "Yes?"

"Get the centerpiece, would you?"

The china turkey, our Thanksgiving centerpiece for as long as I could remember, was kept on a high shelf. I pulled out the step stool and climbed up to get it. Mom hovered, fretting that I'd break it, so I handed it down to her.

"Okay?" I asked, before I let go.

"Yes." She smiled at my carefulness. "Could you wash it for me, please? It's pretty dusty."

I climbed down and took the turkey back. Mom handed me a plastic dishpan so it wouldn't get chipped in the sink. I ran hot water into the pan and squeezed in dishwashing liquid, watching dust dissolve from the bird's colorful plumage. A few bubbles drifted up, reminding me how I'd loved blowing rainbow soap bubbles when I was little. I realized Mom must have bought me the bubble stuff. I imagined her in the market, stopping her cart, tucking the toy in with the groceries. Did she smile, anticipating my fun?

Maybe if I explained now, she'd understand. If she'd give Richard a chance, she'd see he's a good person.

I was so nervous, I didn't know if I could even talk. But I decided to say it as best I could. I glanced up, expecting to see her still smiling, but she was peering into the oven with a harassed expression.

Maybe another time.

After lunch, I peeled chestnuts and sliced green beans. A tent of noisy rain enveloped the house. Dad and I went out to the carport for an armload of firewood. Some of the wood was damp, so we used some fat pine and a few cones to get it going. The house began to smell like Thanksgiving, the scent of roasting turkey blending with a whiff of smoke from the fireplace.

Dad and I sat on the carpet in front of the hearth and played blackjack for matchsticks, the way he'd taught me when I was having trouble with arithmetic in grade school. He brought out the nut bowl, a cast-iron piece with a squirrel-shaped nutcracker attached. When I was little, I'd named the squirrel Harry. Or maybe Hairy, because he wasn't. When I was ten, that had been hilarious.

"Here's Hairy. Fuzzy Wuzzy wuzza bear," he reminded me.

I gave him the smile he expected. Hairy made me think of the time when Dad and I could talk to each other. I started picking through the nuts, looking for the ones I liked. Hazelnuts, then pecans.

"You always grab the hazelnuts," Dad mock-complained. "What have you got against Brazils?"

"They taste like oil-soaked sawdust." *Even if they were good, I couldn't eat one. Uncle Joseph always calls them "niggertoes." I hope he won't say that today. Every time I see a Brazil nut, I feel ashamed. As if it were me who'd said the word.*

Besides, Brazil nuts don't look like toes at all. Not anyone's, certainly not a black person's. Richard's aren't shaped like that, and his feet are white along the soles, like the palms of his hands.

As we lay together that first afternoon at his apartment, I ran my finger along his hands where the white side met the brown.

"Do you know how we got white hands and feet?" he asked.

"No."

"Once upon a time," he began in a singsong storytelling voice, "all the people were black. But one day, a man came home from hunting, and he had white skin and a strange story. He had found a lake off in the hills that had turned his skin white.

"The people asked him to show them. So, he led the way, and they found the little lake, back there in the woods where no one had ever been before.

"Now, some of those people were greedy, and they pushed and shoved to get to the water first. By the time the others got their turn, there was just enough mud in the lake bed for them to dampen the bottoms of their feet and the palms of their hands. But all the mean people, the greedy people, the ones who shoved, they were white all over."

"Richard?"

"Mmmm?"

"Where did that story come from?"

"I don't know. I learned it from my grandfather."

"Why is it fair for you to talk about white people like we were all the same, but it's wrong if it's the other way around?"

He stroked my back silently for a while.

"I don't know," he said. "It feels different. But maybe everyone who puts a straw on the camel thinks their own straw is different too. Let's try to be you and me, if we're going to be lovers. We won't be your people and my people, just you and me. Promise?"

"Promise."

He stroked my back and shoulder a while longer. I was half asleep when he said, "I had no idea it was your first time."

I was about to tell him it didn't matter, but I fell all the way asleep before I could say it.

"Penny for your thoughts?" asked Dad.

"No sale." I pulled my mind back to the present. "They're worth at least two. More than you can afford."

"Ha. In that case I'll have to win all the rest of your matchsticks."

"Not a chance."

We played for a while longer. "Dad?"

"Mmmm?"

I felt nervous about asking him, too, but I made myself go on this time. "Do you mind about Richard?"

"He's a nice young man," he answered. "We didn't raise you and Sharon to be prejudiced." But he looked into the fire as he said it, not at me.

"Does Mom mind?" I asked.

The doorbell rang. I ran and let Aunt Ruth and Uncle Joseph in out of the rain. Right away, Aunt Ruth looked all around the living room and craned her neck to peer through the arch into the dining room. She'd never done that before. Whatever she expected to see, though, no one was there but Mom, opening the gate-legged dining table out to its full, awkward length. She glanced up from struggling with it.

"Come make yourself useful, Kathy. Come on in, Ruth. Take off your coat and stay awhile."

Mom flicked a linen cloth out and smoothed it over the table like she was making a bed. She arranged candles around the china turkey centerpiece, and I set the table—china, silverware, and wineglasses.

Aunt Ruth went into the kitchen and came out wearing Mom's extra apron. We fetched the cold food from the refrigerator and arranged it like a magazine picture—salad, cranberry sauce, bread sticks, olives, and pickles. Dad opened two bottles of burgundy and put them next to the salad.

The door opened, and Sharon came in with Sam, a sweet-faced, redheaded man who carried a dripping cone of red roses and a bottle of champagne. While Sharon was introducing him around, the doorbell rang again. I opened the door to Richard and a spatter of rain. The wind pushed in ahead of him as he hesitated on the porch.

He was carrying more flowers, white carnations. His face was just as I'd imagined it when I was studying, except that a few raindrops clung to his cheeks. I reached up and brushed them off before I led him into the dining room.

Mom and Dad greeted Richard. The others took turns shaking his hand while I introduced him. They looked him over.

What they saw was a tall young man in a gray suit a few years out of style. His shirt was white. His narrow tie was navy blue. His skin was brown. He stood almost at attention, but his face was open and vulnerable, like a kid who's hoping he won't be chosen last for the team.

"Pleased to meet you," said my uncle. "You a student at Southern?"

"No, LSU. Kathy and I have a class together."

Uncle Joseph frowned a little. He'd said more than once that the black students ought to stay over at Southern. But he just asked, "What's your major?" the way he would ask any student.

"Engineering."

What did you expect, a rock musician? You can relax. He's a professional man. Like Sam.

I took the flowers into the kitchen to put in a bowl for the sideboard. As I was arranging them, Richard's and Sam's together, the rain hammered against the window as the wind turned to the north. I heard a crash as one of our loose shutters banged against the house.

Someone in the dining room cried out, and I rushed in to see what was wrong. One leaf of the table was collapsing, and dishes were falling on the floor like an avalanche. Sam grabbed the leaf and wrestled it back into place. Then Richard came crawling out from under the table. Sam reached down and helped him stand.

Uncle Joseph, Aunt Ruth, Mom, and Dad stood as still as automatons in a power failure. I was afraid someone would laugh, but the only sound was from a bottle of wine gurgling a dark stain onto the carpet.

Sam's eyes were sad as he faced Richard's humiliation.

"'Nam?" he asked.

Richard nodded and turned away.

I took his hand and led him toward the bathroom so he could clean the salad and cranberry sauce off his suit. As we left, I saw Sharon bending to pick shards of the china turkey out of the mess.

After Richard shut the bathroom door, I went back to the dining room, but I hesitated near the doorway. Sam stood near the fireplace, while Uncle Joseph faced him from a few feet away.

"What in hell was that about?" demanded my uncle.

"Vietnam," said Sam.

"What do you mean, 'Vietnam'?"

"In battle, you learn to dive for cover when you hear loud noises. Some people unlearn it slower than others."

"Well, that's no excuse! Not everyone who went to Vietnam acts like that!" Uncle Joseph took a step toward Sam.

Sam didn't back up and didn't raise his voice. "Certainly not my brother. He doesn't act *any* way anymore. He died at Khe Sanh."

"I'm sorry to hear it," my uncle said. "But that boy didn't have any reason to turn the table over!"

"Were you ever on a battlefield? You go to Korea?"

"No. I was too young."

"You were lucky you never had to go to war."

"So?"

"Looks like the war's come to *you* now, doesn't it?" Sam's voice was cold.

Uncle Joseph abruptly turned away. He plunked himself on the couch and grabbed a magazine. Flipping through pages too quickly to read, he ignored Sam. There wasn't anything he could say—Sam had hit the nail on the head. Dad didn't speak up either. He'd had rheumatic fever when he was little, so he'd never even had to think about the draft.

When Richard returned, his apologies were politely brushed aside and talk turned to a plane hijacking—last week's news. The conversation sounded like an amateur play. Mom brought the turkey and the other hot food from the kitchen, and we gathered around the table. I was nearly in tears. Richard sat silent beside me in his stained suit, his face smiling and closed. I hoped no one else noticed he was trembling. We all bowed our heads for Dad to say grace.

"Bless, O Lord, this food to our use and us to thy service, and make us ever mindful of the needs of others. We ask in Jesus's name. Amen."

❧ 8 ❧
December 1974, San Pedro
Lacey

"I WOULD NEVER GOSSIP about one of my tenants," said Marilu Collins. Her bracelets clanked as she shuffled the cards. She had a slithery gold cloth draped over the counter, and a couple of scented candles burning. I didn't know what she meant by "one of my tenants." Kathy was the only tenant she had.

"Of course not," I assured her. Marilu wouldn't gossip—except six days a week and double on Sundays. "That's not the kind of thing I meant at all. I was thinking I'd like to call her family to get her sizes, maybe her favorite color or something. You know, for Christmas."

Anyone with a lick of sense would have seen right through this rigmarole. But I figured it was good enough for present company. I kept it sort of incoherent on purpose. At the very least, she'd cut me some slack because I was a customer. That was why I was "consulting" her—even Marilu might not have told me what I wanted to know if I'd turned up out of the blue, asking questions.

"Oh, does your company give Christmas presents?" Marilu's question caught me by surprise. Here she was, supposed to know all, and she didn't know Mr. Giannini was the biggest tightwad in town?

"No, they don't," I said. Maybe I'd get an Academy Award for this performance. I deserved one. "It's for a personal gift. I like Kathy."

"I do too," said Marilu. "I'm giving her a bead curtain for her apartment."

I hadn't seen Kathy's place, but I did not have her figured for the bead curtain type. I had to fight off the giggles at the idea. If Kathy lived in Marilu's building long enough, she'd be up to her eyebrows in wind chimes and incense burners. No way she could call the Sally Army to come get the junk, either, not with The Mystic Eye herself right downstairs. I made my face as blank as I could.

"That sounds cute. I know she'll love it. Anyway, do you have her folks' address?" I asked. I wasn't exactly being subtle, but Marilu didn't seem to catch on. She put the cards back down on the tablecloth. For the moment, she gave up on her attempt to get me into a mystical frame of mind.

"Well, I do check the mailboxes. Hers is right next to the shop's, and sometimes our mailman makes mistakes."

"Mine does too."

If you would go to hell for lying, my passage was about booked. I quit feeling silly—the air came out of that balloon fast. I hated to sneak, and every time I got involved with Kathy's life, I ended up doing it.

"Oh, they're awful," said Marilu. "I sent a package last month, organic herbs, and it arrived damaged. I had to send a replacement for free."

"I hope they don't mislay my Christmas packages." What a conversation. Now we were commiserating about the Post Office. Well, whatever it took. "Anyway, do you know her family's address?"

"I'll get it for you when I've finished your reading. Concentrate on your question now. You have to give respect to the cards."

I *was* concentrating—on keeping a straight face. Marilu laid out the cards in a cross pattern with another line of cards alongside it. She gazed at the bright pictures as fondly as if they were photos of her best friends.

"Here's your central theme, in the first two cards." She turned one over. "It's the justice card, reversed. You're doing an injustice, or you're worried about one. When they're upside down, they mean the opposite."

Good lord, and here I'd been sure this was something silly I was going along with so I could pump her for the address. But that was my big question in a nutshell: Was I doing a wrong or righting one?

"Here's the five of cups. That's regret, or disappointment."

I hoped I wasn't going to regret what I was doing this minute. But maybe the oracle, or whatever it was, could see Kathy's regrets. By now, I had no doubt she had a good-sized inventory of those. What a mess.

Marilu kept turning over cards, analyzing each one in turn. I could see meanings in some of them, not so much in others. It was like finding shapes in the clouds. Maybe they were there, maybe you made them up. I couldn't decide if Marilu's act was mumbo jumbo or not. I came away from the reading no wiser about the future than before, and with twice as much trouble in mind.

Because I came away with something else—an old address of Kathy's in Gretna, Louisiana. And with two more names and addresses: Sharon Woodbridge Quinn in Baton Rouge—I guessed she'd be Kathy's sister—and a Richard Johnson, care of Louisiana State Penitentiary in Angola.

❧ 9 ❧
November 1972, Baton Rouge
Kathy

A BLUE NORTHER COLD FRONT rode behind the winter rain. The morning after Thanksgiving, I woke to the clicking of the heating system. I was thirsty and headachy from sleeping too warm, so I padded to the kitchen to get a drink of water.

The rooms were closed-curtain dim, with slices of brightness where the sun sneaked in. The ashy smell of last night's fire was like the day after a disaster.

I wanted to talk to Richard, but he didn't have a phone. No classes today, either—I'd have to catch him at home. I dressed quickly and slipped out the back door.

A flash of sunlight caught me as I stepped off the porch. I sneezed. The north wind brought the stink of the paper mill in St. Francisville, the smell of winter. Remembering too late that my gloves were in my other jacket, I pushed my hands into my pockets and picked my way through the mud in the yard to my car, parked on the street.

Richard's neighborhood was like a ghost town—no strolling students, not even many cars parked along Chimes Street. Right across the street from campus was his building, the Ghetto. His apartment was at the far end.

When I knocked, a shadow passed across the pane of his door, and then I didn't see anything for a moment. I was sure he was home, so I knocked again. He cracked the door open and peered out.

"Come out and have breakfast with me," I said.

He stepped out onto the porch, pulling the door closed behind him. I pulled him into my arms and held him to me. After a second, he put his arms around me too, and we stood on the porch in the wind and the bright sun. We were so relieved to have each other back that it didn't occur to us that anyone might be looking.

"I feel like I'm hugging a teddy bear," he said, stepping back. "Come in and take off your coat."

"Let's go get something to eat. I'm starving."

"Come in and I'll fix you some teddy bear food." He laughed and pushed the door open. When we were inside, he shut it and locked it.

I took off my jacket and laid it on the bookcase. I was trying to be cool about the dinner party. *Where do I start? How do I say this?*

Since the kitchen corner was too small for both of us, I sat at the table while he fixed coffee and toast.

"Richard, last night . . . . Well, does that kind of thing happen often?" I started fiddling with some papers on the table, then jerked my hand back. *He'll think I'm prying.*

"Not anymore." He rummaged in a cabinet. "I guess I was nervous about the party, and the noise caught me by surprise."

He set the graniteware coffeepot and two unmatched cups on the table, then went back for the toast. He pulled a couple of paper towels off a roll and laid them carefully beside our places for napkins.

"Not any*more*? You mean you used to do stuff like that all the time?"

"Not every minute." His eyes evaded mine. "Too much, though."

I didn't know what to say next. I tried to cover up my confusion by turning my attention to my breakfast. But after we'd eaten in silence for a few minutes, that seemed worse.

Maybe Richard thought so too. He suddenly looked up from his plate and said, "I don't want to talk about the war."

I still couldn't think of a thing to say. Couldn't find decent words for what I needed to know: *Was it something you saw, or something you did?*

He seemed to read the question in my face. "Okay, if you really want to know, I'll tell you. I was in the artillery. I probably did a lot of damage—hell, I was *supposed* to do a lot of damage—but I never saw it up close. Sometimes I have nightmares where I see what my rounds really do. Sometimes I think I'll go to hell and have to look at that over and over, forever."

A picture exploded into my mind. *Oh, Jesus. Hieronymus Bosch with guns and uniforms.* I pushed it away. "Do you even believe in hell?"

"I was raised a Baptist—they sure believe in it. But I don't know what I believe anymore."

"I'm supposed to be an Episcopalian, but I don't either."

Richard got up and walked back to the kitchen corner, even though we had everything we needed. Then he turned quickly and faced me.

"Kathy, I swear to you, I wasn't another Calley. I hurt a lot of people. But I never did it for fun. I never did what I didn't have to do. I know that's not good enough. I have to live with that, and I know how feeble it sounds to a civilian."

The picture flashed around the edge of my imagination again. I made my mind go blank as I looked into Richard's face. "It doesn't sound feeble to me. If Dad's friends don't have to apologize about World War II, why should it be different for you?"

He turned away, abandoning his unfinished breakfast, letting it get cold. "What if I act like a fool again? You don't have to put up with scenes like that. You may think now that you *can* put up with them, but that won't last." Without a glance my way, he walked to the door and unlocked it.

If this was a hint for me to go, I wasn't taking it. I waited.

He stood for a moment, hand on the doorknob. Then he faced me again.

"Kathy, there's plenty of draft dodgers out there who'll fit into your dinner parties just fine. Why don't you find yourself one?"

I didn't move. "I don't want them. I want you."

He hesitated and then crossed to the bed at the back of the apartment and pulled an imaginary wrinkle out of the bedspread. "What if I freak out again in front of your family?" he asked, glancing sharply at me.

"I don't care," I said. I left my coffee and went to him, pulling him into an awkward hug. "If they believe in peace, if it's not some empty word, let them quit judging everyone. That would be real peaceful."

He drew a deep breath, hoarse and ragged-sounding. Then he relaxed. "It would be a good start," he said. "We're going to have to start there too. Let me show you what I was reading this morning." He sat on the side of the bed and picked up a chipped old book lying facedown near the pillow.

He fanned through it, showing me photographs of country people in worn-out clothes. Beautiful pictures, clear and stark. We sat sideways on the bed, backs propped against the wall, while he read aloud about poor whites in the Depression in

Alabama. About how their neighbors hated them for being different. Both of us knew that these same sad people would have been the first to turn on their black neighbors, on people like Richard's grandfather, farming behind those mules. As Richard read, his voice was shaky.

When he stopped reading, we lay quietly together. The room had only been heated by his cooking, and it grew cold in the silence. We got under the blankets and warmed ourselves with them, and then with each other.

☙

MOM LOOKED UP from fixing sandwiches as I closed the kitchen door behind me. The table was covered with leftovers, the turkey from last night, still intact in places, but with a keel of breastbone emerging. The dark meat was gone from one side, too. She opened a can of cranberry sauce to replace the beautiful sauce she'd made yesterday, the sauce that was ruined when Richard crashed into the table.

"Where were you?" she asked.

"I went to talk to Richard."

"Oh. How is he?" She pulled a slicer out of the knife rack and studied its edge.

"Embarrassed. Upset." I counted out enough slices of bread for Mom, Dad, and me.

"Hand me that sharpener, would you?" She gestured toward the knife sharpener, just out of reach. I passed it to her.

"I'd imagine he *would* be upset," she went on. "How long has he been out of the army, anyway?"

"I'm not sure. A year or so." I watched her hone the knife with an expert air. Any live turkey in its right mind would have gotten out of there in a hurry.

"Isn't it time he got over the war?" She tried to slice the turkey but the knife still wasn't right. She frowned at it. Or maybe that frown was for Richard and me.

"I think he is, mostly. He was nervous about meeting everyone last night, and then the bang sort of took him by surprise."

"*Mostly?* How long does it take?" She hacked at the turkey, then slammed the knife down on the counter with a disgusted expression.

"Everyone's different, I guess. You can't set a timetable."

"Is he seeing someone about it?"

"I'm sure he knows the VA and the Student Health Service are there."

"They won't do much. Why not someone private?"

"He's going to school on the GI bill, Mom. He can't afford a therapist."

"Why don't his parents pay?" She opened the refrigerator, and shut it hard without putting anything in or taking anything out.

"They're mad at him about the war."

"But they're army, aren't they? Why would they be mad?"

"His dad wanted him to be an officer. When he enlisted as a private, it was a sort of a slap in the face for his father. They don't talk too much anymore."

"I don't understand. If his son was a draft dodger, I'd get it. But just because he wasn't an officer?"

"Believe me, Mom, it matters. Especially since they're black."

I assembled some messy-looking sandwiches while Mom fussed with rewrapping the bread. She looked at that wrapper as if the answer to all Richard's problems might be printed on it, right next to the list of ingredients.

"Kathy, are you sure you want to get involved in this? I mean, he's a nice young man, but I don't know why you can't find someone with a little more in common. . . ." She broke off.

"I already am involved. I thought it was you and Dad who taught me to stick by my friends." *Did you mean white friends, Mom? Is that what you had in mind?*

"We want you to be happy. And I definitely think he should see a psychologist. Maybe you should too."

She grabbed the platter and draped parsley over the sandwiches. I didn't think it made them look much better, but I kept my mouth shut. She shoved the dish at me without another word. Then she left, turning in the doorway only to say, "I'm getting a headache. I don't think I want dinner after all. Take care of your dad, would you?"

☙

WITH THANKSGIVING BEHIND US, it was time to start studying for finals. My art classes were graded on projects, but I had tests for the academic classes, and tests scared me. And Richard, majoring in engineering, had a much more difficult exam period to look forward to. We both had a lot to do.

Neither of us wanted to spend much time apart. But trying to study at his place was no good—we needed to talk, to touch each other, to make love. We could only study if we went to the university library, separated by the table—even there, our eyes would meet, our fingertips lightly brush. Sometimes I'd steal a look at Richard as he studied. It was amazing how sexy he seemed when he was concentrating on his book. I stored those glimpses and took them out to savor at home, like cookies from a secret hoard.

I might catch Richard smiling a lover's smile into his book, or he might turn to me with a serious gaze, as if I were an engineering formula he needed to learn. He was unpredictable, moody. His face changed like a kaleidoscope, first one pattern, then another. Sometimes his eyes were luminous, like an agate in water. Then they'd turn dull as a dry pebble. *Sometimes he's not even here—he's back in Vietnam.*

But he was special and familiar, and all I wanted.

Other couples studied in the library, probably for reasons much the same as ours. They too glanced and touched and then turned back to books. Like them, we had "our" table. Like them, we barely looked beyond it. I stopped thinking everyone was staring.

But one day I had a creepy feeling that I'd never had before. When I looked up, it took a minute to find the reason: a guy in a green corduroy coat. He seemed young, maybe another student. He was half-hidden behind the stacks, but I realized he was watching us, not looking for a book. I wondered if he thought we couldn't see him. Then I wondered if he knew we could. My skin tightened with a fear so primitive, it astonished me. I forced myself to look away.

Richard seemed down that day, so I didn't mention what I'd seen. When I looked up again, the guy was gone.

The next day, Richard studied alone in the library while I took an English exam. We met late in the afternoon, and he didn't say anything about a man in a green coat or anyone else. He looked tired and discouraged.

I didn't keep Green Coat on my mind either. I had other problems: Aunt Ruth had called and invited us to Christmas dinner. All except Richard. Not, my aunt had hurried to add, because he was black. No, not at all. It was because of his dive under the table at Thanksgiving, nothing more.

"I'm not going if you can't," I told him.

"Hang on—I'm not so sure that's a good idea. If you don't, you'll make your whole family angry."

"So?"

"I don't think it's worth it. Do you? What if we could work it out gradually with them? Please go, Kathy. It's not worth getting into a family fight over just one evening."

"Sharon and Sam aren't going."

"That's their choice. I appreciate it, too. But let's give your family a chance to accept us, okay? Maybe all they need is a little time." He stared off down the quadrangle.

The scared feeling started to come back. "Do you see someone you know?"

"I guess not." He looked wary. *Maybe school is getting to him. Maybe it's my family. Or maybe he saw someone in a dark coat that could have been green corduroy, about fifty feet away. That's what I think I saw, but I'm not sure.*

I reached out to hug him and then remembered the long walk down the hill to the parking lot. I wondered if the man in the green coat would be watching me from the shadows.

I drove home so wrapped up in my problems, it's a good thing no one got in my way.

In the kitchen, Mom looked up from pouring beef stew into a tureen. She pointed the spoon handle at a pot on the stove. "See if the rice is done," she said. "It better be. I don't want this to get cold. Sharon and Sam are coming."

I bit a grain of rice to test it for doneness. It was soft, so I fetched a bowl and ladled it in. The table was already set. As I found a serving spoon, Sharon and Sam arrived. I called to Dad that dinner was on the table.

"Why aren't you going to your aunt's party?" asked Mom as soon as we all sat down.

Sharon fussed with the bread basket. "Because Richard wasn't invited. We didn't think it was right."

"Ruth and Joseph didn't care for him. I mean, ducking under the table . . . ." Mom ladled stew onto Dad's plate and reached for Sam's.

"If you'd invited him half a dozen times, and he did something weird every time, they might have a point," Sharon said. "But isn't just once a bit extreme? Even in baseball, you get three strikes before you're out."

"Ruth and Joseph have a right to decide their own guest list," Mom said. Her tone was final and—I thought—satisfied.

Sharon wasn't buying it. "The guests have a right to send regrets, too," she said. "We don't think they're telling the whole story about why he's not invited." Her face was red and her voice was high and angry.

Dad glanced at Mom, Mom glared at Sharon. Sam looked down at his plate. No one looked my way. It was probably just as well. The more I thought about the party, the angrier I got.

Aunt Ruth used to understand me better than Mom did. Like the time I bought that bathing suit. The one with ruffles on the front so I could pretend I had breasts. Mom laughed at me, but Aunt Ruth said it was pretty.

I used to tell her secrets, things I wouldn't tell Mom. Boys I liked, and how I spent most of the Junior Prom in the ladies' room, afraid no one would ask me to dance. She always told me it would all work out. She must have thought I'd grow up to be like her. Well, no thanks, Benedict-Arnold-Judas-Iscariot-Aunt-Ruth.

My heart started to pound, and my stomach heaved as I looked at the slippery chunks of beef and carrot on my plate. I was afraid to open my mouth.

Sam spoke up unexpectedly.

"Almost everyone has problems. If you limited your guest list to people who've never had any, you'd have some small parties."

"Did you specialize in psychiatry, Sam?" asked Dad.

Sam laughed. "No, I'm an oncologist. But the effects of stress play out in every medical specialty. I think it's a mistake to limit our friends to people who look like winners. Not to mention that putting someone down doesn't make me feel good."

"Well, I may agree," said Dad. "But I can't tell my sister-in-law who to invite to her Christmas party." His words echoed Mom's. *Dad? I can't believe you're saying this. You were always the one who told us segregation was wrong.*

"I guess I seem a bit pushy. You must think I'm the nerviest date Sharon's ever had," Sam said. "But I'm counting myself as family because we were planning to announce our engagement at this party."

A pink sunrise of happiness dawned on Mom's face. Even Dad, who seldom showed much emotion, looked pleased. I felt happy for Sharon. *They're perfect together.*

"So, why not come and announce it?" asked my dad.

"If I can say so without offense, that wouldn't be the way we'd want to start our marriage. We talked it over and decided to handle it informally, without a big to-do."

He slipped a small box from his pocket and opened it. Reaching around the dishes, he put his ring on Sharon's finger.

I wanted to hug them both. But I had a catch in my throat, too. *They're the way it's supposed to be. I'm not—and I don't know how to change that.*

❧ 10 ❧
December 1974, San Pedro
Lacey

IF I HADN'T BEEN SO WORRIED about that prison address, I might have given up, because it was no easy job to find Kathy's sister. There were fifteen Quinns in the public library's Baton Rouge phone book, all men's names except for a couple of listings that were just initials. I copied every last one. Over the next few days, I called thirteen of them, asking for Sharon. Finally I got the right one—Sam Quinn, M.D. A woman answered the phone. It was Sharon.

I had tried to plan what to say, but I was nervous anyway. If there ever was a fool rushing in where angels feared to tread, that fool's name was Lacey Greer.

I started by telling her who I was, and bumped up my importance at Giannini's—made myself sound like a real supervisor instead of the secretary. Then I trotted out the lie about Christmas presents again.

"She likes books," said Sharon. "She's never cared that much about clothes."

No surprise there. "What kind of books? Does she collect cookbooks?" I asked.

Sharon laughed. "No cookbooks, for sure. She likes poetry. And folktales. Plays. Oh, wait, maybe not. Better get something lighter. That might be best right now."

Well, here was the thin end of the wedge. "Oh, I'm sorry. Is something the matter? I thought she looked sort of sad."

"Our father passed away this fall."

"I'm so sorry. No wonder Kathy looks sad."

Sharon hesitated. I was afraid she might be thinking she didn't know me, and I didn't want that idea to get too big.

"I've been concerned about her. I have a daughter almost the same age as Kathy. I guess you never stop being a mom." I didn't add that my daughter had mentioned once or twice that maybe it was time for me to consider doing just that. "I'd like to help if I can. She's so far from home. Although she did live in Gretna for a while, didn't she? So, maybe she's used to being on her own."

"She wasn't exactly on her own," Sharon said. "She was living with friends."

Friends like maybe one Richard Johnson, currently domiciled in Angola at the expense of the State of Louisiana?

"Well, let me give you my address and phone number," I said. "Please do let me know if there's anything I can do. Oh, and please don't tell Kathy I called. It's a surprise."

I didn't want to push it too far the first time I talked to her. If I was right about Kathy, I figured Sharon would be calling me before too long.

❧ 11 ❧
December 1972, Baton Rouge
Kathy

ON THE NIGHT of Aunt Ruth's party, we wrapped ourselves in Christmas cheer as thin as the shiny paper around our packages. My aunt and uncle lived in one of the newer subdivisions, a few miles away from us. As Dad drove us to their house, I kept my mouth shut. I didn't want to ruin Christmas for everyone, but I was miserable—hurt, angry, and coming down with a cold.

Dad parked the car in front of their house, and I climbed out, surveying the yard with a bitter eye. It was the same every year: a mob of electric elves, Santas, and reindeer, topped off with a manger scene. *Did they ever notice that one of the Wise Men is black? Gee, there goes the neighborhood. I hope it makes the yardman laugh when he puts it up.*

We dragged our grocery bags of gifts out of the trunk and juggled them up the walk. Uncle Joseph let us in and went back to the kitchen for Aunt Ruth. While we waited in the hallway, I looked around, trying to see my aunt's house as if I were a stranger. Christmas knickknacks were everywhere. Aunt Ruth had always decorated the house to rival the Christmas issues of women's magazines. One year she even had holiday toilet paper.

I'd taken her decorations for granted when I was younger. Now I had some idea how much work she put into them. Even though I was furious with my aunt, it struck me for the first time:

She wanted kids, but she couldn't have any. Making Christmas a big production is probably the only way it can feel like a holiday at all. She sews one teddy bear after another to put on the mantel because she couldn't have a daughter to make one for.

I gave her a real hug when she came out of the kitchen, and then I remembered my cold. I drew back, confused.

She looked confused too, maybe even offended.

"Sorry," I said, "I'm coming down with a cold. Scared I'll give it to you."

Her face relaxed. "Hey, after Christmas, I wouldn't mind having a good reason to stay in bed for a while. Joe could wait on me!" We laughed. *Uncle Joseph is bringing her breakfast and the morning paper on a tray! The paper has a big headline: Pigs Fly.*

We hurried to join the others in the living room, where the ceiling-scraping artificial tree took up one whole corner and then some. The furniture crowded together and the presents spilled out around the tree. There were so many things, there was hardly any room for us.

Mom, Dad, and I pulled the gifts from our bags and added them to the heap. The gift wrap on the packages I'd brought looked more special than the things I knew were inside. I hoped no one would be disappointed. Probably not, since I gave them the same stuff every year. Aunt Ruth: a Christmas cookie cutter for her collection. Uncle Joseph: fishing flies. A pair of leather gloves for Mom. And for Dad, a gift certificate at the garden store, since he returned anything else he got.

I've always wished I knew what they wanted most and could surprise them with it, with that one magical thing, all unexpected. But I've never been able to guess what it is.

Except this year I do know. What they all want this year is a note that reads, "I will only date people you approve of, from now on.

Love, Kathy." Too bad. That's just what they're not getting. Richard is here to stay.

No one mentioned his name. The gifts were stripped and admired, supper was eaten, the men talked sports, and the women washed the dishes. After a TV special, Christmas was all over for another year.

Next morning I woke at dawn with my cold in miserable full bloom. I could hardly breathe, and I imagined my throat was like hamburger swirling out of the grinder in a butcher shop. I got up and rummaged in the bathroom cabinet for antihistamines left over from the last time someone had been sick, and washed them down with water from the faucet. Then I went back to bed and slept till midmorning.

Dad woke me, knocking at the door and peering in.

"Phone for you," he said. "It's Richard. Oh, Kathy, you look sick. Do you want me to tell him you'll call back?"

"He doesn't have a phone," I rasped, trying to look like I felt better than I did. "Tell him I'll be there in a minute."

I drank a little water to make my voice sound better. Then I put on a robe, stuffed tissues in the pocket, and trailed into the living room where the phone was.

"Hello?" I rasped.

"Uh-oh. I was going to ask how you are, but I guess I don't need to."

"I sound that bad?"

"Worse. It doesn't sound like you'd want to get together today."

"It's not a case of want. I don't think I can go anywhere. Could you come over here?"

"I think I'll wait. Why don't I give you a call tomorrow, and see how you are?"

"Okay." What I wanted to say was, "I love you. I want to spend the day in your bed." But even if I didn't sound like a fairy tale in reverse, the princess who turned into a frog, I was on the living room phone, and Mom could hear every word.

"I have a present for you," Richard said, "You can spend the day imagining what it is."

"I have one for you, too."

"See you tomorrow, then, love. Get better."

I hung up the phone and went back to bed. But I was even sicker the next morning, and for several days I had laryngitis and could barely whisper. Richard called every day and talked to me for a few minutes, a monologue that would start with the weather and finish with how much he loved me, how much he wanted to see me. But even with a good excuse to whisper on the living room phone, I couldn't tell him that he was the only person I wanted to be with anymore. Even the day Mom and Dad went to the sales, and I was all alone, I couldn't say it, not in my parents' house.

I didn't get a chance to see him again until the afternoon of New Year's Day. I left Dad and Uncle Joseph watching football, Mom already starting dinner. Aunt Ruth, down with my cold, had stayed home. I told Dad I was going out for a while, and drove to East Chimes Street.

Once again, the neighborhood looked almost deserted. I supposed everyone else was watching the game. Richard, who didn't like sports any more than I did, was happy to walk around campus with me.

I was still sniffling a bit, and I got tired quicker than I expected. It was warm for January, and not windy, so we sat on a bench in the sun.

"I missed you this week," he said.

I felt a little flare of happiness. "I hope you got a lot of studying done," I said.

"That was the silver lining." He looked up as the campanile interrupted to chime the quarter hour, dee-dah-dee-DAH. "How was Christmas?"

"Dull. I hope I'm not like that when I'm older."

"Like what?"

"Closed. Doing the same thing every year. Doing the same thing every *day.*"

"If you want something different, you're sure to find it." *He said "you," not "we."* My happiness evaporated.

I kept my tone light. "Is that the Sibyl's pronouncement for 1973?"

"It is." His face sparkled with one of his all-over smiles, and I felt better. "I have your present. Happy New Year, love." He gave me a package that looked as if a six-year-old had wrapped it. I took the paper off tenderly—I couldn't stand to tear it. I opened the box.

A fine silver chain with a single pearl pendant. Now I could have something from Richard with me all the time. Something secret, against my skin. He fastened it carefully around my neck.

"I love it," I said. "I brought yours, but it's in the car."

"Let's go get it—I can't wait."

We walked back to the car, and I watched anxiously as he unwrapped the book I'd bought him. *Will you like it?* But he smiled when he saw what it was.

"Oh, Eliot. I love Eliot. Thank you, sweetheart." He kissed me, and I hoped I didn't taste too much like cough drops.

"Sharon and Sam got engaged for Christmas," I told him.

"Hey, that's great. Tell them congratulations from me."

We wound our way back to his apartment, hand in hand. I hoped the man in the green coat was home watching the game.

As we trailed up the balcony to his apartment, a red tabby kitten ran out, squeaking. Richard picked it up.

"Is it yours?" I asked.

"It's a stray. I feed it when it comes around, though." The squeaking turned to squalling. He scratched the kitten's head and put it down. It followed us into the apartment, and Richard poured a dish of milk for it.

"What's its name?" I said.

"I don't know. It's not mine."

"It has other ideas. What's your name?" I asked the kitten. It looked up from the dish and mewed.

"*Mew* it is. What else do you feed it?"

"Scraps."

I stroked its head as it went back to lapping up the milk. He looked at the kitten ruefully. "I was hoping we'd make love."

"I don't feel good right now," I said. "Could you hold me for a while?"

We stretched out on his bed, and Mew curled up in the crook of my arm. We kept each other warm, knowing that the next time would be exciting, but now, for once, just touching, just holding. The kitten purred. We all fell asleep.

When I finally drove away from Richard's apartment building, the evening star was coming clear in a sky like a stained-glass window. I didn't want to go. The house in Magnolia Woods would be bright and warm, filled with the smells of cooking. But I didn't feel I was headed home this time. Home was the apartment, or wherever Richard happened to be. Home was behind me. I was going to visit my parents.

Richard's pearl was smooth against my skin, smooth and cool. In my happiness over his beautiful gift, I brushed aside the old wives' tale that pearls mean tears to come.

෴

THE ATMOSPHERE AT HOME was lighter, now that the holidays were over. The house began to be filled with Dad's gardening catalogs, his midwinter dreams—a part of the year I loved.

He had almost decided to put in the asparagus bed he'd been wanting for several years. It was a big project, since our heavy clay soil all had to be dug out and replaced with sand. He couldn't do that kind of work himself, so he'd have to hire someone.

And he'd plant tomatoes, of course, and herbs. New varieties of tomato had to be considered, the bright pictures in the catalogs compared with memories of the summer before. He'd found a place out on Highland Road that sold native azaleas, delicate and fragrant. He'd have to plant them early, though, and this meant making up his mind with less backtracking than usual.

Planning for good meals to come, for the fragrance of tomato vines and herbs on still summer afternoons, felt much more festive than Christmas. Dad sat each night in the living room, surrounded by pictures of rose arbors, tulip beds, and prize vegetables. I had always helped him with the garden, from planning to harvest. But this year, I couldn't get into it. This year, I only wanted to be with Richard.

I saw the guy in the green coat somewhere almost every day, watching from around a corner in the Union or down a library aisle. He was almost always there, half-hidden, staring at us. He never spoke.

Once, I tried to stare him down. Without breaking his gaze for a second, he raised one hand and pointed his finger in imitation of a gun, the way little boys do when they're playing cowboy. It should have been ridiculous, but my mouth went dry, and I looked quickly away.

One day when we were having lunch off campus, I asked Richard if he'd seen the man.

"Oh, yes," said Richard, buttering a piece of bread.

"You don't sound too worried."

"I'm not—not a lot. Has he ever done anything but look?"

"No, but it's weird. I'm starting to imagine he's there even when I can't see him. He gives me chills."

"I don't see what we could do about it."

"Maybe we should complain to campus security," I said.

"About what? All he's doing is walking around the campus at the same time we are."

"He's doing a lot more than walking around the campus. He's harassing us. We could complain about that."

"You think campus security would listen to *us*?"

"Maybe we should quit hanging around so much. We could study at my parents' house, or else at your place."

"I don't think either one is going to work. Even if it weren't a problem for me to get to your house, I don't think your mom wants to see that much of me. And we already tried my place, remember?"

"We could try again."

He shook his head. "It wouldn't work. Besides, he probably knows where I live. He could watch the door from that fig tree behind the building."

"So, what do we do?" The idea of Green Coat lurking behind the apartment gave me chills.

"Ignore him. He'll get bored."

"Why don't we transfer to LSUNO next year? People in New Orleans aren't like this."

"It would be more expensive for you if you weren't living at home," Richard said.

"About the same for you, though. I'll get a job or a loan or something. We can't stay here—even if that guy does get bored, there's more just like him."

"Not many."

I knew he was wrong about that. There was an area to one side of the Union where students were allowed to make speeches to anyone who'd listen. The ones who preached racism from their soap boxes were a minority, but there were more than a few. "There are dozens of them. I've quit walking past the Free Speech Alley because they make me mad. Any one of them could be the next one to follow us around. Or worse."

"Well, I guess I *would* rather live in New Orleans anyway. Maybe next year."

That was all he would say about it. Maybe someday, maybe some—other—day. But I was worried about Green Coat, and about Richard—and I was starting to worry about next year. I'd been using birth control foam from the drugstore, a brand that claimed to be "98% effective." Who expects to be part of a minority of 2 percent?

One day in January, after the start of the new semester, we went to lunch at a pizza place downtown. The restaurant was dark and salty smelling, cheese and pepperoni. While we waited for our pizza, we ate peanuts and drank Cokes. I did a quick mood check on Richard—he looked relaxed enough for me to bring up something serious, so I took a deep breath, my heart pounding. *I have no idea how to say this, but I'd better tell him something.*

But I missed my moment—he spoke first. "I think I'm going to change my major."

Can't tell him now. I felt almost as relieved as if I'd just gotten my period. "Why? You never said you didn't like engineering."

"I guess I started in engineering because that's what my father always wanted. But I don't fit in over there. It's not grades. I'm just not the type."

"I thought you liked it."

"I do, but I'm not crazy about engineers. They're mostly people who'd rather deal with things than people."

"So, what do you want to major in?"

"I don't know. Maybe government or law, somewhere I might make a difference. . . . I don't know. . . . I'm probably talking crazy."

"Maybe psych?"

"If I went into psych, maybe I could do something to help other veterans. God knows, I have enough problems—moods, nightmares—but I'm pretty mild, considering. Or even in law, maybe I could do something. Lots of those guys get into all kinds of trouble."

"I didn't know you had nightmares."

"Kathy, I don't want to dump all that stuff on you. I don't want to be some invalid you feel sorry for."

"Damn it, Richard, that's the last thing on my mind."

The waiter came with the pizza. Talk got lost for the moment in hot olives and stringy cheese.

As we ate, I watched Richard in the dim light of the restaurant. *He's happy now—his face is sweet and open. I want to trail my fingers over his soft hair and smooth face. Why is it so sexy, the way he's turned his shirt cuffs back? His wrists and hands. . . . I can tell him at his place, after we make love—that's better.*

He caught my eye and smiled. "Want to go to my place after lunch?"

I nodded. We paid quickly and left. Chimes Street was half dug up and full of yellow construction trucks, so I parked around the corner. As we walked to the apartment, I could only think of holding Richard, loving him. But when he stopped short a few feet from his door, I came out of my dream.

Against the gray of the building were two bright spots. One, on the wall by the door, was a bright red swastika. The other, an orange lump right in front of the door, was Mew. His head was cut off, lying on the porch beside him.

I turned and ran. When I reached the corner of the building, I realized Richard wasn't behind me. I looked back—he was standing frozen at the door.

"Richard!"

He looked at me for a second as if he had no idea who I was. Then he walked slowly toward me. I wanted to scream with fear and impatience.

Green Coat is somewhere, watching this.

I grabbed his hand and jerked him along University Avenue and around the corner to my parking place. I didn't know what else to do, so I drove us to my parents' house. Richard looked out the side window all the way there, as if he were interested in the scenery. He laid his hands on his knees, but they wouldn't stay still—once I saw him clasp them together, but when he laid them back on his lap, they started shaking again. I couldn't think of anything to say to comfort him—I wanted *him* to take care of *me*.

When we got home, I sobbed out the story. Mom got up and left the room without a word. Dad called the police. They told him there was nothing they could do.

"Nothing they *will* do is more like it," he added as he told us what they'd said. "I'm sorry, Richard."

"Yes, sir."

"Richard . . . ." Dad ran his hand over his face like he had a headache. "I don't want to be rude, but I wish you wouldn't call me 'sir.'"

"I'm sorry, Dr. Woodbridge. I didn't mean it that way. It's just a habit from the army."

"Not your fault. Richard, why don't you stay in the guest room here tonight? You can't go back there. We'll think of something in the morning." Dad didn't look like he expected a solution then or anytime. He tried to smile, to be a good host. He looked kind of like a gargoyle.

After dinner, Richard and I sat in the living room while Dad moved quietly around in the kitchen. I was too keyed up to go to bed.

Richard found the morning paper in a basket by the couch and scanned the front-page section. As if the news was important. *I don't believe this. He isn't even taking me seriously now.* "He'll be back—he'll do something else."

"What if he does? Now that I'm on my guard, I don't think a teenage redneck can do much to me."

"There's fifty more like him, especially if you get into a fight. Don't get all macho on me. I'm sure you've heard the white supremacist types ranting every chance they get."

"Who hasn't? I've seen other students shout them down, too. I doubt many people would go along with them. Fifty is a wild exaggeration."

"It doesn't take fifty. Two or three is enough to get us killed."

"Aren't you being a little dramatic?" He opened the paper, dismissing my concern with the flick of its pages.

"I think having Mew's head cut off was a little dramatic too." *Jesus. . . . What would these guys do to me when I started looking pregnant? What would they do to a baby?* I started crying again. "I'd be afraid to visit you, wondering who was hiding in the bushes."

He put his arms around me, but I just cried more. "I want to get out of here," I said, when I finally got my breath. "Let's go to New Orleans now. I can't stand this."

"We'd have to drop out of school."

"We can start up again in the fall at NO. Richard, *please*. Maybe this guy doesn't scare you. But what makes you think it's you he's after? He and his buddies could just as easily attack me. I'm afraid all the time—even when I don't see him, I'm sure he's hiding somewhere. Please let's go to New Orleans."

Dad came into the room. From the kitchen, he'd heard every word.

"Kathy, the two of you have to face facts," he said. "Your relationship has some risks. Anywhere. Much as I like you personally, Richard."

Richard folded the newspaper neatly and stood up. "Thanks, Dr. Woodbridge. I think I'll say good night now. I should let you and Kathy talk this over in private." He went back toward the guest room, and I heard the door shut softly.

Dad turned to me. That was when he tried to persuade me that the time hadn't come yet when Richard and I could live together without being afraid. Maybe I should have listened, but he said his piece and I said mine, and in the end, I went to my room and slammed the door behind me.

In the morning, Sharon and Sam came over. Dad went to the garden shed and got a shovel. *They're going to bury Mew. Under the fig tree, where he liked to lie in the shade.*

I pulled Richard aside just inside the back door.

"I'm going to New Orleans," I whispered. "Richard, I'm pregnant. I can't stay here. Please come with me."

His eyes went as blank as Little Orphan Annie's.

"Ready, Richard?" Dad called from the carport. Without a word, Richard turned and left.

When they came back, they had Richard's clothes and books. I gathered my own things, and we packed my Volkswagen solid. Sharon offered to give us some of her household stuff, but there wasn't any more room in the car.

Dad shook his head, but he pushed some money into my hand. I tried to give it back, but he wouldn't take it. Sam, Sharon, and Dad watched us drive away, waving as if everything were all right. Mom didn't even come out to say good-bye.

It hadn't seemed like a good time to announce the baby.

Part 3

❧ 12 ❧
February 1973, New Orleans
Kathy

ONCE WE GOT SETTLED in New Orleans, we started to relax. Maybe we would have been out of place in the suburbs, but the French Quarter was full of all kinds of people: artists, dropouts, sailors on shore leave, even a few leftover hippies. Besides the transients, there were old-time residents of New Orleans, small tradesmen mostly, whose families had kept the same shops and stands for years.

I went to work for one of them, Eddie Graziano. He had a produce stand in the French Market. He sold the best of everything. Some of the vegetables were real homegrown, from his cousins' truck farm in Mississippi. Even when he bought at the wholesale market, he was fussy about quality. He wouldn't let me buy, just weigh and bag and make change.

For his regulars, he still observed the custom of *lagniappe*, "a little something extra." It was a sort of bonus—if you bought your beans from Eddie, he'd throw in the herbs to cook them with.

The stand was on the sidewalk, right in the arcade of the market. I perched on a wooden stool when there wasn't any business, but I didn't get to do it much. Eddie had a constant stream of customers and friends, and a lot of people who were both.

"No to*mah*toes, Eddie?" complained a blue-rinsed lady with a shivering black toy poodle.

"Lucille, it's February. The tomatoes all taste like papier-mâché. I can't be giving you that kind of junk. I'd just as soon shut up the stand and go home."

She sighed in agreement. "What about alligator pears?"

Eddie glanced at me, but I knew that was the local word for avocados. We had some good Hass ones from California, and I helped her choose the closest to ripe. Eddie tucked a bunch of thyme into the bag and glanced at the dog. "Better put Midnight's coat on him or take him home," he advised her. "I think it's coming on to rain."

"You're a fussbudget, Eddie. You've been a fussbudget for more years than I care to count." She laughed, but she swooped the dog up into the mink crook of her arm.

As I watched her tapping along down the street in her spike heels, I hoped she could manage to hold onto Midnight and her sack of vegetables both.

Eddie smiled at me, and I tried to smile back. I didn't feel well—I'd come to work almost as tired as I'd been when I left the day before. I felt queasy, too—the fumes of Eddie's kerosene heater cut through the coffee scent from the Morning Call and the clay smell of the river. Gusts of wind added a sharp whiff of the fish market along the way. I breathed shallowly and tried not to think about it.

A tall man in a trench coat jaywalked toward us across Chartres, waving to Eddie. He came into the arcade, and Eddie shook his hand. The man glanced at me.

"Got a new girlfriend, Eddie?" he asked.

"Naw, this is Kathy," said Eddie. "Kathy's got too much class to be my girlfriend."

"Not surprising," said the man. "Most any girl does."

Eddie mock-punched him on the shoulder. "Kathy, this is Buddy. You've got too much class to be *his* girlfriend, too, so don't give him a chance."

Buddy picked out some satsumas, and I weighed them for him. Eddie threw in a spray of kumquats.

Richard appeared in the arcade. "*There's* my boyfriend," I said. I introduced them.

"How ya doin'?" said Eddie. "You want to take a break, Kathy?"

"Just a few minutes to get a cup of coffee."

"You go ahead. I'll mind the stand. Good to meet you," he added in Richard's direction.

We walked past a praline store, where the plywood mammy sign made me cringe. In the Café Du Monde, we sat outside on iron chairs, leaning out of the waiter's way as he plunked down our coffee and beignets.

"How's the job going?" Richard asked, pocketing his change.

"Fine, I like Eddie." I pulled my jacket a little tighter around me and quickly sipped the coffee to warm me up.

"I got one today," Richard smiled, but his face still looked strained and unhappy.

"A job? Where?"

"Store fixture place. I do the hardware."

It didn't sound interesting to me. I couldn't think of anything to say about the job. We were both quiet for a while, sipping coffee.

"Listen, Kathy," Richard said. "I did the best I could, but I'm not making much money. There just aren't any good jobs for high school graduates. And we can't bring up a baby in a rooming house. How in hell are we going to afford to live?"

I checked the people at the next table. They didn't seem to be paying attention.

"I'm not going to talk about it." I cut him off, sick and empty. *He's hinting at an abortion. He doesn't want our child. Maybe he doesn't want me either, anymore.*

The waiter brushed past us to take an order from another table. Richard ran his hand over his face, leaving a smear of powdered sugar on his chin. He leaned toward me, keeping his voice low.

"Kathy, you don't have the slightest idea about being a mother. Much less the mother of a black baby," Richard said. "Think it over. You know you don't have to keep it."

"I can't believe you want me to get an abortion because our baby is black." I turned away from him.

"It's not because the baby is black. It's because you don't know what you're getting into." He raised his voice as a bus roared by, and a group on the sidewalk peered our way.

I looked at them, then sharply at him to warn him to keep his voice down. "That's what my mother said about you and me. I never thought you'd be singing the same tune."

"That's another thing—you aren't going to get any grandmotherly help from her, that's for sure."

"What about *your* mom?" I asked.

Taboo subject. He drew back and said nothing. One of the Quarter's tourist carriages stopped at the curb. Richard looked at the mule pulling it, and the mule looked at him. *Their expressions aren't all that different.*

"I'll bet my parents get over it one second after they see their grandchild," I said. "Any problem will be in the past, unless you hang onto it."

"Maybe so. But what about everyone else? What about the guy who ran us out of Baton Rouge?"

"Guess we can't ask him to babysit. So what?"

"Kathy, this baby is *black*. I don't think you understand what that means."

"What do you think I'm going to do? Have an abortion, walk away from you, and get on with my life as a white girl? That would be the stupidest, most awful thing I've ever done. *No*."

Richard shrugged. I didn't know if I'd convinced him or if he was just giving up for the time being. We finished our coffee and walked to Eddie's stand more or less reconciled. He gave me a quick hug and left me to get back to work.

"That's your boyfriend, huh?" asked Eddie.

"Uh-huh."

He dragged out an open wood crate of lettuce and undid the wires. I started putting them into our display baskets while Eddie fetched a cardboard box.

Rummaging in the box, Eddie pulled out a bunch of carrots and frowned at it. "He good to you?" he asked.

"Oh, yes. Always."

Eddie looked after Richard. He shook his head. "I missed a lot. My mother wouldn't have liked me to date a girl who wasn't Catholic, let alone black or anything like that. I never liked any of the girls my mother liked."

"So, you never married?" I took the box of carrots and arranged bunches of them around the lettuces.

"No, I lived with Mama till she passed away. Eighty-six, she was." He sounded proud for a minute, then sad again. "I'm alone now. I wish I'd looked around more. I think your generation has it right. Stuff like that shouldn't matter."

The lettuces were loose-headed, ruby leaf. The label on the box said "California." Most of our produce was local, but I guessed it was too cold to grow lettuce around here now. *Would California be a good place for us and our baby?* Eddie was looking at me, waiting for me to say something.

"Not everyone has it yet," I told him. "We got chased out of Baton Rouge by someone who didn't like to see a black guy and a white girl together."

"Don't let it get you, doll," Eddie said. "Think about the good people, let the others go. Just stay out of their way—some of those rednecks are dangerous. I'm not putting Baton Rouge down, but New Orleans is probably better for a couple like you and Richard."

"We kind of thought we might not be the oddest people in the Quarter," I said.

Eddie laughed. "That's for sure!"

"My father says it's too soon for couples like us."

"No one wants to see their kids on the front lines, I guess."

That made me feel a little hopeful. If Dad was just being protective, he wouldn't want to be the one to hurt me. Or my baby. I set the last of the vegetables out in the display and picked up some broken leaves that had fallen on the pavement. Keeping my voice casual, I asked, "You think that's all it is?"

"Well, I don't know your dad. But he raised you right—he can't be that much of a racist. People get cautious when it comes to their kids. Most likely he only wants the best for you." He closed the boxes and shoved them under the counter.

"Richard *is* the best."

Eddie shrugged and wiped his hands on a paper towel. "If that's true, your father'll see it before long. . . . Look out, here comes Estelle."

Estelle was one of our wackier customers. I thought she had a crush on Eddie. She came every day—she swore she could tell the difference when she got her vegetables "fresh that day." Eddie didn't tell her that he didn't buy most of the produce the same day himself. And her flirting was lost on him. In my opinion, all his talk about missing a wife and kids was just fantasy. He liked being an old bachelor.

That night at home, I felt wary, cut off from Richard. *Don't hint anymore about an abortion. I want you to marry me. To want to marry me, not just a shotgun wedding. I want children.*

Even when I was little, baby dolls were my favorites, and everyone thought that was fine. Now, it's all changed. It's not cool anymore to want a husband and baby. But that's what I want. It's not fair.

But he didn't start up again, only asked if Eddie had anything to say after he'd seen us together.

"He said Dad probably wants to make sure I'm okay, that he's not really against us."

I pushed aside the window curtain and looked at the row of cottages across the street. Their windows were lit. Every house, every apartment, was complete in itself, cut off from the others. Like spaceships, headed for different stars. I dropped the curtain and turned back to Richard.

He'd picked up the book he'd left on the bed that morning. Looking up, he marked his place with one finger. "I never thought your dad was against us," he said. "You're not twenty-one—he could have stopped you from coming down here."

"How? I'm over eighteen. I can live where I want."

"Well, I knew one guy whose girlfriend was going to move in with him. Her parents committed her to the state mental hospital in Mandeville. They can do that until you're twenty-one."

"Good God. Because they didn't like him?"

"Yeah, it wasn't race. They just didn't like him. Your dad didn't try to stop you, only said he thought you were making a mistake. He even gave you money."

"The baby would change his mind. He wouldn't think his grandchild was a mistake."

"Maybe not, but your mom's another story—sometimes she looks at me like I'm a roach she's found in her soup."

"She's found *two* roaches. I'm the other one, in case you haven't noticed."

"Oh, I noticed. What the hell's her problem, anyway?"

You're asking me *for an answer to that one?* "I don't know," I said. "By the time I came along, she already had a daughter. The position was taken. I got closer to Aunt Ruth."

"But you're not close anymore, huh? Well, at least you have your dad. But I don't think anyone in your family, including him, would have a problem if you decided on an abortion."

℘

EARLY, COLD, St. Valentine's Day morning. I pulled myself out of bed sighing. Wednesday: Eddie's day to go to the Wholesale Market. Which meant I had to get over to the stand and take care of things. Getting ready, I tiptoed. Richard was sleeping, finally—he'd been thrashing and crying out for most of the night. I eased the door shut as I left the room. I had to feel my way along the stairs—the light was out in the hall again. Outside, a chilling fog turned everything to shades of gray. The row of cottages across Bourbon was like a huddle of shivering stray cats.

I zipped my jacket to the top and burrowed my hands into its pockets. Just time for a cup of coffee at the French Market. The front yard of the Ursuline Convent was a dark hole on the Chartres Street sidewalk. I heard teasing music, damped and tinny.

On the corner, a newsboy stood in a patch of swirling mist, light as angel hair. A tiny transistor radio at his feet tinkled downriver banjo, joined by Dixieland—"Washington Square." An oldie that made my mind go back to the sixties. And beyond: *All the banjos and trumpets that must have been played in the Quarter, going back a century or more. It hasn't changed much, not in this block, not this morning. Maybe I should buy a paper, just to see what date would be on it.*

Time meant nothing in the Café Du Monde either. Dawn was silvering, but day or night made no difference there. They never closed, and they only served coffee and doughnuts—if I closed my eyes, I could imagine any time at all. *Frying oil, the raw scent of powdered sugar, black-roasted coffee and steaming milk. Scrape of chairs, crash of dishes, and blurred foghorns out on the river. It's always been like this and it always will be.*

The awning dripped, and I pulled my chair closer in. I shook off my eerie mood. Whatever year it was, it was morning.

I had to get over to the stand, and I wanted to find a present for Richard today, too. Something for Valentine's Day, something beautiful for almost no money. I sighed. Antiques and jewelry glittered in the windows of Royal Street, but those shops were no use to me. I finished my coffee and stood up, flicking back worries as I flicked back my hair.

As I walked down Chartres to the stand, I saw Eddie's truck parked at the curb. He finished stacking wood crates on the sidewalk, waved quickly, and pulled away. I got started putting out stock. If February tomatoes were no good, neither was much else at that time of year. We had apples, navel oranges, winter squash, onions, and peanuts in the shell. We were starting to get some spring asparagus, but it was expensive. The hot, bittersweet smells of tomatoes and eggplants and Italian parsley were still to come.

I could see my breath in the cold. September seemed so far away. *But everything will be different then. We'll have a house with a tree, and a garden like Dad's. An orange kitten lapping a saucer of milk by the back door and chasing its tail. I'll be a real mother, not like Mom. I'll go to the yard and pick good things to eat, fresh from the garden. My little girl will run to me, and I'll hug her.*

My foot slipped on an onion skin on the market cobblestones. It was almost time to open. I set a weight on my stack of paper bags in case the wind came up, and arranged mirlitons, carrots, and red onions in an eye-catching design. Estelle was sure to want asparagus, so I put aside the best bunch for her.

There wasn't much business that morning, not as cold as it was. I tidied up the stand and made more patterns with apples and oranges. Eddie came back just before ten, swearing under his breath about underripe tomatoes and imported strawberries.

"Hey, the way you got all those vegetables—that looks good!"

I could feel my face turn red. "Oh, well, I got to fooling with them, you know, things were slow—"

"I'm serious, it's pretty. Makes us stand out. Looks high class or something, maybe. Like those 'great restaurants' books."

"Well, thanks. Oh, and I put asparagus aside for Estelle. You know she won't turn up until noon, but then she'll want a good bunch. What was good at the market?"

"Not much."

"Then I guess there's not much to unload."

"You guess wrong. We gotta have something to sell, even if it's awful."

Eddie was exaggerating. He had some good spring vegetables, shallots, and some baby lettuce, and a few more fruits than last week. You could chart the seasons inch by inch, working for Eddie.

We finished a few minutes before noon. By then, the day had warmed up enough for me to eat my sack lunch in Jackson Square.

As I ate, fat beggar pigeons flocked around my feet. They scattered when I brushed crumbs off my lap, but mobbed their way back, pushing and squabbling. Thinking of pigeons as "squab-ling" made me smile as I stood and started across the square.

I had no clear destination, just window-shopping in hopes of finding something good for Richard's gift. Street artists had their pitches all along Pirates' Alley, their work hanging from the wrought-iron fence of the St. Louis Cathedral. I loafed along, looking at the pictures. One of the artists was doing a portrait, with people standing behind him, looking over his shoulder.

Another was sitting idle in a canvas captain's chair. I looked at his pictures. *Can I afford a little one?*

The artist smiled at me. "Draw your portrait for ten dollars."

I didn't have ten dollars. "Oh, no," I said, embarrassed.

He leaned over to whisper. "I'll do it for free, if you want."

Is he coming on to me? "Oh, no thanks."

He looked at me sharply. *He knows what I thought.* "That way, people will watch, and I'll get some business. And you get a free portrait," he explained, still whispering. He nodded towards the next pitch, where one of the onlookers was taking the model's chair.

"Okay," I agreed. *I sure made a fool of myself there.* This would solve the problem of Richard's present, if it was any good. And if it wasn't, I hadn't lost anything but time.

I sat in his other canvas chair and tried to look casual for the picture. He started talking right away.

"I'm Tex," he announced. "What's your name?"

"Kathy." I looked more closely at his drawings hanging along the fence. Mostly portraits, and they looked better than a lot of the artwork in Pirates' Alley, more like real people. A few courtyard scenes and moss-draped plantations for the tourists. At least there was nothing on black velvet.

"Where you from?"

"Here. I live over on Bourbon Street."

"Where on Bourbon?" *Does he think I'm a stripper? One of those women who do bumps and grinds out on the sidewalk? Maybe he is coming on to me.*

"Up by Esplanade." The opposite end from the clubs.

He picked up his charcoal and started a sketch. "Quiet up there."

"That's why we chose it."

"We?" He glanced back and forth from me to the paper. His hand never stopped.

"My boyfriend and I. We wanted a place where people would leave us alone."

"I'd say you have it. What do you do? Have I seen you around?"

"I work for Eddie Graziano, over in the French Market. I don't think I've seen you."

"I don't know him. I never shop in the Market."

"I don't either, except what Eddie gives me. Too expensive."

"Tourist trap, that's what it is. You ever do any modeling?"

Modeling? Do you mean nude? "Oh, no," I said, in the same nervous way as when he'd asked if I wanted a free portrait.

"Just for portraits." *He guessed what I was thinking again.* "I have a class, well, several classes I teach at night. I live over on Dumaine. You interested?"

I hesitated. Maybe he was paying a little. On the other hand, I liked to be with Richard at night. Still, if he was paying . . . .

"Five bucks and dinner, if you want to try it."

He finished the picture and sprayed it with fixative from a can. As he showed it to me with a flourish, two women came up to admire his work. The portrait looked like me, and looked like he had somehow caught me about to say something, too. The face in the picture almost moved. One of the women sat down in the model's chair as soon as I got up.

He rolled the picture, taped it lightly, and handed it to me with a card that said "Tex Smallman, Artist."

"Thanks," I said. "It's great." I wondered when a person got to put "artist" on their card. Did someone official give them permission, or did they decide one day, "Hey, I'm an artist," and call up the print shop and order them?

He looked up as he started on the woman's picture. "Nice meeting you, Kathy. Let me know about the modeling. I'm here every day. Or you can call me."

I took the roll of paper back to the rooming house and found a red ribbon to wrap around it to make it look like a present.

Richard wouldn't be home for a while, so I had some time to tidy the room. We had a tiny closet, bulgy with hangers and pegs, and a chest of drawers with a double row of books on top. Our table had a single-burner hot plate and stacks of dishes and packaged food. I opened a box of instant macaroni and cheese for dinner and fetched some water from the bathroom down the hall to cook it in.

Richard came in as I got back to the room. He looked tired and closed-in, hands crammed into his pockets and shoulders hunched. He sat on the bed and watched me stir the cheese powder into the saucepan.

"Take off your coat and stay a while," I offered, trying to lighten things up.

He didn't answer, only stared blankly at the steam coming off the pan.

"I got you a present." I handed him the rolled-up picture, with its red ribbon. He opened it slowly.

"Oh, sweetheart, it's beautiful." He focused on the paper for a couple of seconds, then looked blank again.

"The artist did it for free," I said. "He wants me to model for his portrait class."

"I can see he would." His face twisted up.

"What's wrong?"

"Oh, God, Kathy, you're so beautiful, but over there . . . ." *He means Vietnam.* "They loved their people too, and I destroyed them."

"Is that what you were having nightmares about last night?"

"I was dreaming faces I saw there, little kids . . . little brown faces, Montagnards." He turned away, but I knew he was crying.

"Montagnards?"

"Hill people. We went through a village one day—they didn't beg like the other kids, only stood by the side of the road, stood in the pits and craters from our shells and watched us go by."

I waited for more. He said nothing. "Richard?"

"They had dark faces and curly hair, oh, God, they looked like my cousins. I couldn't pretend anymore that it wasn't people I was killing."

He went to the window and looked down onto the quiet street, still holding the picture carefully, as if it were his picture of the past. *He's seeing that mountain road in Vietnam.* "I think about shells, my shells, falling on those kids. When I close my eyes, I see theirs looking at me."

The macaroni was starting to sizzle and burn. I took the pot off the hot plate.

"You didn't do anything you didn't have to do."

"That's not true. I could have been a CO."

"Yes, and gone to prison. Isn't that what happened to most of the conscientious objectors?"

"I could have gone to Canada. I should have done something, anything but go over there and kill people . . . women and kids. . . . I can't believe I wanted to impress my father that much." He set the picture gently on the chest of drawers.

Oh, damn. Me and my present—it's like the presents I used to make at school for Mom when I was little. She hid them. And the next time the art teacher gave us a project, I'd make her something else. They were never good enough. And I never stopped trying.

Is there anything I can give him to make him happy? To make him want me?

I put my arms around him. "Richard, you did the best you knew. If you'd known different, you'd have *done* different. That's all anyone has. It's not your fault there was a war."

"That's the thing about turning into someone you hate. It usually isn't your fault. Except it is."

He shoved me away and scrambled out of the room. The door banged behind him. I sat on the bed a few minutes, and then spooned some of the macaroni into a bowl and tried to eat. But I didn't feel hungry anymore, and the burned flavor had seeped all the way through and ruined the whole thing.

❧ 13 ❧
January 1975, San Pedro
Lacey

CALIFORNIA'S JANUARY DRIZZLE had washed away all the holiday glitter by the time I finally got a call about Kathy. It wasn't Sharon. It was a man who'd gotten my number from her.

"Hello, my name is Eddie Graziano," he began. "You don't know me, but I'm a friend of Kathy Woodbridge. She used to work for me in New Orleans. Her sister Sharon gave me your number."

Not a southern accent. Almost like Brooklyn. In New Orleans, they call it "Irish Channel," that accent. When I'd stayed with Tante Eloise, I'd met plenty of people who talked like that. White, blue-collar, family lived in New Orleans since Noah was a kid.

"Nice to talk to you. How's Sharon doing?" Trying to find out what he wanted without seeming too inquisitive.

"She's fine. Except that she's worried about Kathy."

Well, that made at least three of us.

"I was sorry to hear that their dad passed away," I said. I was careful not to tip my hand that Sharon hadn't confided in me and neither had Kathy.

"Sharon told me you'd called her, and we decided to talk to you. We're both worried about Kathy. In fact, all her friends are worried."

"I'll be happy to help any way I can."

He hesitated. "I'm not sure what you could do. Before I called Sharon, I had no idea where Kathy was. I guess I just wanted to check up. Kathy's been on my mind a lot."

"You didn't know where she went?"

"No, she bolted. We didn't know what to think. She ran off from Sharon's house in Baton Rouge after her father's funeral. She left a note to say she was going, but she didn't say where. Sharon thought she'd just gone home. But when she didn't hear anything for a while, she called down here and found out we hadn't seen Kathy, either. Kathy's stuff is still here—I guess she never came back."

"When was her father's funeral?" I asked.

"First week of December."

"That's about when she turned up here. How did Sharon find out where she is?"

"Kathy sent a postcard. Nothing on it but her address. Before that, her sister had no idea she'd gone to California."

"I guess Kathy just picked up and hitchhiked, the way kids do."

"Oh, lord. I hope she didn't hitchhike. How is she?"

"She's not real happy, but she's getting by. She has an apartment here in San Pedro. Didn't Sharon tell you all this?"

"More or less, but I wanted to talk to you direct. You see her every day."

"Well, she's not too good, not too bad."

"Listen, could I give you a call from time to time, stay in touch, you know? And give you my number in case something comes up? Her dad's gone now, and her mom . . . . Well, I don't think she'd be much help if Kathy needed anything. And Sharon's good, but she isn't a whole lot older than Kathy."

"That's fine. Actually, my husband and I are planning to be in New Orleans for Mardi Gras. We could get together, if you'd like. Have a cup of coffee or something."

"That would be great! Where are you staying in New Orleans?"

"My husband made the reservations, so I'm not sure. I'll have to get back to you."

I took his number and got off the phone.

That conversation worried me. Eddie's story hung together as far as it went, but it didn't quite make sense. I could see a girl maybe running away after her father's funeral, especially if she didn't get along with her mother. But she was still here, apparently planning to stay. She hadn't even gotten in touch with her friends. And there was the matter of Richard Johnson.

I didn't ask Eddie about that. Best let him tell me in his own time.

❧ 14 ❧
March 1973, New Orleans
Kathy

BY THE LAST WEEK of February, New Orleans was getting crazy. Mardi Gras Day was March 6 that year, and the city was filling up with revelers. I'd seen the parades many times as a child and didn't care about going again. Maybe to a night parade, I'd never gotten to see one of those—drums and flambeaux and the Quarter all lit up. But Richard couldn't stand crowds, and I tried not to imagine what the torches would remind him of. It was better to pretend none of it was happening.

Living with Richard was showing me things about him that I hadn't expected. He had nightmares, not every night, but several times a week. That was bad enough, but his outburst on Valentine's Day hung on in my mind.

It seemed to stay with him, too. He had come back to the room late that night, long after I'd gone to bed. Next morning, neither of us said anything about it. I didn't know what to do. I kept pretending things were normal, but it wasn't easy. As the days wore on, he rarely spoke, and his body in bed at night felt cold and different.

Dragging home on the Friday before Mardi Gras, I worried how we were even going to get through the weekend. We couldn't go away. Even if we had somewhere to go, the traffic was terrible, blocked by parade routes in every direction. Crowds swirled around all the streets now, even our secluded corner. Eddie had asked me to work a few hours on Saturday and I'd agreed, mostly to get out of our room.

On the downstairs hall table was a letter for me—Sharon's handwriting. I grabbed it as I passed by and tore the envelope open on my way up the stairs.

Hi, L'il Sis!

How are you doing in the Big Easy? I bet Mardi Gras is really something if you're right on the spot. What parades did you go to? Save me a doubloon if you get an extra—Sam and I have been too busy to get down there.

I'm going to make some time after Carnival, though. I miss you. Sam and I could visit some weekend. We'll stay at a hotel—I know you don't have guest space yet. Would you have time? What weekend would work for you?

Give our best to Richard. See you soon.

Love,
Sharon

Well, hell. That was all I needed. I missed Sharon, but I didn't want her to see the way things were now. I wondered how long I could put her off.

But when I opened the door to our room, Richard was making dinner. *He looks like himself again.* I tried a smile.

He smiled back thinly, nodding toward the envelope in my hand. "Letter?"

"From Sharon. She says they're too busy to come down right away, but maybe later."

"Probably the best choice anyway—avoid the Carnival craziness."

Oh, what about our own little spell of craziness, the last couple of weeks? We're just pretending it never happened? Let's brush it under the carpet, except we don't have a carpet. I glowered at the rose-patterned linoleum. It was kind of obvious I wasn't about to find any answer down there.

Richard went back to making spaghetti. We spent the evening reading. *I'll hide behind Sylvia Plath and you hide behind T. S. Eliot. The book I gave you for Christmas.*

Next morning I left the room before he woke. I didn't have to be at the stand until late afternoon, but I wanted to be alone. Not that "alone" was going to be easy, the Saturday before Carnival. I could hear bands from a couple of different directions.

I walked toward Esplanade, away from the noise. It was one of my favorite walks. I loved the Quarter, but sometimes got tired of its hard surfaces—pavement and wrought iron and brick, the narrow, medieval feeling that the tourists came for. Esplanade was a wide street, with big trees and a grassy median that the locals called the "neutral ground."

Walking toward the river, I felt the swing of my steps apply a soothing rhythm to my jumpy thoughts. Maybe if I kept walking, I could think of something.

I can't live this way—not for long.

I don't want to leave him. What about the baby?

I love him. Except when he's someone else. I don't love that other Richard.

I don't know what to do. I'm scared.

Step and step again. Crack in the sidewalk, tree root.

The war was supposed to be over when they signed the cease-fire, wasn't it? Why isn't it over for Richard?

Dogwood flowering pink and white over on the median. Pretty.

I want us to be a family. Why is he hanging on to this evil stuff? Richard, reading about sharecroppers, trying to understand. He can't possibly want to think about the war.

End of Esplanade, no sidewalk left. I looked at the face of the Old Mint, closed since forever. It didn't tell me anything. I turned back the way I'd come.

Maybe he doesn't want to think about the war. Maybe he can't stop. Maybe he can't help it.

Dixie cup on the sidewalk. I picked it up and put it into the next trash can.

Why does he feel so guilty about Vietnam? What did he do that he can't just forget?

I walked on for a while without thinking of anything. Then the worries came back.

What if nothing else could ever seem more important? If the bad thing is too big to forget? Well, Mom has a point—in that case, you talk to a psychologist. But no way Richard's going to do that.

Stop at the corner, let the car turn in front of me. Now I could cross.

Well, I'm not a psychologist! If he's too ashamed to talk to someone who could handle it, he can't turn around and dump it all on me. Also, what about the baby? Is it going to grow up with a father who acts like some crazy person?

I looked up, realizing that I'd walked farther than I intended. The expressway was right in front of me. I turned south and sat on a bench in the Municipal Auditorium Park, looking toward

the walls of the old St. Louis Cemeteries, where legend said the
Voodoo Queen was buried.

I'd only been there a few minutes when a tall woman in
a long black dress staggered up. Still drunk from the night
before—that was Mardi Gras for you. She plopped down on
my bench. Just what I needed. *But I'll look mean if I get up and
walk off.*

"Bobby's over there," she said.

She pointed over toward the old St. Louis cemetery. *I don't
know who Bobby is, but if he turns up, I really will leave. Screw it.
I can't deal with two of them.*

I didn't see anyone coming. "Bobby?" I asked.

She laughed harshly. "Don't look for Bobby. He'd be six feet
under if he wasn't buried aboveground. Don't go looking for
Bobby no more." The last word came out as a sob.

I was confused. "I thought this was a just a historic cemetery," I said.

"People never stop dying, you know? But if it wasn't this one,
it was one exactly like it. What difference does it make which
cemetery, anyway? They're all the same. Everyone in them is
dead." Her voice was loud and angry.

I looked her over carefully. *She must have been well-dressed
last night or the night before, whenever she started drinking. She
sure is bizarre now.*

A long-sleeved evening gown draped from a high turtle-
neck scarf to her spike-heeled shoes. Above the scarf, and now
streaked all over it, was heavy pancake makeup. Her eyes were
raccooned with mascara, and one of her false eyelash strips was
coming loose. A teased cone of black hair was sprinkled with
glitter. *Probably supposed to look like stars. Radioactive dandruff
is more like it.*

Real-looking diamonds flashed from her heavy clip-back earrings. In this neighborhood, stones like that would get a drunk woman mugged for sure.

"Did you know we had him a jazz funeral?" she asked, suddenly sociable. "His mama and sister nearly died of embarrassment. *They* aren't jazz types at all. But Bobby was a *musician*. It was right." She frowned again. "They played 'In the Sweet Bye and Bye' on the way to the cemetery. I don't see anything sweet about rotting in a cement box."

I had heard of jazz funerals, but I'd never seen one. She obviously wasn't the person to ask, not right now, anyway. "Maybe you ought to go up to Canal Street, where it's safer," I suggested.

"Maybe I should." She stood up, weaving to balance on those stiletto heels. I wondered what I should do if she passed out on the sidewalk.

"On the way back, they played 'Didn't He Ramble?'" she said. "They most always play that at a jazz funeral. They play happy-sounding stuff on the way back. When I asked why, they said, 'We done all we could for him. Couldn't do no more.'"

She wavered for a second. "But you know what? *I* didn't do all I could for Bobby. *I* wasn't there at the last, when I could maybe have stopped him. I didn't even say anything afterwards. But what could I have done? *He* didn't want them to know about us, either."

Her hand reached out to me as she started singing, "Didn't he ramble, didn't he ramble?" The singing voice was a deep bass. *And that hand is much too big for a woman's. My God.*

The voice switched back to falsetto to say, "Those guys who play that on their saxes, if they think it's a happy song, they must not know the words." Another switch to bass melody—"He rambled till the butchers cut him down."

He lurched toward Canal Street. It was a good thing his back was to me. My mouth was open wide enough to catch flies. As he disappeared around a corner, I imagined Bobby slipping from his mausoleum and through the gates of the cemetery, following him.

I got out of there. I headed uptown, looking for streets with a few more people, trying to shake the feeling that Bobby was around the next corner. *I have enough trouble as it is.*

I walked north on Tulane Avenue, past the Greyhound depot, where an old black man was sitting on a camp stool on the sidewalk, playing a Dobro and singing to nobody.

"Angel got two wings to veil my face, angel got two wings to fly away."

It seemed to mean something, but I wasn't sure what. I didn't have any spare money to drop into the open case at his feet. I tried to smile at him, but his white-glazed eyes told me he didn't see.

I turned away and scrambled along Tulane Avenue, past Charity Hospital, past the prosthetics stores and all-night coffee shops clustered near it. Past the bail bond places around the courthouse. I wondered if people could get bailed out of the hospital, out of illness. Maybe you could buy a bail bond from Death. *Angel got two wings . . . . This is nuts.* With an effort, I pulled myself together and kept going. There were lots of pedestrians on the sidewalks of Tulane Avenue, but I felt like the only person in the world.

Through the Civic Center, past the library, and then I remembered I had to work at the stand that afternoon. Better head back—it was a long walk.

The sidewalk started to get crowded, everyone heading the same way I was. I realized I must have blundered into a parade crowd.

But I wasn't sure where the parade was, so I didn't know how to get away. I kept walking, east and south toward the Quarter. A nightmare mob of people in costumes was in my way now. I brushed against an eight-foot-high chicken carrying a tall drink, a man wearing a G-string and a Sioux headdress, and a Dracula. *Which are the masks—the faces they have now, or the ones they wear the rest of the year?* I was going to be late.

Six streakers pelted past me kicking aside beer cans, with everyone getting out of their way. I dodged a couple in blackface and pushed through a group of laughing purple tarantulas. A passed-out Tinkerbell lay on the sidewalk beside a pool of hot-pink vomit. *Man or woman?* I was near panic. I kept pushing past.

Distant yelling and drums told me the parade was coming my way. I had to get across Canal Street before the floats reached me, or I'd be held up for hours. A cop blew his whistle at me as I slipped through the barrier and ran across Canal. The crowds thinned as I got into the Quarter, but I was panting as I headed up Decatur toward Eddie and safety.

He waved happily when he saw me coming, then his face pulled into worry lines when I got closer.

"What's the matter, doll?"

"Carnival crowd. Like a nightmare."

"Nightmare?" Eddie frowned.

"There was a drunk man in the Municipal Auditorium Park. Only I thought it was a woman." Somehow, this didn't sound as scary as it had been. I tried to explain. "He had on a sort of covered-up gown. I really fell for it."

"Some of those guys are real good," said Eddie. "No way you could tell, especially at Carnival." He shook his head. "What's the matter, doll? You've seen men in drag before, I'm sure."

"Well, yes, but not that convincing." I had been to a gay bar on Halloween with my friend Jimmy. Some of the guys were more or less in drag, but they didn't come close to looking like women. Especially when they pulled the beanbags out of their bras and threw them at each other. "Mostly, it's what she . . . he . . . said. He said he hadn't done everything he could for Bobby."

"Who's Bobby?"

"His lover, I think. He said Bobby was in the cemetery. I think he committed suicide."

Eddie looked up sharply. "So?"

"Richard's upset about the war," I admitted. I wasn't sure I was making sense, but Eddie seemed to get the gist of it, at least.

"You afraid he might do something?"

"I don't know."

Two customers came up, bought strawberries, and took their change. Eddie turned back to me. "He ever hit you?"

"No. He doesn't do anything, doesn't even talk. But he has nightmares."

"You talk to your mother and dad about it?"

"I don't want to."

Eddie rubbed his eyes. He watched a couple of women check out the satsumas, ready to answer questions, but they moved on down the arcade. "Why stay with him, doll?" he asked. "You don't have to put up with that. Girl like you, you could have almost any fellow in town."

"I don't *want* to. Anyway, I'm pregnant."

"Oh, lord."

A middle-aged man with a Midwestern accent interrupted to ask where to buy "real New Orleans coffee." Eddie waved him over to the Morning Call. "So, Richard's going through some kind of shell shock, you're scared, and you don't know what to do. And you got a baby on the way."

"That's it." *He understands. Thank God someone does.*

"When's it due?"

"September."

"We have a little time, then. I have a neighbor was in the war. Australian fellow. He's sure to know more than you and me. Let me see what he says."

"Richard won't go to a psychologist. I asked."

"Martin's not one. But he'll know something. Meantime, keep cool. Don't tell Richard we talked. I mean it."

When I got home that night, Richard was asleep. I took off my coat and slipped into bed beside him. He reached out and held me, and I went to sleep too against his warmth. We woke early and made love for the first time in a long time. *He's Richard again. I want to stay with him no matter what.*

Our Sunday was quiet, with a backdrop of distant, irrelevant parades. We made love again and read aloud to each other, talked about Sharon and Sam's visit. We still didn't say anything about our problems, but I felt easier now that Eddie had something up his sleeve. *Eddie's smart, he knows everybody. If Eddie's on my side, something good will happen.*

He didn't let me down. When I showed up for work Monday morning, he was jubilant. "This is gonna work out good, doll," he said. "I told you about my neighbor Martin that was in the war. Martin Yates. Well, he's got some kind of grant now—he's setting up a puppet theater. *And* he's looking for people to work for him."

"Richard has a job."

"What is it, counting screws or something? He'll take this in a minute. *Also*"—he gave me a sidelong look—"I think *you* should go work for Martin too. I mean, it's not that I don't want you, but I think you and Richard ought to do something together. Of course, you could still work for me sometimes," he added. "And if this doesn't pan out for some reason, you can come back anytime."

I'd worried for a moment that Eddie wanted to get rid of me, but I could feel it wasn't that at all. "Where is it?"

"Out in Gretna. You might want to think about getting a place out there. Easy to come in if you want, and the rents would be a lot cheaper."

"What about the neighborhood? I mean, Richard and I—"

"Gretna? No one in that area will care."

"What about the baby?"

"Martin's got twins. He won't have a problem. Quit worrying, Kathy! It'll be okay."

I was still doubtful. "What would we be doing? Neither of us knows a thing about puppets."

"That's the beauty part. Some of this grant is for education, and it helps that Richard's a veteran. And black. Give it a try—it'll be fun. Also, I told him about Richard and the war stuff, and he's going to do what he can to help. Quiet-like, but I think he knows what he's talking about."

When I told Richard about Eddie's idea that night, he hesitated about two seconds before he decided he wanted to try it. We called Martin from the pay phone in the hall, and he invited us to come and talk to him.

Eddie looked pleased when I told him next day. "I'll be sad to see you go, doll, I really will. But it's the best thing for both of you. And I live right in the neighborhood—I'll still be seeing you around. Take the day off tomorrow, go talk to Martin. If it works out, maybe even find yourself a place to stay."

I took the Volkswagen across the bridge to Gretna on Wednesday afternoon. Richard couldn't get off work, so I went alone. I felt so hopeful, I bought a paper and went early to look for apartments.

Eddie was right about the rents being cheaper—except that the rents for houses and apartments were all more than we were paying for our tiny room. Everything I saw cost more than we could afford. First and last rent in advance, and deposits for cleaning and security—I'd have to ask Dad for money, and I didn't want to. I decided to talk to Martin anyway. We had to start somewhere.

His address turned out to be in an old neighborhood near the levee. His house was a raised cottage with a long stairway leading to its porch.

When the door opened, I peered through the screen at the place I expected to see a face. I was looking a couple of feet too high. A man smiled at me from his wheelchair as I adjusted my gaze. *How'd he get up those steps?* He had navy blue eyes and curly black hair—"Black Irish," my dad would have said. He looked about thirty-five.

"Martin?"

"You must be Kathy." He pushed the screen open and I edged through. "Come on in. You picked a good time—my wife's taken the kids to the zoo. Have a seat on the couch there—push some of their junk aside."

His living room looked like it might *be* a zoo. Toys were everywhere. Unusual, beautiful toys, almost all handmade. Ornate building blocks, wooden animals, and dolls—not one of them from a factory, as far as I could see.

I elbowed out of my jacket and sat down, moving a carved horse carefully to the coffee table. "It's beautiful." A block palace filled most of the table. Each block was exquisitely carved and painted. Martin laughed as he saw me taking it all in.

"My wife's an artist, and we're both puppeteers—and of course, we're getting started in business, so we have to economize. And the boys are twins, so we need twice as many of everything. We make all their stuff." If this was economy, I felt sorry for rich kids. And better about Richard and me.

"So, you and your boyfriend want to work for us. We need help with everything, almost. I don't suppose you've ever done anything with puppets before?"

"No, we haven't. But we'll work hard, I promise. I'm sure we can learn."

He smiled. "We can teach you. We don't really expect experience. We work long hours, though, and you'll also have to practice on your own to be any good. Where do you live?"

"We're in the Quarter now, but we want to move. Do you know of any apartments for rent in this neighborhood? I looked around this morning, but I didn't see anything we could afford."

"Well, one of the neighbors, Francine Boudreaux, has a mother-in-law house in her backyard. A while back, she was talking about renting it, but she couldn't advertise since it's not zoned for rental. Maybe she still wants to—I doubt she'd charge much. It's just one big room, and it's not fancy."

"Can I look at it?"

"I happen to know she's not at home at the moment—in fact, she's with my family at the zoo. She and my wife are friends—they like to speak French together."

"Is your wife French?"

"No, Vietnamese. Francine's a Creole. I sometimes wonder what kind of French they could have in common, but if their rate of talking is anything to go by, it must be quite a bit. Anyway, when they get back, I'll ask Francine about the house."

"Richard, my boyfriend, is a Vietnam vet." *Is your wife angry about the war? I think I'd be.*

"Eddie told me," Martin said. "I'm not a vet, but I was a journalist over there. That's where Thu and I met. We left in '68 when I got injured."

Pretend he didn't say anything about his injury. Change the subject. "Eddie said you're from Australia."

"I am. Yes. We came to the United States for medical treatment for me. But we decided to stay for a while."

"Do you do puppets from Vietnam?"

"There and everywhere. Would you like to see some?"

"Oh, *yes.*"

He showed me to a workroom at the back of the house. Puppets of all sorts were everywhere, even some figures that didn't look like puppets at all. There was an odd little flat man like a big paper doll, with a curly red stocking cap. At the tip of the cap was a small light.

"What's this one?" I asked.

"That's Beberuhi. He's Turkish. The light is to help him search for truth." He laughed. "Frankly, I'd think you might need a brighter one to find it. He never does—maybe that's why."

"He's flat," I said.

"A shadow puppet. He's held up between a light and a screen, and the audience sees his shadow on the screen from the other side. Traditionally, shadow puppets are opaque, but I've modified him with colored bits, kind of a stained-glass effect. Also, it's not traditional to have a real light on his cap.

I picked up a carved wooden puppet that wasn't strung yet. "Who's this?"

"He's not actually a folk puppet. He's a conventional mario-nette for a character in an Arab folktale. It's sort of a mixed approach. They wouldn't use a marionette in those countries."

"Why not?" I couldn't see anything wrong with the puppet.

"In some Islamic countries, it's unacceptable to make images of living creatures. It varies. We use traditional puppets like the shadow puppets if we can, otherwise we adapt them."

"Why would you have to?"

"So the puppets won't seem too odd at first. When Thu and I came here, we noticed that most Americans don't understand other cultures. We thought that might be one reason for the war, so we started the puppet project. In fact, the main group sponsoring us is a peace organization."

"Where do you perform?"

"Mostly in schools now, but we'd like to found a permanent theater for the public. Maybe have a puppetry school or at least some classes." His voice was wistful, filled with his dream.

He pushed his wheelchair away from the worktable and led me back to the living room. "When can you start work?" he asked, as I picked up my purse and coat.

"Monday."

"Good enough. I'll talk to Francine tonight. Call me tomor-row and I'll let you know. You can move in over the weekend if she says yes—and if you like the place, of course. I'm looking forward to having some help. This thing is starting to get out of control." The satisfaction in his voice belied his words.

I headed back across the bridge to New Orleans. *Everyone's going home, but that building downtown is blinking awake with lights. Switch on the car lights to see me home, turn on the lights, exactly like the puppet looking for truth.*

❦

"Oh, Richard, it's great!" I burst into our room, leaving the door open behind me. Richard, sitting on the bed reading, looked up with a smile.

"They have all these puppets from all over the world, and they make their kids' toys, and there's even a place for us to live. . . ." I realized I was being incoherent. I turned and shut the door and started over.

"They're starting a puppet theater to teach kids about other cultures. Martin's Australian, well, you knew that. He's in a wheelchair. I didn't meet his wife and kids—she's from Vietnam. They met over there."

"She's *Vietnamese?*" Richard asked. His hands fumbled at the book, his expression startled, stiffening. "Hold on, Kathy. No way I can do this. No way." The book dropped on the floor with a bang that made Richard jump. He looked like a cornered animal.

I was stunned. "What do you mean, you can't do it?"

"I can't face her. I can't, not after the war. Why don't you see that? We'll find something else." He wouldn't even look at me.

"Like what? Sorting screws for the rest of your life, so you won't meet anyone inconvenient? No. *I* won't live like that."

"I can't do it."

"You can talk to them once, anyway. If she's angry or hostile, we won't do it. But if not, I don't see why you'd have a problem. I mean it, Richard. You have to give it a try, at least. You owe it to the baby." *Not fair, and I don't care.*

Richard opened his mouth and then shut it. We didn't say another word about it all evening. In fact, we hardly said anything at all.

When I called Martin the next morning, he suggested that we come over and look at the house.

"There's a kind of problem," I told him. "Richard doesn't think he can face your wife, on account of the war."

"Oh. *That* problem. That one's happened before. Don't worry, I'll talk to him. Come over about seven?"

Richard was still giving me the silent treatment when it was time to go to Gretna. He plopped himself into the passenger seat of the car and gazed out the side window. I thought he was sulking. But as I turned onto the bridge, he reached to turn on the car's heater and I saw his hand was shaking. Shaking as it had on Thanksgiving, his face as closed and scared as it had been that day.

I love him, but it isn't going to be enough. We have to get away from the war. He has to stop this. And I can't make that happen all by myself. What do I say now? He probably thinks I'm sulking too.

I parked on Martin's street, and we trailed single file up the stairs to his house like a couple of strangers who'd just happened to arrive at the same time. The door was answered by a toddler who ran away to get a grown-up, leaving us on the porch. Martin let us in.

"Hi, there," he greeted us. "Meet Dominic." The little boy peek-a-booed from behind Martin's chair. "He has a twin brother, Joss. They're identical, but you'll learn to tell them apart before long. Go get Mommy, please, Dom."

Martin held his hand out to Richard. "Martin Yates," he offered. "I'm glad to meet you."

"Richard Johnson." Richard shook Martin's hand, but his voice sounded perfunctory. "Martin, I need—"

He broke off as Thu came into the room, both children tagging after. She was thin and dark, about my height. She must have been cooking—a blue denim chef's apron was wrapped around her, tied in a half-bow at the front. Her long black hair was pulled back into a ponytail at the nape of her neck. She smiled at us, preoccupied by the children dancing behind her.

"Thu, I'd like you to meet Kathy and Richard—they're going to work with us on the puppets," Martin said.

Richard turned to Thu and extended his hand politely. "I'm happy to meet you, Thu."

She looked down. After a second's hesitation, she shook his hand. Richard looked like he'd been slapped.

"Come on out the back way," Martin broke in. "We're going to see Francine's house, honey. Back in a few."

He led us out through the kitchen, down a ramp to the driveway. "Couldn't stand to mess up the house with a ramp in front," he said. "So, now the kitchen door has turned *into* the front."

We followed him down the drive to the street.

"I can't do this, Martin," Richard burst out as soon as we were a few steps from the house. "How could I work with Thu? She didn't even want to shake my hand. Not that I blame her."

Martin rolled on a moment without speaking. Camphor trees leaned over the sidewalk, their roots making the pavement crooked and pitched. In the summer, they would be a shade tunnel—now they were black sticks.

"My wife doesn't even know you were a soldier," Martin said. "I haven't discussed it with her yet. All she knows about you is that you're going to help us with the puppets."

"What do you mean, she doesn't know? She wouldn't even look me in the eye!"

Martin laughed. "It's not the custom in Vietnam to look people directly in the eye. Shaking hands isn't the custom either, especially for women. Of course, Thu knows it's what we do

here, but it's not second nature to her yet. 'Scuse me." His chair
darted down a driveway, crossed the street in the intersection,
and returned to the sidewalk on the other side.

We scrambled to catch up with him. "This is a bummer," he
grumbled, waving back at the too-high curb. "The funny thing
is, people are so uncomfortable talking about it that it's hard to
get anything done. I get a double whammy 'cause I was injured
in the war and no one wants to hear about that either."

Richard winced. "You're a veteran?"

"Not me. I was a journalist until the Tet Offensive."

"At Tet, huh? Where were you?"

*He's opening up a little—still cautious. But two men talking
about their war. He'll at least give this a chance.*

"Hue," Martin said. "I was wounded by 'friendly fire,' they
called it. Didn't feel too damn friendly, tell you the truth."

"At least you weren't in the army. That's why I'm worried
about Thu. How could anyone forgive that?"

Martin looked up at Richard. "In the army or out, nobody's
innocent. War does things to people, even the ones who never
get near the fighting. Maybe my project can teach a few people
to enjoy different cultures rather than fear them.

"Anyway, I hope you won't let us down. We need help, and
Eddie said you'd be perfect. And Thu wouldn't think you were
an enemy. You ought to talk to her sometime."

He turned toward a Victorian cottage, where a dumpy little
woman was silhouetted against the porch light. "Hi, Francine.
Richard and Kathy are here."

"Hey there," she called, clinging to the gingerbread railing
as she picked her way down the steps. Up close, she looked like
a grandmother in a children's book—gray hair worn in a scrag-
gly bun, sweet brown eyes. *Is she black, or what?* She was neatly

dressed in dark, old-lady clothes, except her shoes were four-inch red heels. She walked in them with teetery caution as she led us up the driveway to a house in the backyard.

"Now, this isn't fancy at all. I don't know if you'd want it or not. My Tante Beatrice lived here for years when my parents had the place. You two go on in and take a look. I want to talk to Martin."

The little house was two steps above the yard, with a porch running all along the front. The door opened into a big room with a small kitchen in one corner. That was it, except for the bathroom and a big closet. The furniture was sparse and dowdy—a bed with a chenille bedspread and a doily-covered chest of drawers. No sofa or armchairs, and no space for them, either—not if we put in a crib and a bookcase.

But it was bigger than our room in the Quarter, and it had lots of windows and a yard for the baby. I looked at Richard and he shrugged and then smiled and put his arms around me. We hurried out into the yard where Martin and Francine were waiting.

"It's perfect," I told them.

Francine bent down and pulled a weed. When she straightened up, she laughed, a little awkwardly. "Doggone weeds. They spring up overnight, I swear." She dusted off her hands. "I never rented this before, you know. Would seventy-five a month be too much?"

Seventy-five a month was cheap. I could have hugged her for being so kind. My voice wouldn't work for a minute, so it was Richard who said, "That's fine, Mrs. . . . ."

"Call me Francine," she told him. "But make out the check to Francine Boudreaux."

Richard pulled out his checkbook and started writing. "How do you spell *Boudreaux*?"

"*B, o, u, d, r, e, a, u, x*. You mean, you're not Creole?"

"No, we've been living in Baton Rouge, but my family's Army. I grew up all over the country. Why?"

"Oh. I thought you looked sort of Creole. Never mind. When do you want to move in?"

"Would tomorrow evening be too soon?" I asked.

"I'll get it cleaned for you." She handed me a key.

"See you then. Good night," I called as we headed down the drive, ambling alongside Martin's chair. Francine was working on the weeds again. No doubt they'd come back the next time it rained, but at least for now, they had met their match.

Wish I could turn her loose on Richard's nightmares.

✵ 15 ✵
January 1975, San Pedro
Lacey

I WAS KNITTING a Fair Isle afghan that winter, working on it in the evenings while Willis sat in his recliner and watched TV. I had to lay the colors out along the couch to keep from getting tangled like a fly in a spiderweb.

We usually talked for a while before we put the TV on—told how it went that day, that kind of thing. Sometimes I'd tell Willis about the office, and he'd get a good laugh out of George's dumb antics. But when I told him about Eddie's phone call, he didn't think it was funny.

"I don't understand what you're doing at all, honey," he complained, pulling his hand back from the television knob. Its blank screen reflected us, as if we were the entertainment that evening. "What is it, you going through the change or something?"

This was not the way to get on my good side. "What's that supposed to mean?"

"It's supposed to mean I think you've lost your mind. Phone calls to Louisiana—you some kind of investigator now? Sneaking off to The Mystic Eye, pumping Marilu Collins for whatever she might know. Which is what, exactly? You think this girl pals with her nutty landlady?"

I knitted a little faster. "I got Kathy's old address in Gretna," I said. "And her sister's address and phone number in Baton Rouge."

"Yes, and then got five bucks added to the damn phone bill. For what? None of this is any of your business."

"Just walk by on the other side, is that what we're supposed to do?" I finished with the white, picked up the green, and started again.

"It's not your *business,* Lacey. Ever since Angela went up to Berkeley—no, ever since she *said* she was going—you've been acting like a crazy woman. You're just messing around with Kathy as a replacement for mothering Angie. Maybe you're even mad at Angela, getting back at her for moving out. I think you ought to see a doctor or something. This empty-nest stuff is getting out of hand. Angela was floored when she came home and found she'd been kicked out of her room."

Tears rushed to my eyes. "She wasn't kicked out. She *moved* out. *I* was the one who got pushed out."

Willis sat back in his recliner and closed his eyes. He was quiet for a couple of minutes. I'm sure he counted at least to ten, and maybe he got in a quick prayer for patience after that. Maybe not, though. Willis always said that every time he prayed for patience, the Lord sent him a bunch of trials to help him develop some.

"What do you mean?" Willis sounded more worried than angry now.

"You don't know what it's like—you have your work. How do you think you'd feel if you had to retire? My job doesn't mean a lot to me, but raising Angela did, and now it's all done. She doesn't need me anymore."

"First place, *I* need you. What do you think I have the business *for?* It's for us. Second place, what makes you think Angela doesn't need you?"

"Well, she could hardly wait to move out." When I checked my knitting, I saw it was much too tight. I was going to have to pick out everything I'd done. I laid it in my lap. Better do it later.

"So what?" said Willis. "It's her time to do that. Doesn't mean she doesn't need you. She needs you to show her how to be a grown woman. Later on, she'll need you to help her pick a husband. Then to show her how to be a mother herself."

"She doesn't need me for that. She's seen all that, just growing up."

Willis leaned forward in his chair. "You haven't shown her how to let go of an almost-grown daughter yet. Bet she'll need to know *that* someday. How to grow old. Way I see it, honey, we're a step ahead of her. Everything in life, she'll see us get there first."

Willis could always make me feel better when I was down. I even managed a little smile. "I guess I'm still her mother," I said. "Brought her into the world, and someday, I'll teach her how to leave it, I guess. Guess I wouldn't have it any different."

He sat back, looking relieved but still wary. "So, now this waif comes along, and you want to fix all her problems. Maybe you ought to join the Big Sisters or something."

"If I did that, I'd be doing the same thing I'm doing for Kathy. What's the difference?"

Willis rubbed the heels of his hands across his eyelids, the way he did when he hadn't gotten enough sleep. "The difference is that you wouldn't have to sneak around. And it wouldn't have to be on Pacific Avenue, either. My shop is about two blocks from Marilu's. I'd a lot rather you didn't mess with my neighbors."

I hadn't thought of that. He did have a point. "I'm sorry, honey. I wasn't thinking," I admitted. "I didn't mean to embarrass you. All the same, I think it's only right for me to help if I can. And it does get my mind off my 'empty nest' for now."

"Well, okay. You want to see if you can help Kathy, fair enough. But that'll be over before long, you know. You'll fix Kathy's problems, she'll say thanks, and then she'll want to live her own life, same as Angela."

That hadn't occurred to me, either. "So, what do I do, Willis? Surely it's not crazy to want to help other people."

"Like I said, I think you ought to volunteer for the Big Sisters. Or even go to work for them. Better yet, why don't you go back to school?"

"Go back to school? You mean, apply to college?"

"Sure, why not? If you want to do this kind of stuff, get a degree in social work or something. You're wasted at Giannini's." He got up and came over to the couch. "Got room for me?"

I set the afghan tangle aside. Willis sat next to me and put his arm around my shoulders. I squeezed his hand.

"I bet *I* can distract you," said Willis. "Let's make this year's trip to the Mardi Gras into a second honeymoon." He put on a comic-sexy look—wiggled his eyebrows and did his best to leer. I laughed.

"I sort of set it up to get together with Kathy's friends while we're there," I said.

His expression changed to eye-rolling resignation. "You want me to spend my vacation doing that?"

"Not for long, I promise. I'll trade you. If you'll come along on this, I'll go to the parades with you."

"*You'll* go to the parades? Sounds to me like a piecrust promise—made to be broken. Believe *that* one when I see it."

"I'll do it if you'll help me with Kathy's friends," I said.

"Okay, you got a deal."

Now I was going to have to go to the damned parades—couldn't say I hadn't gotten myself into that one, me and my big mouth. I could see us standing in the rain on Canal Street while the floats sailed by, yelling, "Throw me somethin', mister!" at the top of our lungs. And then saying the same thing silently to Eddie Graziano in Gretna, trying to figure out what was going on.

Some second honeymoon.

❧ 16 ❧
March 1973, New Orleans
Kathy

"YOU'RE MOVING *AGAIN*?" my mother snapped.

The wind huffed and puffed against the sides of the phone booth like the Big Bad Wolf. I kept the folding door shut by leaning on it.

"We never intended to stay in a rooming house permanently," I said. The booth had initials scratched into its aluminum frame. "JL + CP." *Good luck to them. Whoever they are.*

Mom sighed loudly. "I suppose not. But when are you going to settle down? You can't *drift*."

Some papers flew by. *They* weren't drifting. They were really moving. Maybe Mom would be happy if I did that, just flew away.

I tried to keep my voice friendly. "We're not drifting. We got better jobs. We're going to work for a puppet theater."

"*Puppet* theater. . . . What in the world are you *doing*, Kathy? Birthday parties, that kind of thing?"

"No, we do international folk tales. It's for world peace."

"Oh, for pity's sake, that's even worse. With birthday parties, at least you might meet people. Are you turning into hippies?"

I sighed. "No, Mom, we're not turning into hippies. Just doing something we believe in."

"You've always been so *difficult,* Kathy. Why don't you get something with the city?"

"We *will* be working for the city a lot. We'll be performing in schools."

"It doesn't sound like much of an opportunity. And why Gretna? That's so far away from everything."

"In Gretna, we can afford a house. And we need one, because, well, we're having a baby." A motorcycle passed, drowning out Mom's answer. If there was one.

"Mom?"

"I heard you. Kathy, aside from everything else, you are too young to have a baby."

"The baby's even younger, Mom."

"I don't feel well. Maybe you'd better talk to your dad."

She put the phone down, and a loud, confused conversation filtered through it from the other end. I hung up as gently as if the receiver were made of Limoges porcelain. Called Sharon, but she wasn't home. I'd send her a postcard and tell her. Too bad Mom would get to her first.

Back in the room, Richard was putting books into a couple of toilet paper cartons I'd scrounged at the market. He gestured toward the boxes, grinning. "Was this a commentary on our taste in literature?"

"No, just the only cardboard boxes I could find."

He reached over and squeezed my hand. He still seemed doubtful about it all, but at least he was going to try.

"Want me to go get a pizza or something?" I asked. It was getting on for dinnertime, and he'd packed the food.

"Pizza, the mover's friend," he agreed. "Got money?"

"Uh-huh. What kind of toppings?"

"Whatever you like." He turned back to the boxes with tape and scissors. Toppings—uh-oh. I was in my fourth month, and I felt nauseated a lot. Not in the morning, and not by any specific thing. Something would smell funny all of a sudden, and then it would be queasy time.

I was starting to bulge, too. So far, I looked more chubby than pregnant. That wouldn't last much longer—all my clothes were getting tight. At least we'd have more money, working for Martin. There were probably lots of maternity things at the Salvation Army anyway.

They'd have baby furniture, too. I'd have to take pink and blue both, whatever I could get, but maybe I could make it pretty so it wouldn't look hand-me-down. I went over the furnishings of Francine's house in my mind. Tante Beatrice hadn't had a crib or a changing table, of course. The idea made me smile.

This is more like I want it to be. With the house and the baby, and Richard trying to be happy.

I got a mushroom pizza and brought it back to the room. After we ate, we packed the car and headed over to Gretna.

One last stop: at the Market, to say good-bye to Eddie. "It's not good-bye, doll," he said as I hugged him. "I live on the next street—Martin will show you. You take care of my girl, now," he told Richard, squeezing his shoulder. "And I want to be that baby's *godfather.*"

He gave us a big bag of fruits and vegetables as a housewarming present. I could see it was stuffed with the best of everything, and my throat closed up like it was wrapped with a tight scarf. Once again, we drove across the bridge, with Richard holding the brown paper bag in his lap.

It didn't take long to unpack our Volkswagen-full of possessions. Francine had left a box of kitchenware and linens sitting in the corner on the kitchenette, with a note: "Thought you might use these." The room was clean and the doilies were gone. There was a vase of homegrown flowers on the table. To keep from bursting into tears, I made the bed with Francine's linens and put the kitchen things away. I set each thing in place so carefully, so perfectly straight, I might have been tending a shrine.

It rained in the night, the wind rattling the window sash and water drumming on the roof. I woke and held Richard as he slept, feeling the coziness of being out of the storm. I was drifting, almost asleep, when the baby moved for the first time. I caught my breath, surprised and scared. *I'm a mother.* And then Richard, still sleeping, laid his arm across me and pulled me to him. I lulled into his arms, listening to the rain slacken, and finally slept too in the warmth beside him.

I woke to Richard's quiet rustlings in the kitchen and the smell of cooking. It was still raining. Richard had lit the heater, but the room wasn't warm yet. I wrapped myself in a fuzzy robe as he poured me a cup of coffee. He was already dressed. Oatmeal steamed in a saucepan on the back burner, and on the front one was a skillet full of sausages he was stabbing with a table fork. A small pop of grease caught his finger.

"Damn," he said, without much interest, glancing at his hand. He didn't bother to get a longer fork.

I looked at the sausages and decided not to have any. Better not think of them as food at all. "I felt the baby move last night," I told him, to change the subject.

"Are you okay?"

He sounded confused. *I wanted you to be excited and happy.* "Sure I am, it's what's supposed to happen."

"Oh. I'm sorry. This is sort of a lot to take in."

"Don't worry, it's not a problem," I told him. *It is a problem. I want you to want us, not put up with us.* But pushing him wasn't going to help. *Change the subject.*

"So, what's on for today?" I asked.

"We're all set here. I thought we might go over to Martin's after breakfast, see what he needs?"

"It *is* Saturday."

"I don't think he's got a nine-to-five operation."

His eagerness surprised me. I had expected resistance and awkwardness. I dressed in a clean shirt and yesterday's jeans, leaving the snap and about an inch of the zipper undone so I could fit into them. We didn't have an umbrella, but Richard was pacing, impatient to get going, so we left anyway, trying to run between the raindrops.

We waited awhile on the front porch after we knocked. We could hear the children inside, hear Martin and Thu, but no one answered for a minute or so. When Martin did let us in, he laughed.

"Better use the kitchen door like we do. Almost didn't realize you were here. Good thing the porch is covered. I wish you'd get a phone, by the way. It would make it a lot easier to work with you."

"Oh," said Richard. "I guess it would." I looked at him sharply, surprised at his quick agreement. We hadn't even considered it before.

We draggled, dripping, into the living room. Thu glanced up from the couch, where she was persuading one of the twins to eat a piece of toast. The other twin came in with a beautiful phoenix kite. He sat beside his brother, reached for a slice of toast on the coffee table, and brushed against a steaming cup. It turned over and rolled, spreading tea across the surface. Thu mopped it up with a napkin and smiled at us. "It looks like I'm making tea. Would you like some?"

"Please." Hot anything sounded good to me. She gestured at the dining table, and we sat around it. She disappeared into the kitchen.

Martin set his chair at the end of the table. "I gather you've never done much with puppets before," he said.

"Well, no," Richard admitted.

"No sweat. We'll start at the beginning. First you need to see the different kinds of puppets and get a feel for what they do. We use all sorts—glove puppets, shadow, rod, marionettes—so you're going to have to learn fast."

"We'll practice a lot," I promised.

He didn't answer right away, and I waited, afraid to say more. I hoped he wasn't reconsidering hiring us. Finally, he met my eyes and smiled.

"Thu's whole family is puppeteers, so she's learned all this since she was little. I had to get it the same way you will, quickly. She's still a far better puppeteer than I am. Probably always will be, too," he added as she came in with the tea. "There's also the matter of talent."

"Practice," she admonished. He smiled. *Maybe someday Richard and I will have in-jokes too.*

"That's the key," Martin said. "Practice at home, and then rehearse here with us. Eddie said you'd been at college. What were you studying?"

"Engineering," said Richard.

"Art," I chimed in.

Their faces lit up. "You'll both be *very* useful," Martin said.

Thu turned to me. "Once you get settled, let's get together and go over the art side of the theater—the scenery and costumes and so on. I can really use some help with that."

"What will I be doing?" Richard asked.

"Maybe your engineering will come in handy on some of the special effects," said Martin. "But both of you will mostly be operating puppets. I hope you can learn quickly, too. We can really use the extra hands."

Richard nodded. "Can I see some of the puppets?" he asked.

"Oh, yes. That's what we want to do first thing. We'll start with a couple of marionettes—they're probably more familiar to you."

Thu opened a cabinet and took out a clown and a bear. She handed the clown to Martin.

Both marionettes bowed to us, and then the clown juggled, did a flip, and danced. But the bear looked unimpressed. It nibbled at its paw and then scratched behind an ear. The clown gyrated wildly and the bear turned its back. The clown approached the bear and tapped its shoulder. The bear scratched again and lay down. It curled up to go to sleep.

The clown shook the bear's shoulder and pushed it back upright. I knew a puppet couldn't have facial expressions, but I could swear the bear looked bored and annoyed by the clown's persistence. Finally it gave in, shrugged, and gazed at the sky with "Enough, already!" in every line of its pose. And dropped to all fours, once again an ordinary bear.

The whole performance took less than five minutes. When it was over, I looked around, startled. Everything was much too big. I wanted the magic world of the puppets to go on and on, wanted to live there.

Richard was bright-eyed and silent. *He forgot about being a soldier for a few minutes. He looks like a kid.* The sudden turning-over feeling inside of me may have been the baby again, or maybe it was love, I couldn't tell.

එ

IT WAS A MONTH into our apprenticeship with Martin, and he and I were watching Richard and Thu block out the action of *The Legend of Savitri*. Pieces of costume littered the coffee table, along with assorted props, teacups, books, and notepads. Martin took the narrator's lines. Reading, he lost his Australian accent completely. He began spinning the story with a bewitching tone of "once upon a time."

> NARRATOR: Long ago, in the land of India, there lived a king named Aswapati who wanted a child more than any other of the world's blessings.

The curtain opened. For this rehearsal, the stage was bare except for an altar. The final scenery would have to show a private room, one where the king would go to pray. I made a note to check the library for ideas about Indian interiors. Or maybe I could simplify it, since the scene was short? Martin and Thu would have opinions about that. I scribbled a note to myself in the margin of my script.

Aswapati entered from stage left. Richard's hours of practice with the marionette were paying off. When we'd first begun rehearsing *Savitri*, Aswapati had walked like Frankenstein, but now he moved fairly normally.

> ASWAPATI: I have many wives, but none are blessed with children. For long years I have prayed to the goddess Savitri, morning and evening. My hope is nearly threadbare. Still, I will continue to pray. Surely the goddess will send me a child.

Aswapati knelt with a faint thump. Martin marked the rehearsal script, though I knew Richard wouldn't have to be reminded to work on the move. Aswapati would be praying morning and evening, all right. He would kneel and get up, kneel and get up, until Richard was satisfied with his performance.

> SAVITRI: *(rising from behind the altar)* I am Savitri, the daughter of the sun. King Aswapati, you have been faithful in your prayers. Your wish is granted. You will be the father of a baby girl.
> ASWAPATI: Oh, goddess, thank you! My daughter shall be named Savitri, after you!

Richard's voice was a soft monotone, stumbling on the foreign name. It was obvious he was reading the lines. Martin made another note in his script as the curtain closed.

> NARRATOR: Savitri grew to be a mirror for the beauty and wisdom of the goddess.

The curtain opened again on what I knew would be a garden scene. I wondered how I was going to design scenery to change from indoors to outdoors that quickly. I made another note in my script.

A young woman puppet entered from stage right, and Aswapati again from the left.

> ASWAPATI: Daughter, you are of age to marry.
> SAVITRI: But, Father, no man has asked for my hand.
> ASWAPATI: They do not dare. They turn away from your radiance. Still, you must have a husband.

SAVITRI: How shall we find him?
ASWAPATI: You must go out into the world, Savitri.
You must find the man who is worthy of you.

Aswapati stood stiffly at attention, facing the audience. Richard's voice had been louder as he delivered the last line of the scene, but he still spoke in a self-conscious monotone.

Martin broke in before Richard and Thu began the next scene. "Richard, bring Aswapati downstage and make him look more troubled. This isn't just heroics."

"Heroics?" Richard's head appeared around one side of the stage, his face wrinkled in confusion. "I didn't know he was being heroic at all."

Thu peered around the other side. They looked like marionettes themselves—the Indian puppets were controlled partly with strings from metal bands around the puppeteers' heads.

Martin looked up from his script. "Heroism isn't conflict," he said. "It's going to meet your fate."

"Without fear," Richard put in.

"Good God, no! *With* fear. But going anyway," said Martin.

Richard considered that a moment. "How do I make a marionette look troubled?" he asked.

"Hold the gestures close to the body at first. A person who's sad or pressured pulls in. Then when he sends her to find a husband, show the thought in an outward movement of his arm as you turn the head. Make it slow at first and then more confident," said Martin.

"If the body and head are right," Thu added, "the audience will imagine the facial expressions." Richard bobbed back behind the curtains.

The next scene showed Savitri and her retinue. Several attendants, strung as a group, followed her.

> SAVITRI: I have traveled so far, and yet I have found no suitable husband. I will stop and rest at this hermitage.
> *(TEACHER enters from stage left.)*
> SAVITRI: *(aside)* Perhaps the teacher here will guide me in my quest.
> TEACHER: Welcome!
> SAVITRI: *(bows her head in reverence)* I thank you. *(gesturing offstage)* Teacher, who are these men approaching?
> TEACHER: That is Prince Satyavan and his father, a king with no kingdom, for he was conquered and blinded. Satyavan is well-named "Son of Truth"— he is a man of great virtue.

"Take a break," called Martin. After a moment, Richard and Thu emerged from backstage. Thu eased into the kitchen, and I heard the kettle scrape onto the stove. Richard slumped on the couch.

"You can't expect to get everything at once," said Martin. "Actually, you're doing well with the puppets. I can tell you're practicing a lot."

Richard nodded. It was true—he'd worked hard. Every couple of days, he traded the puppets he'd taken home for new ones of a different type. He'd work on his own for a while, then with me, then go back to Thu or Martin with questions. I loved the puppets, but Richard went far beyond that. Even now, taking a break, he was unconscious of me, immersed in the *Savitri* script. His expression was like Martin's, intense and absorbed. He'd forgotten me.

Maybe he'd look at me if I were like Savitri, beautiful and brave. But I don't even want to be like her. All I want is my own home, and the sun coming into the baby's room through new curtains. Why would anyone love a housewife with her baby and her dumb curtains?

I rubbed my eyes so hard I saw blue fireworks.

Thu brought in a tray with a teapot and steaming cups of tea, a welcome distraction. She passed the cups around.

Martin turned to Richard. "Why don't you concentrate on the marionettes for a while, instead of trying to get all the different puppets at once?"

"Okay."

"When you practice, do you do the lines or only the motions?"

"Just the motions."

"So, you're not practicing the lines at all."

"Well, I would feel foolish, talking to myself."

"Better to feel foolish when you're practicing than to sound foolish when we're performing."

I was afraid Martin's candor would hurt Richard's feelings. But Richard smiled. "I'll need a script, then," was all he said.

"Don't stick to the script too tightly, though, or you'll sound theatrical." Martin grabbed the nearest puppet, which was a glove puppet depicting a dog. "Here, let me show you."

"I am so *angry!*" the dog said, as Martin worked its head and front paws. "My people *shut me out of the house.* I can't get *in!* I have a right to lie in my own bed, not out here in the mud! It's 'pretty puppy' this and 'baby' that, but what happens when I'm inconvenient? 'Out you go, good dog.' Who in *hell* do they think they are?" His voice vibrated with fury.

Once again, I had the illusion that the puppet's face moved, and every gesture was completely canine. I thought of every dog I'd ever seen, and I felt an echo of all the anger I'd ever felt. Martin stripped the dog off his hand and laid it back on the table.

"Take any one of the puppets and go through the catalog of emotions with it," he said. "There are only a few. The basic ones are fear, anger, shame, love, and joy. Get those down, and then you can go on to variations and subtleties. You feel a lot less foolish after you've done it a few times. In fact, awkwardness is probably nine-tenths of what's wrong to begin with. Do the verbal practice with one that's easy to move, so you're not trying to get too much down at once." Martin smiled at Richard to soften his criticism.

Richard sipped his tea. Steam from the cup curled around his face like dragon breath. He didn't look upset by Martin's remarks. He looked interested, professional.

I picked up a carved wooden fish from the coffee table. "You made this?" I asked Thu.

"Oh, yes. It isn't difficult." She poured more of the fragrant tea into her cup, and gestured slightly toward mine. I held it out, and Thu refilled it.

"Do you think you could teach me?" I sipped carefully, afraid of burning my tongue.

"Of course. I'll be glad to show you. Remind me next time we get together to work on the sets, and I'll get you started. It would be wonderful if you learned to carve—you could help with the puppet heads and hands."

"I never tried it before. I don't know if I'd be able to do it. . . ." I left the thought dangling.

Thu smiled. "I never did it before the first time either," she said. "I'm sure you can do it. You're very talented. You can use my tools at first, and then I'll help you find some of your own."

The idea of carving was exciting. Drawing was recording, but carving an animal would be almost like creating a live one. I looked at the fish again, wondering if I could make something like that.

Or when I'd even have time to try. I didn't practice with the puppets as much as Richard did, but I did spend a good bit of time on it. And somehow I always ended up doing most of the housework, although Richard kept saying he was going to help. And I'd decided to take Tex up on the modeling offer, if he still wanted me.

"The Baby"—I was starting to think about it a lot now. I needed a name. Richard wouldn't discuss it, so I started turning over names in my mind. I didn't want to think up boys' names and girls' both, so I thought of all the ones that would be good for either. Chris was one, but I knew a Chris I didn't like. Robin, Jackie, Kelly, Lee . . . .

Richard and I gathered the day's load of puppets and carried them home. We looked like parents already, and the thought made me smile—today we were parents of Prince Satyavan, a dancing girl, a boy hand puppet, and a horse. Tomorrow's children might be a frog, a warrior, or a god.

I made chili and corn bread for dinner. Eating the spicy food, I watched the sky darken behind the misted-up windows. While Richard washed the dishes, I called Tex. He asked me to model Tuesday nights, and I made a note on the kitchen calendar.

Richard sponged off the table, whistling the music from one of the clown routines. The prince's gold robes glittered on the chair in the corner. Richard took out the garbage, and I opened a library book about how to be a good mother. It was pretty dog-eared, and I imagined the city being full of wonderful mothers who had read every word. Richard bustled back, letting the screen door slap shut behind him, and took up a puppet.

> TEACHER: That is Prince Satyavan and his father, a king with no kingdom, for he was conquered and blinded. Satyavan is well-named "Son of Truth"— he is a man of great virtue.
> SAVITRI: Satyavan is the one I will marry.

I blinked. I hadn't expected Richard to do the women's voices. And the falsetto reminded me of the man at the cemetery.

> ASWAPATI: Daughter, you must choose a different husband. I have learned from a holy man that Satyavan will die a year from today.
> SAVITRI: Even so, I will marry Satyavan.

ᴄ⍥

"WHY DON'T YOU GET MARRIED?" asked Sharon.

"I don't think Richard wants to," I said. I had picked a time when he was away to make this phone call, knowing how it was likely to go.

"He *does* know he's going to be a father?"

"It would be kind of hard to hide it at this point."

"I don't think it's fair to you. Don't you mind?"

I felt like crying, but I didn't want Sharon to hear that. When we were kids, the only time she ever got in a real fight was when I got picked on at school. "Yes," I said. "But I'm afraid to push it."

"Dad and Mom are upset."

"I knew about Mom. She wants me to get an abortion. I guess she doesn't realize it's too late for that."

"Well, Dad thinks you should get married. It's certainly not too late for *that*."

"Maybe we will someday. I don't think this is a good time to mention it." *Don't cry. Don't let her know how much it hurts that he doesn't want me that way.* "It's the war, Sharon. He went through some awful stuff. Let it be."

"Well, can Sam and I still visit?"

"Sure you can. When?"

"Let's see, it's April third. Not this month. Sam's got a conference and a million other things. Early May?"

I thought about our rehearsal schedule. "May is fine. Do you still want to stay at the Monteleone?"

"Let me talk to Sam. He might not want to stay in the Quarter. Especially now that you're out in Gretna."

"When are *you* getting married, by the way? Speaking of marriage." I felt a twist of jealousy. *Why can Sharon get married and not me?*

"Probably after Christmas. Mom wanted us to wait a while longer so she'd have time to organize a big wedding, but we don't care about that."

"Poor Mom. One daughter too fast, one too slow."

"She should have had a third one. Then one could be j-u-u-u-s-t right." Sharon laughed at her mimicry of a record of "Goldilocks" we'd had when we were little.

"If Mom had a hundred daughters, none of them would *ever* be right. I gotta go now. Doing some portrait modeling over in the Quarter."

"Love you, Sis. Don't let it get you down—it'll work out."
Sharon had been in the middle of quarrels between Mom and
me more than once.

"Eventually. Love you." I hung up.

I drove across the bridge and found a parking spot in the
Quarter. Tex's apartment on Dumaine was in a quiet, run-down
building with a dry fountain in the courtyard. The class was starting as I got there. Waving me to the only comfortable-looking
chair in the place, Tex draped a black Spanish shawl around my
shoulders and adjusted a light.

It was hard to keep still for so long. At first I wanted to
squirm. My nose itched, but I knew I wasn't supposed to move.
Then, in the light's halo, I fell into a near-trance. The fidgets
dropped away, and my mind drifted back to Richard and the
puppets, to the tale of Savitri.

> NARRATOR: Savitri and Satyavan lived in married
> bliss for one year. And the time approached that
> Savitri knew was appointed for Satyavan's death.
> For three days and three nights, she knelt at the
> altar in prayer.
> *(Curtain opens to show SAVITRI kneeling at the altar.
> SATYAVAN enters from stage left, hesitates, then goes
> to SAVITRI.)*
> SATYAVAN: My love, it is good to fast and pray,
> but you must not forget to rest. Are you troubled
> over something?
> SAVITRI: *(rising to her feet)* Yes, but I may not
> speak of it.
> SATYAVAN: Then I will leave you to your prayers
> and go to the forest for the day.

SAVITRI: I will go to the forest with you.
SATYAVAN: Will you abandon your prayers, then,
   my love?
SAVITRI: I will never do that. *(aside)* He does not
   know his fate. I will not leave him, wherever he
   goes.
(SAVITRI and SATYAVAN exit stage right.)

I had another quick scene change at that point. The altar
and the other trappings of an Indian interior had to be replaced
by a believable forest. I wondered if I could use Indian music
between scenes to distract the audience while I managed the
scenery. Even an extra half a minute would make a big difference. *I have the same problem as Savitri—needing to buy a little
time. Only it's not quite as important for a puppet show as when
you're trying to save your husband's life.*

The curtain would open on Savitri and Satyavan walking
through the forest. Or maybe it could open on the empty set,
and the two of them could walk onto the stage. That would work
better—Satyavan could stumble, to show he was ill.

SAVITRI: We have walked many miles.
SATYAVAN: Yes, I am very tired. I will rest for a
   while. *(lies down)*

What would Savitri do then? She might stand near him, or
she might sit beside him. She knew he was about to die—surely
she'd want to touch him one last time. But then she'd have to look
up, startled, as Yama, the god of death, appeared on the stage.

Thu would be operating Savitri, and I knew she'd make her
look frightened but determined. Maybe Savitri would flinch a

little, but she would stand her ground as Yama came and claimed Satyavan's soul. This was a prop detail that I had yet to work out—Satyavan's soul was to be a tiny likeness of him, concealed somehow in his costume. It would have its own string, and be able to be switched from Satyavan to Yama. Maybe Thu would know how to do that.

Yama would then turn and walk away, but Savitri would follow.

> YAMA: *(turning to SAVITRI)* Go back, Princess. I go to the Land of the Dead. Go back. Your husband's time has come, and yours has not.
> SAVITRI: I will not go back. It is my duty to stay beside my husband.
> YAMA: Savitri, you are brave and loving. But your duty to your husband is over. I will grant you three favors, but none may be the life of Satyavan.
> SAVITRI: Yama, I ask that you restore my husband's father to all that was his, his kingdom and his sight.
> YAMA: I will grant that. And what else do you ask?
> SAVITRI: Yama, I am my father's only child. Grant that he may have many more children.
> YAMA: Yes, I will grant that. And what will your last favor be, Princess?
> SAVITRI: Yama, grant that I may have many children—the children of Satyavan.
> YAMA: Savitri, you are as clever as you are brave. I have no choice but to release your husband.

Richard had struggled with the emotions in the play and how to express them. His acting *was* improving, but he wasn't going to win any Academy Awards yet. There were still the basic emotion exercises to do with the hand puppet. Maybe he'd do that this evening, while I wasn't there to make him self-conscious.

The class took a break and I looked at the portraits. Some of them were awkward, and these were more or less alike. The good ones all looked like me, but not like each other, as if each artist had seen a different Kathy behind my face. I thought that portraits were a bit like puppetry, trying to get to something that was there but hard to see.

I picked up a charcoal stub and sketched a face on the back of a scrap of paper while the others chatted over coffee. Tex came up and considered my picture.

"Ever had art lessons before?"

"In high school I did. It was my major in college, but I didn't stay there long. I do scenery for the puppet theater where I work. And one of my bosses is teaching me to carve."

"You want to take lessons here? You're not bad at all."

"I don't think I'd have the money."

"You could swap for more modeling."

I considered it. I liked the thought of having an art class. It would mean being away from home one evening a week—but Richard and I had gone from hardly seeing each other to spending a little too much time together. Maybe a few hours apart would be good for both of us.

"Okay, I'll give it a try." We dropped the subject as the others came to their places and waited for me to take my place.

But I thought for the rest of the evening about all the new things in my life. Mom was mad because I'd dropped out of school—she kept saying I'd never go back, not with a child to care for. She probably didn't like being a grandmother anyway, and a black grandchild was just too much to take. *Faculty-wife*

*tea: "How are your sweet daughters doing, Virginia?" "Oh, just
fine, Sharon is marrying a doctor!" "And what about the cute little
blonde?" "She's living with a black boy in New Orleans. They're
having a baby." Uh-huh.*

I wished she could at least see that what I was doing now was
better than school. In a way, it was like a real art school—carving,
drawing, and making the sets and costumes for the puppets. Even
better, because I was learning the puppets themselves, and the
folklore that went with them, and about the cultures that the folklore came from. Those things were more important than what I'd
found in college courses, too. Especially if Martin was right, that
the puppets would make people understand each other better.

I was also learning some things that I'd rather not think
about. Martin's folktales were pretty idealistic. About brave, clever
people like Savitri. I wasn't like her. *All I want is to be close to
someone, to belong to someone. To Richard. But why would anyone
want me? If Yama came through the forest toward me, Richard or
no Richard, I'd run. I'd feel guilty about it, but I can't imagine
doing anything else.*

The evening finished late. Back home, I parked the car on
the night-quiet street and walked softly past Francine's darkened
house. As I reached our place, Richard's voice startled me, not
loud but charged with feeling.

"I'm scared, I'm so scared. I'm trapped. I can't get out. I want
out. *Oh, God, let me out!*"

I dropped my purse on purpose just outside the door. I
thought if he heard me coming, he could get himself together
before I had to look at his face. As I came in, he was taking the
boy glove puppet off his hand. He looked shocked, and not one
bit glad to see me.

He's done some good work on the problem of expressing emotion. But if that's how he feels about being a father, I guess we won't be getting married, will we?

❧ 17 ❧
February 1975, San Pedro
Lacey

I CALLED EDDIE a couple of weeks before Mardi Gras to let him know our schedule in New Orleans.

"You know, I've been thinking," he said, "and I talked it over with my friend Francine. She asked me to invite you to stay at her place instead of going to a hotel."

"Oh, Eddie, I couldn't possibly intrude on her. I mean, she doesn't know us—we'd just be underfoot."

"It wouldn't be an intrusion. I'm sure it wouldn't. Francine has a mother-in-law house in her backyard, so you'd really be on your own. As a matter of fact, it's where Kathy lived. Francine never rented it to anyone else. She keeps hoping Kathy will come back."

"Would it be okay if I talk it over with my husband and call you later?"

"Sure. Just let me know. And we'll get together while you're here, either way."

I thought staying with Kathy's friends was a great idea, but I had no idea how Willis would feel. He'd be glad to save the money, but he might think Gretna was a little too far from downtown. He also might be uncomfortable about staying with people he didn't know, private house or no private house.

But the main concern was slowly dawning. I did know about southern hospitality, but these people seemed surprisingly eager to take us in, considering they didn't know us from Adam.

I'd launched this Mama Fix-It campaign believing that Kathy's problems were likely to be kid ones—misunderstandings I could clear up without much trouble. Even after I'd seen her the day of the Christmas Faire, I'd thought she was probably overreacting to situations that would look manageable to an adult.

But Eddie was no kid. He sounded like he'd been around the block a few times. And his voice had an edge of desperation that made me wonder if I was going to be able to help at all.

What had I gotten myself into?

❧ 18 ❧
April 1973, New Orleans
Kathy

"Is FRANCINE BLACK?" asked Richard.

Thu, Martin, and Eddie looked up, surprised at the odd question right after Martin's usual table grace. We were having dinner at the picnic table in our yard, bundled in sweaters and jackets. It was my idea—I didn't want to wait any longer to invite them over, and Martin's chair couldn't get into the house because of the steps. I was serving steaming gumbo, fresh homemade bread, and hot tea to make up for the chilly April dusk.

Eddie raised an eyebrow. "Yes and no," he said. "She's a Creole."

Richard tore a chunk off the braided loaf and passed me the basket. "Is that different?" he asked.

"Depends. There are French Creoles, black Creoles, and Creoles of Color. Goes back a lot of years here. Francine's what you'd call a Creole of Color. The old *gens de couleur libre*," Eddie said.

Richard frowned. "I have no idea what that means," he said.

"Free people of color," Thu translated. "Which color are they talking about?" She kept an eye on Dom and Joss as they scampered around, chasing an early lightning bug.

Eddie snorted. "*Color* always means *black*, Thu," he answered. "Pass the bread, would you, Kathy?"

I started the basket toward Eddie. Eager hands reached in all along the way, but there was plenty. I poured tea into mugs and passed them, too.

"So, exactly who is a Creole?" Richard asked.

Eddie laughed. "Seems like it's anyone who says they are." He took Martin's bowl and ladled gumbo into it from the pot.

"She asked if *I* was one." Richard looked confused. He held out his bowl as if Eddie could fill it with information along with the soup.

"She *does* tend to include people," said Eddie. With all the soup bowls filled, he sat down and tasted from his. "Why don't you ask her about it?" He took some filé and passed the jar to Thu. She sprinkled it on top of the gumbo, as the rest of us were doing, and then squinted at the label. In the dimming light, she gave up quickly and passed it to Richard.

"I thought she might be offended," Richard said.

"Francine?" Eddie laughed. "Not her. Francine's a typical Creole. Proud as Lucifer, every one of them. The only problem with asking about Creoles is that she'll talk your ear off, half of it in French." He looked around. "She coming tonight?"

"No, she's off at her daughter's. She said to ask you for some tomatoes and okra, when you get a chance," I told him.

Eddie's spoon stopped halfway to his mouth. "Tomatoes and okra! Where am I going to get decent tomatoes and okra, middle of April?"

I shrugged. "I think that's her problem, too."

"What do you do with okra?" asked Thu. She loved good cooking as much as any New Orleanian, and was starting to experiment with local specialties. I wasn't sure how she would fit okra into her repertoire, though, and sort of hoped she'd lose interest.

"Roll it in cornmeal and fry it, that's the best," offered Eddie. "Otherwise, it tends to come out slimy. You can thicken gumbo with it, too." He swirled his spoon through the gumbo, checking the ingredients. "Kathy doesn't have any in this one, though."

"No," I said quickly. "I don't like it. I used filé instead."

"We use filé too," said Thu. "Gumbo is like bouillabaisse. I didn't know it could be thickened with okra."

She called in French to the boys, who were getting excited chasing the bug. I knew vaguely that France had held Vietnam for a while.

Will she mind if I ask? "Is your family French as well as Vietnamese?" I ventured.

"Oh, no. But the French were in Vietnam for a hundred years or more. My family were artists in Hue and Saigon. We had partly a French education."

"Do you mind my asking?" She didn't sound as if she did, but Mom had always said not to ask personal questions.

"Not at all. In fact, I'd rather you did. Why does no one ask? Like Richard, being afraid to ask about Francine. Why is it?" Dom and Joss ran to her, and she tousled their hair and gave them soup and bread.

"You never know if people might have a chip on their shoulder," I said.

"Chip?" Thu's English was so fluent, I tended to forget she didn't know all the idioms.

"Might be sort of sensitive," I explained. "Or ready to get mad about it for their own reasons."

Martin looked up from his plate. "Same thing with the wheelchair," he said. "Parents tell their kids not to stare at people in wheelchairs. So, nobody looks at all. Everyone I see just happens to be looking the other way." He laughed. "I always wanted to turn heads—guess I forgot to specify which direction."

"It's like being a veteran," Richard said. "No one wants to think about it. I swear, I might as well be a leper." Suddenly he looked at Thu in horror, realizing what he'd admitted.

She was unperturbed. "I *thought* you'd been a soldier. So have most of the men in my country, and not only this generation, either. Over the years, some of my family have been on one side, some on the other. That part is hard."

She looked straight at Richard with trouble in her face. "This is our misfortune, all of us. But even Uncle Ho said our quarrel is not with the American people."

"Uncle Ho?" he asked, hoarsely.

"Ho Chi Minh," she explained.

"Ho Chi Minh was your uncle?" Eddie exclaimed.

"Not like an uncle here. In Vietnam, we believe we're all related. So, we say "sister," "aunt," "uncle," depending on the person's status. It's polite." Thu looked around to see whether we understood.

"Actually," said Eddie, "I feel that way about this neighborhood. Most of us are like family. Back in my mother's day, it was true *most* places, but here it's not gone yet."

"We're sort of a motley family," Martin objected. "An Italian, a black soldier, a gimp Aussie, a Vietnamese, a *gens de couleur libre,* and Kathy. . . . What are you, Kathy?"

I scraped the last of the gumbo from my bowl. "Worst thing of all. A Yankee."

"You are?" Martin looked up in surprise. "You have a southern accent."

"I was born in Illinois. My dad moved us south when he got hired at LSU."

"I'll never tell. Provided you give me one million dollars in a plain brown bag." He put out his hand for the loot.

I laughed. "You can't blackmail me. I'm a relative. We're the Motley family."

"The Motley family," said Eddie. "I like it! That's who we are—the Motley family!" He raised his mug in a toast.

"How can we just say we're a family?" asked Richard.

"Same way a person can just say they're a Creole, I guess. Who has the right to tell us we're not?" Eddie countered. We all raised our mugs.

I reached out to touch Dom's silky hair. We *were* sort of a mixed bunch. *Maybe that's why, for once, I feel like I belong.*

"The baby will be even more mixed," I said without thinking. *Me and my big mouth—Richard will be mad.*

"Baby?" asked Martin. He and Thu each picked up a twin. "Congratulations! I thought you were getting a bit stout. But, you know, I didn't want to say anything. . . ."

"In case I had a chip on my shoulder," I agreed.

"To the youngest Motley!" Martin said, raising his mug. All the mugs were raised again—except for Richard's.

"When's it due?" Martin asked.

"September."

"What are you going to name it?" asked Thu.

"We haven't decided." *No "we" about it—Richard won't discuss the baby at all. I hope they don't notice how withdrawn he looks all of a sudden.*

"You need a name," said Martin. "Which names are you considering?"

"Maybe one for either a boy or a girl. That way, we'll have one no matter which it is."

Martin considered this. "Like Jo or Jamie?" he asked.

"Jamie! We didn't think of that. I like Jamie."

I smiled at Martin, and he bowed from his chair. "Do I get to be the godfather?"

"Eddie already has dibs. Do you get two?"

"Only if it's a boy," said Martin. "Hey, Eddie—you knew and you didn't tell? Not fair, buddy." Martin turned back to me. "You'd better quit hauling the sets and props around like you have been, or neither one of us will be a godfather."

"Lord, Martin, I'm not made out of glass." I looked at Richard. *How is he taking all this? He looks a million miles away.* The conversation dropped, and he came out of his reverie.

"I need to work some more with the shadow puppets," he mumbled. I wondered if he'd heard us at all. Eddie clinked his knife on his glass.

"Attention, all members of the Motley family! You are invited to attend Easter Vigil service at Our Lady of Lourdes next Saturday night with Francine and me. Please come. It's a Motley family tradition."

Thu laughed. "How can it be a tradition when you formed the Motley family ten minutes ago, Eddie?"

"I formed the traditions at the same time."

"I can't wait to find out what the other ones are," she said.

"One is the annual family reunion," Eddie announced. "This is the first."

"Richard and I aren't Catholic," I said, getting back to his invitation. "I'm Episcopalian and Richard's a Baptist."

Eddie turned to Richard. "Do they have Easter Vigil at the Baptist Church?"

"I don't think so."

"So, come with us."

It didn't seem completely logical, but that wasn't any reason not to go. I gathered the empty bowls, and wrapped the leftover bread in a napkin. Richard was off in his own thoughts again—probably puppets. The boys had dropped off to sleep. The gumbo was gone, and everyone was starting to shiver. We said good night. The first Motley family reunion was over.

の

THE NEIGHBORHOOD WAS BUSY Saturday night as Richard and I walked to Martin's house. The circles of light from the porches almost-but-not-quite touched, like flower heads in the sweet clover chains I braided as a little girl. Doors of houses and doors of cars closed softly, and a voice called, "Let's go, let's go now." All the walkers were headed the same way.

Richard and I were awkward, churchgoing-solemn. Richard wore his gray graduation suit, and I had on a secondhand maternity dress. I was at an in-between stage—maternity clothes swamped me, but nothing else was comfortable. Francine had given me a lace circle to cover my head, like the one she was wearing. They made me think of Tante Beatrice's doilies.

Thu answered Richard's knock. I'd never seen her wear anything but jeans and a T-shirt before, but here she was, stunning in a silky red *ao dai*. A black mantilla floated over her hair. Eddie and Francine had already arrived, so we started for Our Lady of Lourdes right away.

Dom was whining because it was Joss's turn to ride in Martin's lap, so Richard took him from Thu and carried him piggyback. Dom laughed with glee to be riding so high, and the others laughed too. I was startled and then touched by their casualness. Like we were headed over to a friend's place.

The church was dark as we approached, but the lawn outside the front door was crowded. We waited quietly. The crowd passed around unlit candles.

A group near the entrance of the church stood around something that looked like a small table. A flame struck, faded, steadied. A fire sprang up in the bowl-like top of the table.

A huge candle was lit, and people began filing through the doors. Altar boys scurried with tapers to spread the light to the congregation's candles. Waves of light followed the great candle's progress to the altar. A voice came out of the dim, singing strongly and alone:

"Rejoice, heavenly powers! Sing, choirs of angels!"

The points of flame pushed back the darkness, and I felt goose bumps on my arms. Richard, intent beside me, had the face of an African angel. I couldn't see the singer from where I sat, but I heard every word, so distinct that he might have been singing especially for me:

"The night will be as clear as day: it will become my light, my joy. The power of this holy night dispels all evil, washes guilt away, restores lost innocence, brings mourners joy; it casts out hatred, brings us peace, and humbles earthly pride. Night truly blessed when heaven is wedded to earth, and man is reconciled with God!"

I gripped the candle until my nails made crescents in the wax. Lost innocence brought back, and peace—was that what Easter was about? Could a soldier ever be innocent again? The tears running down my cheeks were almost as hot as the wax drips that rolled burning over my hand. I didn't wipe either away.

Readings and prayers and songs followed, and I sat and stood and knelt with the others. When they said, "I will take you out of the nations; I will gather you from all the countries and bring you back into your own land," I looked secretly at Thu. Did she miss her country? Was it gone forever, destroyed by our guns and chemicals? Richard had helped to do that.

I have too—I've never protested the war. It's never felt real to me until now. Martin was right. No one is innocent. That's why Richard cries in his sleep. That's why he's afraid to be a father.

"I will give you a new heart and put a new spirit in you; I will remove from you your heart of stone and give you a heart of flesh."

A new heart and a new spirit. . . . My baby, my Jamie, she has *to grow up in a different world from this one we've made.* I knelt in silent anguish, thinking of the women whose children hadn't been able to do that. *What can anyone do to change it? The puppets are supposed to be for peace, but what can they do? Savitri, eighteen inches high, stands in front of a tank. It rolls over her without even a bump.*

The priest held up the circle of bread. "Behold the Lamb of God who takes away the sins of the world."

"Lord, I am not worthy to receive you," the congregation answered. "But only say the word and I shall be healed."

After Mass, we trailed home, exhausted. Richard put his arm around me as we walked alone though the night.

⟨⟩

APRIL ENDED with early heat that year. Every time I looked, Francine's rosebushes had popped out more flowers—they reminded me of a jack-in-the-box. Hummingbirds dipped in and out of the red ones all day, and after the sun went down, lightning bugs made neon processions.

We were learning *The Snow Queen* with the puppets. Martin had proposed it the week before, as we sat around his living room after a rehearsal.

"You're the boss," Richard had said.

Martin shook his head. "Not that kind of boss. I want us to decide together." He kept the stack of scripts in his lap.

"So, why do it?" Richard asked.

"Because we need a strong Christmas piece, and I think it has a good message."

It sounded convincing to me. "So, why *not* do it?" I asked.

Martin opened the top script and riffled the pages. "It's not a folktale. It's a literary fairy tale. It doesn't have the international flavor that we plan to specialize in."

"Are there any Christmas pieces that do?" I asked.

"I don't know of any." Martin shrugged and handed the scripts around.

We voted unanimously to do it.

Rehearsals of *The Snow Queen* began in earnest the next day. Now we were putting the production together, using temporary puppets while we made the permanent ones. Christmas seemed remote, almost impossible, in the blossoming heat of New Orleans. I would have given anything for some of the ice and snow in the story.

I thought of the last line: "It was summer—warm, beautiful summer." *Easy for a Danish man to say. He should have tried being pregnant in a tropical climate.* September could hurry up, as far as I was concerned.

I borrowed Thu's sewing machine and sewed puppet costumes with the breeze of a fan right on me. I had to weigh down the pattern pieces to keep them from blowing away. The costumes reminded me of doll dresses I'd made with Aunt Ruth. I wondered if she ever missed me.

Richard came in from the yard, carrying a box. "We need to practice today—can you do the costumes later?"

I sighed. There was so much to do later and so little later to do it in. It was only a couple of days until Sharon's and Sam's visit. I needed to buy food and clean house and do the laundry. And cook.

And I had an assignment for Tex's drawing class—I was working my way though an odd old book of drawing exercises. This week's assignment was to draw something while looking only at the model, not at the drawing. It sounded impossible. And for Thu's woodcarving lesson, I was supposed to carve a chain out of a single piece of wood, which also sounded impossible. And I had backdrops to do for *The Snow Queen,* under Thu's watchful eye.

But Richard was right—practice came first. We had to at least go through it once before rehearsal with Martin and Thu this afternoon. I put aside the costumes as Richard pulled puppets out of the box. We used the table as a stage.

NARRATOR: Once upon a time, a demon made a mirror in which everything was reflected as evil. Everyone who looked into it believed it showed the world as it really was. And that was bad, but still worse was to come. For, one day it broke, and the pieces flew everywhere. All who were caught by one of the shards saw the world in the likeness of that mirror.

With the glove puppets, it was easy to do fast vignettes of people dressed in clothes of all nations, jeering and criticizing each other and everything around them. We both talked at once in a babble of discord. I picked up the story again.

NARRATOR: In a large city, there lived two friends, a boy named Kay and a girl named Gerda. One day when they were playing, Kay felt something strike him in the heart, and a cold splinter pierced his eye. He cried out and Gerda ran to help him.

Too stiff. "This last bit should be dialogue, not narration," I commented. I marked the script for revision.

KAY: You are very ugly. Why should I spend time with you? I can find a much more beautiful girl. *(turns and leaves)*

The Gerda puppet reached her hand out as if to draw him back, then lifted it to wipe her cheek.

The phone rang.

With the hand that wasn't being Kay, Richard got it. He passed it to me.

"Hey, doll. Francine says she doesn't mind if I build a ramp up to your porch so Martin's chair can get in the door," Eddie said. "Is it okay with you?"

"Good idea." I didn't want to have any more picnic dinners. It was warm enough now for a picnic, but the mosquitoes knew that as well as we did.

"This afternoon work for you? I've got the wood and everything."

"This afternoon's fine. I need to go to the market anyway. Sharon and Sam are coming, day after tomorrow."

"I'll bring you some vegetables, then. See you later."

I told Richard what Eddie had said, then set the sleigh and Kay's sled on the table. "The next scene shows kids playing in the snow. I don't know what to do to get a realistic snow effect. We have snowflakes, but I can't dump them like garbage out of a truck."

Richard laughed. "Any ideas?"

"Maybe some kind of sifter? Maybe a net?

"What would make them fall out?"

"I could jiggle it," I suggested.

"I don't see how, unless you can grow a third hand. Even with glove puppets, you can't tend to a net."

"What about a mechanical sifter?" I wasn't sure how this would work, but there had to be some way to do it.

"Noisy. Fasten a string to your toe and tap your foot."

I considered this bizarre solution. "It would make me too stationary. But a foot-operated device is a good idea. Something with a pedal, or a stirrup thing that I could get out of when I needed to."

I was developing into the scenery and special effects person, which suited me fine. And a scriptwriter. Of course, I liked operating the puppets as well, but Richard had far more talent than I did. Neither of us was like Thu, who had mastered it all. Of course, she'd been doing it a lot longer than we had.

We settled the boy puppets onto our hands and went on with the dialogue.

> BOY 1: Let's tie our sleds to the carriage! The horses will pull us through the streets!
> BOY 2: Don't let the coachman see us!

I had constructed sleigh-and-horse combinations to glide across the stage. I managed these while Richard's boy puppets sneaked rides behind them, laughing and playing.

When they were offstage, we had a brief break that would be filled with music and falling snow—provided I could work out a good way to make that happen. The seconds without puppets would be effective, but they'd also give us a chance to set up for the remainder of the scene.

I marked my script to insert a music cue for Kay to appear onstage alone, carrying his sled. From the other direction, a great white sleigh appeared, with a driver muffled in a furry white coat.

"*Ermine*," Richard said, studying the script. "What does that mean besides *white?*"

"It has small black markings."

"Could anyone *tell* from the audience?"

"Probably not. But I'll do them anyway. *I'll* know, even if no one else does."

Richard struggled to make Kay tie his sled to the sleigh runners. A hand puppet didn't make for convenient knotting, but we couldn't have the ties dangling. I'd have to work something out to make them stick. Something that would hold when Kay, tiring of the game, found he couldn't escape.

"So, he yells 'Stop!' and 'Let me go!' And then what?" Richard, juggling props, had lost his place in the script.

"That's the cue for more snow." I marked my script. It looked like I was going to have a busy foot, twitching the net to make a blizzard. It would probably take a second person to pull the sleigh and manage the lights.

NARRATOR: The great sleigh slipped along faster and faster. The wind whipped at Kay's cheeks and tore his hat away.

"How do we manage the hat?" he asked.

"I'll put a string on it."

He laughed. "Which one-man-band did you hire to do all this?"

"I have an idea it's going to be me." It was true. When it came to special effects, everyone expected me to do magic. And I loved figuring out the effects, along with the scenery and props to go with them.

"You could get a second job at Preservation Hall."

"My first job already takes up all my second-job time."

NARRATOR: All at once, the flurries cleared and the sleigh drew to a halt. A tall figure rose slowly from its high seat. Snowflakes glittered on her crown, and a diamond flashed from her cloak like ice. It was the Snow Queen.

"That ought to sound scarier. Richard? If I don't get to the market this minute, I'll be late for rehearsal with Thu and Martin."

"I thought Eddie was bringing food," he said indistinctly, hunting under the table for Kay's hat.

"Vegetables, Richard. Last time I checked, you hadn't turned vegetarian, and I know Sharon and Sam haven't." I kissed him quickly and got out of there.

When I got back with the groceries, Eddie and Richard were laying out the framing for a platform and ramp. They took the bags from my arms and heaved them onto the porch. With the steps gone, it wasn't easy for me to get myself up. I decided to try to manage some of the housekeeping chores before rehearsal. Richard was going to have to take the clothes to the Laundromat—I was out of time.

I wanted everything to be perfect for Sharon, wanted to show her I wasn't a hippie like Mom said. I scrubbed angrily at a stain on the sink. *Mom should try something like this for a change—try and see how perfect she could make things without the big new house in Magnolia Woods and the twice-a-week maid. Try working full time and then some, and taking classes too. I'd like to see her try living with a man who woke up with battle nightmares night after night. Try being pregnant—well, she did that, twice. Probably she wished she'd quit after once.* I slapped the dishcloth on the counter.

"Hey, what's wrong?" Richard asked behind me. I hadn't heard him come in.

"Mom thinks we're hippies."

"Why that in particular? I mean, we don't use drugs or any of the rest of it. Aren't hippies passé anyway?"

"Mom doesn't know that."

"Guess not. But why hippies? We're serious artists. We don't do anything but work."

"She doesn't think it's work."

"Hell, in that case, let's get her down here to move scenery. If she thinks it isn't work, she'll have a ball."

Picturing my mother as a stagehand made me laugh so hard, I collapsed into a chair.

"That's what you call serious?" I gasped.

"No, but I'm glad you can see the funny side. I hate to see you quarrel with your folks. I wish now I hadn't been so self-righteous with my parents. They were wrong about a lot of things, but I was too, and so what? I wish Mama was going to be around to see the baby."

A flood of relief took me by surprise. He wanted his mother to see Jamie. "Could you make up with them?" I suggested.

"I don't think so. Sergeant Johnson made it clear that I was dishonorably discharged from the family."

"But what *happened?*" I pushed out the other chair for him to sit down and talk to me, but he ignored it. He got out the laundry bag and went into the bathroom.

His voice came muffled around the door. "I joined the March on Washington."

"The one where they threw their medals over the fence?" I called.

"I didn't have any medals to throw. But yes, that one."

"Why didn't you tell me before?"

"I never talk about the war. Somehow it dirties everything it touches."

"Even the protests?"

He came back dragging the bag. "Even that. I can't explain it too well, Kathy. I finally quit trying."

"I can see where your marching on Washington might bother your dad. Do you wish you hadn't done it?"

"No way," he said, without a second's hesitation. "But I wish I hadn't been such a sanctimonious little shit when I told him. That's what I mean by *dirties.* I was being a warrior. I had to win." He opened a cabinet and took out the box of detergent.

"Do you think your mom would care, with a grandchild on the way?"

"Maybe not," he said, pausing in the doorway with the bag of dirty clothes. "But there's another angle. Racism doesn't work all one way, you know. They're not exactly going to be happy that I chose a white girl." He went out, careful to keep the screen from banging behind him.

My shock about what he'd said was followed by another shock at my own attitude. *If I don't have even a little bit of racism myself, why did I think they'd be glad to have me in their family? Mom may not be as far away as I thought. Maybe some of her is right here in my head.*

QUEEN (to KAY): Why are you afraid? *(embraces KAY and kisses him)*

KAY: Why is it so cold? My heart is a lump of ice! Am I dying? *(pause)* But wait! Now I'm not cold anymore. *(touches SNOW QUEEN'S face)* You're the most beautiful woman I've ever seen.

⅔ 19 ⅗
February 1975, San Pedro
Lacey

KATHY WAS NERVOUS about handling the office by herself. "What if there's a bid?" she asked.

"I'm only going for a week," I said. "There isn't anything right now, and if something does come up, they'll be doing the estimating on it for days. Don't worry about it."

"Where are you and Willis going?"

"New Orleans. We decided to go to Mardi Gras." I didn't mention that I was planning to see her friends.

Just the same, she looked startled. She opened her mouth and then shut it again without a word. After an awkward couple of seconds, she excused herself and went to the restroom. When she got back, I pretended I hadn't noticed a thing.

The day before I left, she crawfished around the subject again. "I thought you didn't like Carnival?"

"I don't. I usually spend most of the time with my aunt. That and making sure Antoine's and Brennan's haven't slipped in the past year. This time, it's our twenty-fifth wedding anniversary, so Willis is calling it a second honeymoon."

Since Willis had brought up the issue of lying and sneaking, I was trying to be more aware of cutting corners. I hadn't exactly reformed overnight, though. If anything, I was mastering the art of truthful lying, for want of a better term. Using the literal facts to misrepresent the situation, like I was doing now. In my book, that was even worse.

Kathy relaxed a little. She even tried to cheer me up. "Oh, a second honeymoon! Neat! Did you get some pretty clothes?"

"Yeah—a glamorous new umbrella and some sexy galoshes," I said, pretending a sour attitude. Actually, I *had* bought a few things. If Willis wanted a second honeymoon, I was ready to be the bride.

"Lacey?"

"Uh-huh?" I came back from my daydreams about what Willis would say when he saw me in my new things.

"Well, I don't mean to be too personal or anything . . . ." She didn't finish.

"But?" Her expression was so troubled, I just wanted to hug her like a little girl.

"Lacey, how do you make a marriage work out right?" Her voice was low, so no one would overhear.

I sighed. "Kathy, there has been more BS talked about that one subject than any other I know. Lately, seems like everyone thinks you have to not hold in your feelings. So, what you read is that the right way to do a marriage is to yell every time you get mad. And then, guess what? It doesn't work."

"What would you do if the other person had a lot of problems?"

"Get him to get help."

"What if he wouldn't?"

"You'd probably have to leave him. No way a woman can do a relationship on her own. A man either, but it's the women who think they ought to."

She nodded without saying anything.

"You can't stay with someone who's not good to you, Kathy," I told her. "You're sure to have your differences, but you both should be happy most of the time. And any man who raises his hand to you, well, he's not much of a man."

The phone rang. "Giannini Construction, good afternoon," I said brightly, my eyes on Kathy.

She looked like she was close to tears. I wondered what kind of problems this Richard Johnson had. Enough to put him in Angola, anyway. And I wondered where Kathy's mother had been while Kathy was finding out about him the hard way.

❦ 20 ❦
May 1973, New Orleans
Kathy

"So, what's this one about?" asked Sam, turning the Snow Queen puppet over in his hands. I had done a good job on her. The "diamond" on her cloak was right over her heart. I planned to pick it up with a blue spotlight as she rose from the sleigh. I hoped it would make a cold flash.

"It's from *The Snow Queen,* a Hans Christian Andersen story," I told him. "There's a mirror that shows everything as evil. It breaks, and pieces fly all over the world. People who touch a piece of it see only the distortions the mirror shows them."

Sam laughed. "Sounds like my morning paper."

I went on. "The main characters are a boy named Kay and a girl named Gerda. A piece of the mirror gets in Kay's eye, and another piece in his heart. He starts mistreating Gerda, then goes off with the beautiful Snow Queen.

"The queen imprisons Kay in her snow palace and turns his heart to ice, but Gerda follows him to the ends of the earth—that's how the story reads. And her tears wash the sliver out of his eye so he can see things again as they are. And she kisses him, and his heart melts and he comes back to life," I told him.

"Sounds like Snow White, except the gender roles are reversed."

"I guess it is, a little."

"Well, it's always comforting to know someone will go to the ends of the earth for you," Sharon said.

The visit was going well—Sam and Sharon were fascinated with the puppets. Since they were staying in a hotel, they had no idea about Richard's nightmares or the mornings when he seemed to have a piece of the Snow Queen's mirror in *his* eye. With Sam and Sharon, he was charming, and part of the time I was sure he was acting. *Good thing he can act well enough to pull this off. Wonder if his acting is going to make problems between us in the long run.* I put it out of my mind.

"What's this one?" Sam picked up a marionette in the dress of the early nineteenth century.

"That's Jean Lafitte," Richard told him. "You know, the pirate. Lafitte's blacksmith shop, and all that. He's part of the Louisiana History segment."

Sam raised his eyebrows. "A pirate? Isn't this supposed to be about peace?" He investigated the puppet's drooping mustache and elegant clothes, careful not to mess it up.

"Oh, it is," said Richard. "Because Lafitte was a complicated fellow. First of all, he didn't do anything violent himself."

"Just paid someone else to do it?" Sharon asked.

Richard nodded. "It wasn't only him and his pirates—lots of the merchants of New Orleans made big profits from his crimes. We're trying to show that violence can be indirect. It's an important point."

Sam took the controls and tried to make the puppet walk, but he didn't know how. Jean Lafitte staggered with his arms splayed and his butt in the air. "What else did he do?" Sam asked.

"At one point, Governor Claiborne offered a $500 reward for his capture. Lafitte turned around and offered $2,500 for Claiborne."

Sam snorted. "Impudent bastard." Jean Lafitte flailed around, flopping like a duck.

"That he was," Richard said. "But in the end, he was one of the heroes of the Battle of New Orleans. And he was pardoned by the president."

"So, why would a pirate run a blacksmith shop?" Sam asked. Jean waved a hand. Sam was starting to understand how the controls worked.

"It was a front," Richard said, nodding at Sam's progress as a puppeteer. "Lafitte pretended to run the blacksmith shop, and customers came in and made purchases, but what they were buying wasn't iron grillwork. It was 'black ivory,' smuggled slaves."

Sharon frowned. "Is that something you really want to show kids?"

"That's bothered me, too," I said. "Martin and I are working out how to get it into the script. Or whether we *should* get it in."

"Did Lafitte reform after he was pardoned?" asked Sharon.

"Not for long," I admitted. "Maybe we'll end with the pardon, though. Show that a person who's done wrong can make up for it."

"Isn't that bending the facts a bit?" Sam asked.

Richard thought for a moment. "This isn't a full biography of Jean Lafitte. The point *is* an honest one, though, because people *can* reform."

Sam set Jean Lafitte back into the box. "Do you ever do anything but puppets?"

"Let's do something else right now," I said. "Let's go to the Quarter and get lemon ices at Brocato's."

"I'd rather have spumone," said Sam.

We called Thu and Martin, but they didn't want to drive over to New Orleans. Martin asked us to bring back some ice cream. They were having a dinner for us four and the rest of the Motley family that evening, so I volunteered to go by Eddie's stand and pick up vegetables.

"Are all the shows as serious as the Snow Queen one and the Jean Lafitte?" asked Sam as we walked down Royal Street.

"Oh, no," said Richard. "There's the Nasruddin one. He's sometimes a fool and sometimes a trickster. And the shadow puppets include Hacivat and Karagöz—they're funny, too. The story behind them is political, because the sultan had them killed for joking too much. Then he missed them, so a dervish made puppets to tell their jokes."

"Do you go looking for this sort of stuff?" Sam sounded frustrated. I glanced sharply at him—it wasn't like Sam to make a fuss over something unless it was important to him. I couldn't imagine why the puppets would be.

"What do you mean?" asked Richard.

"Well . . . negative. Slavery, and tyranny, and the mirror that makes you see everything twisted. It's all so *grim.*"

"Someone has to face the way things are and try to change them," Richard said.

"Maybe, but you'll never do it by scolding." Sam stopped in the middle of the sidewalk, as if he could make his point better if he didn't have to walk at the same time. Sharon took his hand and pulled him back into step with us.

"What do you suggest?" Richard asked.

"Well, hell, I'm not a puppeteer. Maybe you know best. But if I went to a puppet show, I'd be hoping the show would have a magical feeling. The stories you're telling, it's almost like you're going out looking for misery."

"Don't have to," Richard told him. "It's everywhere."

"Story of our times?" asked Sam.

"Story of our species," Richard said. "Don't blame me. I didn't make the world."

Our species was on its good behavior that afternoon in the Quarter. Whoever made the world, it didn't look so awful. Cheerful crowds meandered and window-shopped and stared into the ferny courtyards through antique wrought-iron gates. *Did any of those gates come from Jean Lafitte's blacksmith shop?*

I shuddered as we passed the corner of Royal and Governor Nicholls, the Lalaurie house trimmed with its own edging of iron lace. No one in early New Orleans suspected—but when a fire broke out, the firemen found slaves in prison cells. And a torture room. The owners fled, and black ghosts had haunted the place ever since. As I researched Louisiana history for the theater, though, I'd learned that a charitable group had used the house during the Depression. For years, they fed and cared for anyone who asked for help. No one remembered that. I sighed. Maybe Sam had a point.

Richard broke into my thoughts. "Getting tired, sweetheart?"

"I guess so. Let's go on to Eddie's and then take the ferry home."

Later, on the boat, we got out of the car to watch the brown water of the river slide past. Richard told Sam and Sharon more about the theater.

"We're putting together a set of the Nasruddin stories for some comic relief. A few of them are funny, almost like jokes. In one, he's told he has to pay for truth. When he protests, the seller reminds him that the price of a thing is set by its scarcity."

Richard chuckled. "In another, he goes to get a drink of water and his friend asks him to bring a cup back. He comes back without it, and tells the friend, 'After I got my own drink, I found you weren't thirsty anymore.'

"But my favorite so far is the one where he's asked what fate is. He answers that fate is like a weaving, the visible threads intertwined with invisible ones. He points to a man going off to be hanged. 'Is it his fate to be hanged because one man saw him commit the crime, or because another gave him the money to buy a knife? Or is it because of all the good folk who didn't stop him?'"

"Too dark," objected Sam. "That one will never do for comic relief. You need to lighten up! You know, it's like in my profession. It's awful to lose a kid to cancer. People think doctors are so detached, but that's not so for me. But I can't let it stop me. Because there's always someone else I *can* help. You can get sidetracked on the negative stuff and never see anything else. And then, I'm sorry, but you're worthless to anyone, including yourself." *He sounds angry. Almost, anyway.*

We scrambled back into the car as the west bank of the river approached, and then drove off the ferry into the streets of Algiers, our next-door town. I thought about Sam's words as I drove.

He was right. I worried about everything—Richard, the baby, my parents. I worried almost constantly. But Thu and Martin had worse problems than we did, and they'd both survived terrible losses. And they seemed much less burdened than Richard and me. *What about that? Why am I working for peace when I haven't made peace with myself?*

When Martin opened the door that evening, the smell of good food tumbled out to meet us. Thu had cooked a rice dish, spicy and almost familiar. Sharon and I went back to the kitchen to help her.

"What is this?" I asked, stealing a before-dinner taste from a copper pot.

"It's called *Com Chien Thap Cam*. Of course, I couldn't get Vietnamese rice."

"What difference would that make?" Sharon asked.

Thu looked surprised. "Oh, it makes an enormous difference. Rice of each area has its own flavor. When people move away from their own village, they miss the taste of their own rice almost more than anything else."

I lifted the lid of a big saucepan. "What's this?"

Thu, rinsing vegetables at the sink, turned to see what I was looking at. "Oh, it's *pho*. You'd call it beef noodle soup."

Eddie and Francine came into the kitchen. "Hey, dirty rice!" Eddie exclaimed.

Thu flew to her pot and surveyed the contents. "Where?"

"Right there in the pot—dirty rice."

"It's not dirty! What are you talking about, Eddie?" Thu's face was set in a deep scowl, an expression I'd never seen from her before.

"Oh, no, I didn't mean it was *dirty*, Thu. I'm sorry—I meant it was 'dirty rice.' It's a Creole dish."

"That's the name of a *dish*?" She was still suspicious. "What is it?"

"Oh, rice with stuff in it. Vegetables and onions and giblets, maybe shrimp or crawdads. Or maybe that's a pilau. Mama never taught me how to cook. I call them all 'dirty rice.'"

"Giblets? Crawdads? Pilau?" Thu was floundering in new words.

Francine laughed. "Tell you later, honey. He said it—his mama didn't teach him *nothin'* about cooking. I'll show you. This *Com* whatever-you-call-it, it *is* a lot like pilau. *Dirty rice*." She shot Eddie a look of mock disgust. "Bet you don't even know how to get you a cup of coffee."

"Of course I do," Eddie said, with injured dignity.

"Oh? How?" Francine put her fists on her ample hips and surveyed Eddie like he was a little kid trying to get away with something.

"Go to the Café Du Monde and tell the waiter, 'One cup of café au lait, please.'"

Thu laughed, her hurt feelings forgotten. She brought the food to the table and the Motleys gathered around. The boys sat on chairs stacked with thick books.

All of us bowed our heads, and Martin said, "Bless us, O Lord, and these Thy gifts which we are about to receive from Thy bounty through Christ our Lord."

"Amen."

Hot braided bread and a tangy salad went around. The rice dish had shrimp, sausage, mushrooms, and buttery scallions. It was delicious.

"What do you two do?" asked Martin.

"I'm an accountant and Sam's a doctor," Sharon answered.

"What kind of doctor?" Francine asked Sam.

"I'm a pediatric oncologist. I specialize in cancer and leukemia in children." Judging from Francine's expression, she wished she hadn't asked.

"I hope you like seafood." Thu, gesturing toward the rice dish, changed the subject gracefully.

"Lord, yes. Delicious. What kind of dish is it?" asked Sam.

"Vietnamese."

"You're from Vietnam?"

"I am—Martin's Australian."

"I think they can tell, honey," Martin said. He'd worked on his accent so it wouldn't distract from the puppet performances, but a little of it was still left.

"Actually, yes." Sam smiled. "How did you meet each other?"

"I was a journalist over there until 1968."

"And then?"

"We lived in Hue," Martin said. "It's in central Vietnam, the old Imperial City. It's a university town as well, a sort of cultural and historic center. It had been quiet up until '68, almost as if the war couldn't come there. Thu was running her family's marionette theater, and I was doing freelance writing and learning the puppets. When Tet came, the war roared in."

"A siege, wasn't it?" Sam asked.

"A massacre. House-to-house fighting, soldiers everywhere. I was outside in the street—fortunately not too far away. I was trying to get back, but I got shot. I crawled inside and Thu hid me."

"You mean they searched your house?" Sharon sounded horrified.

"We were in the theater. But yes, they searched. More than once. Somehow, they knew a foreigner was attached to the place."

"Where did you hide?" Sam asked.

Martin returned his question with another one. "Do you know what water puppets are?"

Sam shook his head.

"They're a folk tradition in the north of Vietnam," Martin explained. "Puppeteers stand in hip-deep water and manipulate the puppets with the water surface as a stage floor. Each family of puppeteers has a unique version. They hold their secrets so closely that they won't even teach their daughters, because women marry outside the family."

"Is that the kind of puppets you had? I thought you said Thu was managing the theater."

"She was," Martin said, "but we didn't have water puppets. Thu's family wasn't that kind of puppeteer. We wanted to do

water puppets, though, and we'd hired a young man named
Minh who knew one tradition. He was from the north, and his
whole family had been wiped out in the war. He thought he
might as well teach us, under the circumstances.

"We built a tank under the stage and fixed the stage floor to
be removable. No one knew—we wanted the opening to be a
surprise. No one else but Minh knew it was there. We hadn't
filled it with water yet. That was where we hid, in the tank."
Martin turned to Thu. "Why don't you tell the rest."

"It was raining and very cold for Hue," said Thu. "Martin was
delirious most of the time. I thought he was dying, but I didn't
dare try to get help. I crept out once to get food and water and
something to keep us warm. The only food we had in the theater
was a tray of traditional Tet foods, dried fruits and vegetables,
mostly sweet, and candied ginger. There were no blankets, so I
grabbed a bolt of gold velvet I'd bought to make robes for kings
and gods. I filled a couple of big vases with water, pushed it all
back into the tank, and then crawled in and set the flooring
piece back down."

She broke off, and gave Sam a rare direct-in-the-eyes look.

"What happened then?" he asked. He was hoarse, as if his
voice didn't want to work. I knew how he felt—I couldn't have
said a word. Richard's chair was pushed back from the group,
his face remote and shadowy.

"For days, Martin tossed on the metal floor of the tank,
wrapped up in the puppets' velvet. I wanted to warm him with
my body, but I was afraid I'd hurt him. I sat in the dark near
him, nauseated from fear and from having nothing to eat but
sweets. The building shook from artillery. At first I was afraid a
shell would hit us, later I almost wished one would. Sometimes
I heard heavy boots running across the stage right above our

heads, sometimes gunshots. We had no way to know who was winning.

"When the noise finally stopped, I crept out into the ruins of the street and found Americans. They medevaced Martin out."

"What happened to Minh?" Sam asked.

"As I helped the men put Martin in the helicopter, I saw in the dim light that the soldiers had machine-gunned even a puppet Martin had left dangling on the stage. Minh was gone. I hope he got away, but we never heard. We did all we could—everything beyond that is fate."

"You went to Australia after that?"

"Yes, and then came here. Have you ever seen Australia? It's very beautiful." Thu fetched a book of photographs, turning the subject away from the tragedies of her country. Relieved at the change, we passed the book around, admiring the pictures.

With dessert, Thu brought out an album of photos by Martin, and we talked about photography, and arts in general, carving, and then the puppets. As we scraped the last morsels from our dessert plates, Martin bowed his head again. We all fumbled to follow suit, even Richard and I, who had never seen grace said after meals, even when we ate with Martin.

"We give Thee thanks, almighty God, for all Thy benefits, Who livest and reignest, world without end."

"Thanks be to God," replied Francine, Thu, and Eddie together.

"May the souls of the faithful departed, through the mercy of God, rest in peace."

"Amen."

We didn't stay long after dinner. Thu wrapped up food for us to take home, and we protested that it was too much even as we looked forward to eating it. Sharon and Sam hugged everyone, bending to put their arms around Martin. We all flocked onto the porch for good-byes. Joss and Dom called "Bye-bye! Bye-bye!" for as long as we could hear—and maybe after, for all we knew.

Part 4

❧ 21 ❧
July 1974, New Orleans
Kathy

JAMIE WAS BORN JULY 23, two months early. It was a panicked night, with Thu driving Richard and me across the bridge to Charity Hospital. Sisters of Charity were the nurses, modern in skills, businesslike in their manner, and dressed for the Middle Ages in long habits and tall white headdresses winged like swans.

The nuns wouldn't let Richard stay with me because we weren't married, but they let Thu stay for a while. I gripped her hand so hard I was afraid I'd break it, and she never complained. I didn't get to see Jamie at all that night. They'd hustled her off to an incubator and took me to a recovery room. I felt empty, and the emptiness was starting to fill with fear. Thu wasn't supposed to visit before I was settled in a ward, but she sneaked in and stood beside me till they found her and made her leave.

"I would be stupid to tell you not to worry, but don't give up," she told me before she left. "Like a dancer on a tightrope—don't look down."

The sister stood adamant in her dark blue habit. Thu lingered a defiant minute and touched my arm. Then she left, stopping once to wave.

"Mrs. Woodbridge," the sister said, "Father Evans would like to baptize your daughter now."

Does that mean she's going to die? "All right," I said. "Her name is Jamie."

"Would you choose a saint's name for the baptism?"

"Catherine," I said. I didn't know many saints' names, but I did know there was a Saint Catherine. I tried to claim my baby by giving her my own name. I was too tired to think anymore. As soon as they moved me to a ward, I fell asleep.

I woke to sunlight and the sound of traffic from the city streets, both coming in through open windows on one side of the ward. There was a line of beds along each of the long walls—I didn't try to count how many. The walls were painted pale green, darker at the bottom to save repainting, like the walls of a bus station. I could smell rubbing alcohol and maybe floor cleaner—whatever else it was that made hospitals all smell the same.

A doctor in a white coat came through the double doors in the middle of the opposite wall. It was Sam.

"What are you doing here?" I yelped.

He made shushing gestures and bent to whisper to me.

"I crashed the party," he said, looking around to make sure no nuns were close enough to overhear.

I almost laughed. Then I remembered Jamie.

"Richard called in the middle of the night. He was so upset that Sharon and I came down here. They wouldn't let us in until visiting hours tonight, but I knew you'd be half scared to death, so I put on my monkey suit." His gesture took in his coat and stethoscope, the professional getup that would let him pass without question in a hospital. "I saw her, and she's pretty little, but she's probably going to be okay."

"The nuns made me have her baptized."

"That's nuns. Don't let it worry you. She'll have to stay in the hospital awhile and she's going to need a lot of care when she gets home. Take care of yourself now, and don't worry."

Two nuns headed our way. Sam bustled out, looking like someone who belonged, but he threw me a wink before he went through the double doors. *Maybe she'll live. Sam thinks she'll live.* I couldn't help crying, even though the ward wasn't private. I didn't sob or sniffle, but tears kept coming like there was no end of them inside. I tried to pull myself together. *Sam said she'll be okay. Sam said she'll be okay.* I stopped crying and started again a couple of times before I was through. As far as I could tell, no one noticed.

There was nothing to read, nothing to do but wait. When the doctor made his rounds, he said I could go home the next day, but that Jamie would have to stay "for a while."

In the afternoon, they finally let me go to the nursery, but there wasn't much to see and almost no light to see in anyway. Jamie's incubator was like some distant country with tubes and wires and equipment everywhere. They wouldn't let me hold her. *Will I ever get to? I wish I could stuff her back inside me so I could grow her a little more.*

I'm losing my mind.

In the evening, Sam came back in ordinary clothes, Sharon with him.

"She's still doing fairly well," he reported. "How's the mama?"

"Tired. It's scary."

"Of course it is," said Sharon. "What can we do for you? You'll be going home tomorrow—how can we help?"

I sighed. It was too much to think about. "I don't know, maybe see what Richard says. Did Mom and Dad come with you?"

"They were getting ready, but then Mom got a headache. Dad said maybe later."

My head felt disbelief, but my insides cramped with shame. *I wish I hadn't asked.* I picked at my blanket and worked on not crying again. That wasn't what Sharon and Sam were here for.

"Get better, Sis," said Sharon, watching me. "We'll be back to pitch in however we can."

The Motleys came in then, but one at a time, as the hospital required. "You missed out," I told Eddie. "They already baptized her. You don't get to be a godfather after all."

"Ah, doesn't that sound like nuns? They couldn't wait, could they? Don't worry, doll. I'm still her godfather, wait and see."

He unpacked a basket of beautiful raspberries, blew me a kiss and left.

The others came in for a quick hug and an update on Jamie. "Sam says she's going to be all right," I told them all.

And then, Richard stood by the bed.

"I saw her," he told me. "I mean, I guess I did. I couldn't see anything but machines."

"That's all I saw, too. They said I could visit her more tomorrow before I go home."

"I'll come get you. Kathy?"

"Mmm?"

"I'm sorry about your parents."

Tears started squeezing out of my eyes again. I took Richard's hand. There weren't any chairs, so he stood by the bed until the nurses made him go home. After that, I ate Eddie's raspberries one at a time while I looked out the window. The last of the evening left the sky, and the neon signs of the city took the place of stars. When the berries were gone, I wiped out the basket and tucked it away.

The hospital was all lit up now. Surely the Motleys could see it all the way from Gretna. *They're looking at us with hopeful faces. Thu is lighting a candle, murmuring a short prayer for Jamie and me.*

I wanted to cry again, but I made myself stop. *Don't look down, Thu said. Don't look down.*

The next day, Richard came in the Volkswagen to take me back to Gretna. I gathered the few things I had and put them in the carrier the hospital gave me. All except the little raspberry basket—I held that by the handle. *I have to get the basket home without breaking it. Except I'm not exactly going home, with Jamie still back here. It's not like going from one place to the other, more like being stretched between the two, thinner and thinner.*

When I got to Gretna, I went straight to bed.

For the next few weeks, I spent most of my time at the hospital, and the rest asleep. Sometimes I did both—slept on a chair in the hospital waiting room until visiting hours started again. Whenever I got a chance, I cheated and sneaked in to look through the nursery window. Some of the nuns let me do it, others would make me go away when they caught me. But I always came back.

When Jamie got to five and a half pounds, the doctors let me take her home. As hard as the past couple of months had been, wanting Jamie to come home and agonizing over every setback, I wasn't ready when the time came. She seemed more like the hospital's baby than mine. I hadn't even bought much for her—I'd been planning to do that in August and September, but I'd spent every day at the hospital instead.

I phoned my parents to tell them she was home.

"Oh, honey, that's great," my dad said. "But you know your mom hasn't been well. She's had a lot of headaches. I think we'd better wait, in case she's got something catching."

His voice sounded stiff, a little cold. I gave up. *If it means so much to them that Jamie's a golden-brown baby instead of a pink one, there's nothing I can say. If they think my daughter is second-rate, they can stay home, for all I care.*

I didn't have any energy to worry about it. I had other problems—I couldn't figure out how to do "mother" right. Because Jamie, premature or not, was a feisty little thing. At first, I didn't know what to do with her. She wouldn't sleep until she was exhausted with crying, and even then, she slept for only a couple of hours—then she'd start crying again. I'd check if she was hungry, if her diaper needed changing. Nothing. The library books I'd read while I was pregnant hadn't covered this. I was sure I was a terrible mother. And Richard was no help at all.

Thu came over with a gift one afternoon about a week after I brought Jamie home. She was in jeans and a T-shirt as usual, immaculate as usual, her waist-length hair loose for once, a shimmering river of black silk. I was still in my bathrobe with my hair uncombed.

I looked at Thu and started crying as hard as the baby. The sink was full of dirty dishes, and the bed was unmade. All I'd had to eat was a couple of crackers from a ripped package that spilled across the table. I had spent most of the morning trying to feed Jamie, to comfort her. I didn't know how to make her happy like other babies, or even how to get her to stop screaming.

"What's this about?" Thu asked. She put her beautifully wrapped present down beside the crackers.

"Oh, Thu, I don't know. She cries all day and almost all night. Maybe she ought to go back to the hospital. Maybe she's sick. I don't know what to do."

"Hmmm. Let me take you now, Jamie?" She picked the baby up from her crib, but Jamie thrashed around and cried harder. "Do you have a blanket or something?"

I gave her a small cotton blanket, and she wrapped Jamie securely in it. The crying stopped. Jamie, wrapped like a papoose, looked out with a surprised expression.

"What did you do?" I asked. If Jamie was surprised, I was astonished.

"Didn't they tell you some babies like to be wrapped up?"

"They didn't tell me much at all. Just to keep her warm and feed her when she cries."

"She doesn't always want food when she cries." Held close to Thu, Jamie cooed sleepily.

"Or change her diaper, I guess."

"That's not all, either."

"What, then?" I felt just as frustrated as before.

"*Xin chào.*" Thu tossed her hair back and smiled at me.

"What?"

"*Xin chào.*"

"What does that mean?"

"Could it be a noise that doesn't mean anything?"

"Well, I assume it's Vietnamese. It didn't sound like French."

"You didn't understand it, so you believe it's a foreign language that you don't know, right?"

"Well, yes." *So?*

"Same thing when Jamie cries. She means different things, and she doesn't speak your language. Like someone who comes here from a foreign country with no English. Everything is strange, no one understands, and she doesn't know how to get what she needs." Jamie was fast asleep.

"So, what am I supposed to do?" I reached out, and Thu laid her in my arms.

"Learn her language. For now. Later, she'll learn yours. But until she can do that, study her expressions and the noises she makes and see what they mean. I'll help you. My two were incredibly different, considering they're twins. Dom was a cranky little boy, Joss was the opposite."

"I'll never figure it out."

"You'll probably understand Jamie better than I do in no time. For one thing, she already knows your voice, from before she was born." She stroked Jamie's head with a gentle finger.

"Thu?"

"Mmm?"

"What does it mean?"

"What does what mean?"

"What you said."

"*Xin chào?* It means hello. See how easy it turns out to be? *Xin chào,* Jamie."

I wouldn't have been one bit surprised if Jamie answered her.

After that, things got better. I learned Jamie's hungry sound and her "something wrong" cry. I learned how to make her smile—at least it looked like a smile to me. It *was* a new language, not all that difficult. I noticed how she paid attention when I really talked to her instead of making baby-talk noises.

When Richard understood what I was doing, he got interested too. He liked to hold her and talk to her, tell her about things. His face was beautiful when he looked at her.

But I didn't trust him. *He said, "You don't have to keep it." And I know what I heard the night I came home from Tex's class. He still hasn't told his parents about us. He still doesn't want to marry me. I know how well he can act now, too.*

I thought about having all my doubts out with him, clearing the air—but how would I know he wasn't acting if he told me there was nothing to worry about? Since I wouldn't believe him if he reassured me, why bring it up?

In fact, I didn't want to do anything to upset Richard, because things were hard enough. Richard wasn't mean, but he had a way of turning away from me right after we'd been especially tender that never stopped tearing me up. *He goes up and down, round and round, like the flying horses of the Pontchartrain Beach carousel when I was little. Up and down, round and round, but there's no gold ring for me this time. No gold ring at all.*

I felt like there was a hole at the middle of everything. But I still had Sam and Sharon, and the Motleys.

And Jamie. I still had Jamie.

❧ 22 ❧
February 1975, New Orleans
Lacey

MOISANT AIRPORT WAS MOBBED the weekend before Carnival. The gate area was packed with people who'd come to meet friends. We would never have found Eddie if he hadn't been holding up a card with "Greer" on it. I'd also given him a sketchy description of us, so he was on the lookout for a tall, middle-aged black couple. So, we got together without much trouble.

Eddie was a skinny guy, no more than five-nine, with short curly hair and dark brown eyes. Even if I hadn't already known his last name was Graziano, I'd have said he was Italian in a second. I took to Eddie right away.

But the crowds in the airport were about enough to make me scream. And the traffic on the highway going into town was crazy. I couldn't understand how Willis could enjoy the crowds, but he watched everything like a kid at his first circus.

Eddie seemed relaxed too, easygoing. He wore casual clothes and seemed to belong in them. He probably hung onto a good suit and a couple of ties forever and didn't realize how out-of-date he looked on the few occasions when he wore them.

"What do you do, Eddie?" I asked, more to get a conversation going than because I thought it would be important.

"I own a vegetable stand in the French Market."

That figured. The car had obviously been cleaned for this trip, but it had a slight perfume of onions.

"We appreciate you fixing us up to stay with your friend," I said. "Also, coming all the way here to get us. I didn't realize it was such a long drive for you."

"You're welcome. Don't see how you could have done it on the bus. The airport's way out of town. And downtown isn't handy to Gretna, either."

"It seems pretty far."

"I guess it's not that much, though," said Eddie, "compared to getting around in Los Angeles."

"We live in San Pedro. It's supposed to be part of L.A., but it's more like a small town. We rarely go into L.A. Have you known Kathy for long?" I slipped that in like it was just more chitchat. Willis shot me a quick look, but then he went back to staring out the window.

"Kathy came to work for me year before last, about this time of year," Eddie told me. "Then Richard needed a job, so I got the two of them together with Martin, over in Gretna."

"Does he have a vegetable business too?"

"No, a puppet theater. Richard had a lot of talent with the puppets, and Kathy was doing all the sets, lighting, even the clerical work. Little of everything. Martin and his wife didn't have anyone before Kathy and Richard, now they're up to six people. That puppet theater is really something. Better than the movies."

Eddie slid off the subject of Kathy as fast as I could coax him back to it. I was about to try one more time when Willis chimed in with some sports nonsense, and they talked about that for the rest of the drive. They kept on and on about a new football stadium that was about to open. As if anyone cared.

I wanted to yell at the both of them, but I smiled and nodded. And the more they talked, the more that smile of mine felt
like something that Giannini's crew had poured into forms and
left to set for about a month.

❧ 23 ❧
May 1973, New Orleans
Kathy

"I HAD A LITTLE NUT TREE.
Nothing would it bear
But a silver apple
And a golden pear."

As I sang, Jamie reached out her hands to me and made gurgly baby noises.

"The King of Spain's daughter
Came to visit me,
And all was because of
My little nut tree."

"Is that a children's song?" asked Thu, balanced precariously on a stepladder with a screwdriver in her hand. She had made Jamie a brightly painted mobile and was hanging it from the ceiling. The ceiling wasn't cooperating. Hunks of it kept flaking out instead of holding the screws.

"I guess so. I remember it from when I was little."

"What does it mean?"

"Nothing I know of. Some of the nursery rhymes have strange meanings, political stuff—'Ring-Around-the-Rosy' is about the

Black Death—but the one I was singing doesn't mean anything, far as I know."

"It sounds like that's just as well."

I laughed.

"Pass me one of those anchors from the toolbox, would you?" Thu fiddled with it, muttering under her breath until the screw eye held. She hung the mobile carefully and picked her way down the ladder. She checked her palms and crossed to the sink to wash her hands.

"Martin's having a party for my birthday, Saturday," she said, drying her hands on the kitchen towel. "Can you and Richard and Jamie come?"

"Happy birthday! I had no idea it was coming up!"

Thu looked surprised. "You didn't?"

"No, how could I?"

She laughed. "I forgot you don't speak Vietnamese. *Thu* means *autumn,* so I guess I assume people will know I was born in the fall."

"Autumn! How beautiful!"

"But can you come?"

I hesitated. Jamie hadn't gone out with other people yet. But Sharon and Sam and the Motleys came over all the time, so what was the difference?

"I guess so. For a while, anyway."

Thu turned to Jamie. "Would you like to come to my party?" Jamie chuckled. She liked Thu.

"Jamie, may I hold you now?" Thu held out her arms, and Jamie reached for her.

"She's such a pretty girl!" said Thu.

I knew parents always thought their child was the most beautiful, but in Jamie's case, it happened to be the truth. Her golden skin was a much prettier color than either Richard's or mine. Her eyes, large and baby-round, were dark brown. Mom had told me once that all newborns have blue eyes, but she must not have ever noticed any babies but white ones. And I'd accepted her remark without looking around to see whether it was true.

From her perch on Thu's shoulder, my beautiful golden baby started to whine.

"Sing some more," suggested Thu. I did.

"Speed, bonnie boat, like a bird on the wing,
Onward, the sailors cry.
Carry the lad that's born to be king
Over the sea to Skye."

"What a lovely song! Is that a children's song, also?" Thu laid Jamie gently in her crib and set her tools back into their slots in her toolbox.

"Hardly. The rest of it is grisly. It's about a war between England and Scotland. Here, let me get the dustpan for that." I kept my voice down, hoping Jamie would sleep for a while.

"Oh, really! I must admit, I never paid much attention to European history in school. When did this happen?" Thu asked.

"A long time ago. Eighteenth century? Something like that." I didn't know a lot about the Skye boat song myself. Vague words and pictures swirled through my mind: Bonnie Prince Charlie, Culloden, Glencoe, the clans. . . . Did tartans come later? I wasn't sure.

"What were they fighting about?" Thu asked.

"Religion, I think. And independence."

"But Scotland is part of Great Britain, isn't it?" She sounded puzzled.

"They lost."

Thu considered this. "Are there any stories we could use for the puppets?"

"I don't think so, but I'll take a look next time I'm at the library. I need to get back to rehearsing, Thu. Here it is November, and we're opening at Christmas! I've probably forgotten everything!"

"I doubt that. But Jamie *is* going to have to let you start working again. I still have baby things from Dom and Joss at home, you know. I'll pull a playpen out, and you can bring her along. Also, could you do some grant forms for the NEA? I could bring them here—I don't think the sound of the typewriter would bother her too much."

"No, don't worry. I can type them. What are we going to do for Thanksgiving dinner?"

"I hadn't thought about it. Of course, I'd be happy to cook, but it wouldn't be traditional American."

"That's fine with me." After the disaster of last year's Norman Rockwell Thanksgiving, I didn't know if I could ever eat turkey and cranberry sauce again. *Com Chien Thap Cam* would be a lot better. So would peanut butter sandwiches, as far as I was concerned.

"I'll ask the others," Thu said. "Maybe we could have a potluck—some traditional, some other dishes. Why don't you invite your sister and Sam, too? We liked them a lot. I'll pull out a high chair for Jamie."

She picked up her toolbox and tiptoed out, blowing a kiss to Jamie, or maybe to me.

The thought of Thanksgiving with the Motleys made me smile. Maybe there'd be a mass at Our Lady of Lourdes. Then we'd sit down to a Motley dinner, fruits and vegetables from

Eddie's stand, Vietnamese food from Thu and Creole from Francine, jokes and fun, shoptalk about the puppets. Dom and Joss and now Jamie in the circle, learning from us every minute. Sharon and Sam were becoming honorary Motleys, and that made me smile too. I opened my cookbook, wondering what I could give them all that would be good enough for what I felt. Good enough for my family, my motley family.

For now, Jamie was fast asleep. I snuggled into a chair with my cookbook and turned the radio on to soft piano music. I was almost feeling sleepy myself when the news came on.

> Today, the House and Senate voted to override President Nixon's veto of the War Powers Resolution, requiring the president to consult with Congress before committing military forces. Unless authorized by a declaration of war, no military involvement can be extended beyond ninety days. Opponents of the war in Vietnam have favored this resolution, believing that it reduces the chance for future conflicts that are not supported by the American people.
>
> In other news, the Chicago Cubs traded Glenn Beckert and a minor league player to the Padres for Jerry Morales.
>
> Stay tuned this evening for a reading from *Black Elk Speaks* in honor of author John Gneisenau Neihardt, who died on Saturday at the age of ninety-two. His book, an account of the history of the Oglala Sioux from the Indian point of view, is known for its historical and spiritual significance. The book describes a great vision of peace and Black Elk's life-long regret that he was not able to fulfill this vision.

To have a vision of peace and then see it slip away . . . .
I wondered about Black Elk, about what he'd done and why
he'd failed. And I wondered if the War Powers Resolution would
fare any better.

I felt chilly as the room grew darker, so I got up to light
the heater and set a kettle on the stove. The door opened, and
Richard edged through with a box of puppets in his arms. I
turned toward him, clinking the kettle against the sink, and was
startled by his face, open and wondering, his eyes like Jamie's.
His love for us reached across the room to me. *How could I ever
have doubted it?*

He stood still for a minute. Then he set the box on the
floor. I went to him and he wrapped me in his arms the way I
always wrapped Jamie. I stayed there for a long time without
saying anything, being held to his warmth, listening to him
breathe.

ↄ

"How do you spell *THAT*?" asked Sharon, pushing a flop of hair
off her face with the back of her pen hand.

We sat facing each other across my table, mid-afternoon
sunlight slanting through the window. It picked up the gleam
of things I'd cleaned when I had the time, and a swirl of dust
bunnies in corners I hadn't gotten around to.

"*B, a, n, h,* new word, *k, h, o, a, i,*" I read from Thu's writing.

"Let me see it." She reached across the table and took the
paper. "What in the world is it?"

"A specialty from Hue. Thu says it's a crepe with pork stuffing."

"Oh." She wrote that and then studied the list for a minute,
frowning. "Well, what's this other one?"

"*Can chua.* Richard and I had that once before at their place. It has fruit and spices and vegetables—it's sour, maybe like Chinese hot and sour soup."

"What was that one she served last time we were here?"

"The soup? *Pho,* I think."

"She said it was beef noodle, but it didn't taste like any beef noodle I ever had."

"It has star anise and ginger in it. I like it too." Sharon hadn't exactly said she'd liked it, but I remembered she'd eaten three bowls of it. In fact, I'd had to snitch the last of it from her.

The conversation was a murmur, because Jamie was finally sleeping. She had caught a cold, probably at Thu's birthday party, and had screamed for about four days, as well as most of the nights between them. Sam said she'd be okay, but I was beginning to wonder whether *I* would.

Sharon was visiting, staying in Francine's guest room. Our current project was fancy menus for the Motleys' Thanksgiving dinner. Sharon's handwriting wasn't real calligraphy, but it looked good.

"Francine's bringing Creole bread pudding with whiskey sauce," I told her.

"I'll save that for the end. What are you making?"

"I can't decide. Got any suggestions?" Cooking was not my specialty.

"Hey, I've got it! S'mores! You were always good at s'mores!" She pretended to write on the menu, giggling. "Let's see. . . . *S,* apostrophe, *m* . . . ."

I shook my head. "Not s'mores. This is a formal dinner. I'll make that rice cereal and marshmallow thing."

"Do you serve that with red or white Kool-Aid?"

I assumed an air of hauteur. "Red, of course. Only a *peasant* would serve white Kool-Aid with marshmallow squares."

Jamie's waking shriek cut through our giggles. I picked her up from her crib, changed her, and held her close to me. Her breathing was stuffed-up and snuffly, and she pushed away her bottle. I used a rubber syringe Sam had provided to clear her nose. She hiccupped for a few minutes and fell back asleep, wheezing and whimpering.

"Sam and I might move down here after we get married," said Sharon. "We both like New Orleans, and Sam has some doctors he might want to partner with."

"That's great!" I loved the idea of having Sharon and Sam in town.

"Also," she went on, more slowly, laying her pen aside, "Dad is thinking of coming down here for a few weeks."

"What for?"

"He wants to see a doctor at Ochsner Hospital."

"Why?" My annoyance with Dad didn't keep me from feeling a stab of fear. "Is he sick?"

"No, not really. But he did have rheumatic fever, and he's having problems. Feeling tired, short of breath, that kind of thing."

"But he was a kid when he had rheumatic fever!"

"Some of the symptoms don't show up much until you get older."

"Did you ask Sam about it?"

"I didn't want to."

Why not? "Where is Dad going to stay?"

"What about here at Francine's?"

I thought a moment. "Things are awkward right now."

Sharon frowned. "I think he needs to see Jamie. Kathy, you and Dad have to work this out. I know they hurt your feelings when Jamie was born. Dad wanted to come, and Mom wouldn't let him. And he shouldn't have given in, and he's sorry he did. Give him another chance, would you? He has to accept his grandchild, and *you* have to accept that he's not perfect." She went back to her lettering.

"What about Mom?" I asked.

Sharon looked up at me with a conspiratorial grin straight from our childhood years. "Divide and conquer."

I had to laugh.

"Gotta go, Sis," said Sharon, packing up her pens. "I promised Sam I'd call at five."

There was a knock at the door, and Sharon opened it. "Hi, Thu. I was just leaving. We're working on menus for Thanksgiving. See you later."

"See you later, Sharon. Hi, Kathy." Thu closed the door behind her and looked around. She took off her coat and hung it carefully over a chair. "How's Jamie?"

"She's asleep. I don't know whether to be happy or worried. If she sleeps now, maybe she'll be up all night again."

"Bad night?"

"Richard couldn't stand it. He went out and slept in the car."

"In the *Volkswagen?*"

Is she surprised because he's so tall and the car is so small, or because he walked out and didn't help me with the baby? Change the subject. "Thu, would you teach me some Vietnamese?"

"What for?"

"No special reason. I'm curious about it. Please?"

"But how are you going to find the time? You have Jamie, and opening is in a few weeks, and you're still trying to learn to carve, *and* . . ."—she fished some papers out of her purse—

"I brought even *more* forms for you to fill out, courtesy of our friends at the National Endowment for the Arts."

"That won't take long, now that I've figured out how to adjust the typewriter."

She put the papers on the table. "Okay, where do you want to start with Vietnamese? I don't have any lesson books or anything."

"You taught me 'hello.' *Xin chào*. Is that right?" I sat down and waved her to a chair, too.

"Well, yes, in a general sense. That means *hello*, but it depends who you're talking to."

I didn't feel like this was a good start—I was confused already. "You say hello differently to different people?"

"It depends on how old the other person is compared to you, how much respect you want to show, how close you are. . . . It's complicated. In a formal situation, you'd say the person's name. For casual, you probably wouldn't." Thu ticked off points on her fingers.

I felt discouraged, but I still wanted to start somewhere. "How would you say hello to me?"

"*Chào bạn*. That would be for a friend of your own age. Or, to an intimate, *chào em*. There's a few different terms."

"How do you say good-bye?"

"*Tạm biệt*."

"Would you make me a list to study?"

"Sure." Thu turned as Richard came in. "Hi, Richard. Is rehearsal over?"

"For now." He went to the kitchen.

"It's almost evening—I'd better see about dinner," Thu said, putting on her coat. "Bye—*tạm biệt*." She closed the door quietly behind her. It *was* later than I'd realized—the sun was pulling back from the window and the room was shadowy. I'd been so wrapped up with Jamie that I hadn't even thought about dinner.

Richard opened the refrigerator and stared into it.

"I wish I didn't run into Thu everywhere," he blurted.

I was startled. "I thought you liked Thu."

"I do, but she sure makes me remember stuff I don't want to. Especially when I have to hear someone speaking Vietnamese in my own home."

"Well, for God's sake, Richard, Thu wasn't a soldier!" I remembered to keep my voice down so I wouldn't wake Jamie.

"That's the point. She wasn't a soldier. Probably most of the people I killed with my M-101 *weren't* soldiers." He fished a loaf of bread out of the refrigerator and tossed it onto the counter. The wrapping opened and bread fanned out over the cutting board. A couple of slices fell on the floor, but Richard didn't pick them up.

I started to do it, but he glared at me, and I stepped back. "Richard, that's *morbid*." I said. "You don't know that you killed anyone."

"True enough, but I sure aimed a howitzer at places where people lived and fired it. What do *you* think happened at the other end, Kathy?"

"Shhhhh! I think you did what you were ordered to do. And I think it's in the past."

"It's *never* in the damn past. I dream about it almost every night—for sure after every time I see Thu. The only reason she wasn't in any danger from me is that no one *ordered* me to shell the town where she lived. If they had, I would've."

His melodrama was getting on my nerves. "I don't think so, Richard. By the time you were in the army, Martin and Thu lived in Sydney, Australia. If someone had ordered you to shell Sydney, I doubt you'd have done it. We weren't at war with Australia."

"Very funny, Kathy. We weren't at war with Vietnam either."

"I bet you could have fooled *them*."

"Probably so." Richard slapped a sandwich together, just one for himself, and sat down at the kitchen table. He didn't ask me if I'd eaten.

"You could have helped me with Jamie last night instead of going off to sleep in the car." *I'm getting tired of you feeling so guilty about the past that you act like a jackass in the present.*

"I couldn't." His voice was loud and flat.

"Don't talk so loud—she'll wake up. *Someone* has to take care of her. What if I'd walked out too?"

"I do remember suggesting that having a baby wasn't going to be easy. Although, I must say, I hadn't counted on your family being so damned racist and hypocritical. Isn't it the grandmother who's supposed to help out? Shame our baby's too *brown* for that. Besides, why would Jamie need anyone but you? All you think about is Jamie, Jamie, Jamie. I'm not sure I live here anymore."

Let it rip. I don't care. "Well, *I'm* not sure who you *are* anymore. I never know who's going to walk through the door, my lover or Mr. Ice. Back when I told you I was pregnant, you wanted me to chuck Jamie away like a Dixie cup. One day you don't seem to have any feelings at all. Then the next day, you love us. Except when you say you love us, I wonder if you're acting. It's *weird*, Richard. I want you to make up your mind and stop jerking me back and forth. Are you in this family or out?"

Richard jumped up out of his chair. *Is he going to hit me? Is he going to leave?* He stood glaring at me for a minute like he didn't know himself which to do. Then he sat down again and huddled over his solo sandwich without another whisper.

You didn't answer my question. Are you in this family or out?

ॐ

"WHAT IN THE WORLD is this all over the clothes?" asked Richard, dragging in a basket from the Laundromat.

He pulled out a pair of jockey shorts, now glitter-bedizened. They looked like a costume for one of the male strippers at the My-Oh-My Club in the Quarter. Or might have, except that these shorts weren't exactly new.

"Uh-oh. I must have left one of the bags of puppet snow in a pocket," I said.

We looked at each other for a minute. *Is he going to explode again?* He shook the shorts provocatively. Flecks of glitter drifted down in exactly the effect I had perfected for the *Snow Queen* production. We both cracked up.

We laughed all the harder because it was such a relief after a week of politeness, going to rehearsal and pretending the fight hadn't happened. Putting on an act for the couple of days left in Sharon's visit, then for Thu and Martin. A giggle emerged from Jamie's direction too, and we both stopped and looked at her enjoying our laugh together. She was growing fast, now, watching us, learning how to be a person.

Thinking I might not have given her too good an example lately, I hugged Richard and kissed the end of his nose. Then I scooped Jamie up and made a raspberry sound on her neck. She squealed and reached for him, and we sat down hard together on the edge of the bed, all three wiggling like puppies.

"Want me to wash the clothes again?" I offered.

"No, let's be spangled for a while. It'll be festive. About time, too." He pulled me to him in a long hug.

"Richard . . . about this week . . . ."

"Let's not start in again. I'm sorry." *Is anything going to change, or does "sorry" just mean you don't want to discuss it?* I tried to hold onto some hope. Maybe he'd think things over. Maybe some of Sam's ideas would sink in. Sam, sweet redheaded Sam, who had to watch kids die of cancer. I hugged Jamie tightly to me.

"Don't squish her," Richard said.

I came back to the present, with Jamie wiggling and starting to whine. I picked her stuffed dog off the bed and handed it to her. "Doggie!" I said in my best mama voice. "Woof woof!" I tickled her, and she waved her arms and giggled. She chewed the toy, drooling a little.

"Dad's coming to New Orleans soon," I told Richard. "Sharon thinks we should encourage him to get to know Jamie."

I set Jamie in her crib and started folding the sparkly clothes—underwear and shirts and jeans. I even knotted the socks into pairs, studying them as if they were important, so I wouldn't have to look Richard in the eye. As I crossed the room to put the clothes away, he took one of the shirts off the pile and put it on. It had a lot of glitter on it.

I remembered a Dylan Thomas poem from English class: "They shall have stars at elbow and foot." It looked like we would too for a while.

Richard watched me fiddle for a minute. "I hope it works out."

To change the subject, I asked, "What do you think I should take to Thanksgiving dinner?"

"Pumpkin pie."

"Francine's already bringing bread pudding."

"Could we bring a main dish?"

"Only if you help cook."

"Okay."

Richard cooked fairly well. No worse than I did, anyway. Neither of us had cooked much lately, though, between Jamie and rehearsals. We were living on sandwiches at the moment, but the production was going to be ready. The costumes and props were all perfect, the lines and all the moves. I didn't like having to be the evil character, so I just pretended I was Mom while I did the Snow Queen. It was convincing and made me feel a little better, too.

Richard broke into my reverie. "What about your mom?"

"What about her?"

"When is *she* coming to see Jamie?"

"I don't know." *I don't even like Mom. Why are you looking at me?*

"*Shit,* Kathy. This is getting old."

"Yes, but at least Dad is coming. I don't want Jamie to grow up not knowing any of her grandparents. I thought you believed in forgiving people."

His faced closed into sullen mulishness. "They have to be sorry first."

"Look, Dad's never even seen her. Let him come once and see her big brown eyes and the way she reaches out for hugs and kisses. If he can reject her then, I'll give up. Just once, okay?"

Richard shrugged, shoulders sparkling with puppet snow.

"Why don't we go for a walk?" I asked. "We haven't gotten out in a long time." I took a glittery sweater from the drawer.

I put Jamie in her stroller and wrapped her up, though it wasn't cold. November in New Orleans was unpredictable—some days wet and chilly, others warm as Indian summer.

Today it was easy to see the year was packing up to go. Leaves from the hackberry trees along the sidewalk were like soggy black tissue wadded up where last week's rain had dropped it. A few late roses still dotted the yards.

I wished Richard could learn from Thu, learn from the way she said, "I *thought* you'd been a soldier." But Thu just made him feel guilty all over again. *He doesn't want to see Thu, because she's Vietnamese. My parents don't want to see Jamie, because she's brown. Even Black Elk couldn't bring peace to his people. But why not?*

The sparkle on Richard's sleeve was like bright confetti. *What if the puppets were here too, walking all around us, a parade of characters from Denmark and India, Africa and China?*

A Vietnamese woman like Thu, a Russian in a fur hat, Immortals and magicians, lovers and saints. Each nation with its own face, its own color, its own stories.

A crowd watches from the curb, smiling and understanding at last that these are only people like themselves. There's Dad, smiling and tapping his foot to the music, his hair ruffled by the autumn breeze. Beside him there's a girl, about the age I was, last time Dad took me to a parade. She stands so straight, just like him, but she's short like me, and her eyes are Richard's eyes. And her skin is golden—you can't tell which of the motley puppet band might tell her story. She belongs to all of them, to Dad, to me. She belongs to herself.

A whimper from Jamie brought me back to reality, and I covered her more tightly in her stroller. I put my dreams away and thought over the things I needed to do. The next few months would be busy, full of projects. Thanksgiving with the Motleys, and Jamie's first Christmas, the opening of the puppet theater. Thu was already talking about plans for Tet, January 23 next year. Nineteen seventy-four, the Year of the Tiger.

❧ 24 ❧

February 1975, New Orleans
Lacey

EDDIE PULLED UP in the driveway of an old wood house trimmed with the kind of gingerbread a Californian would swoon over. Here, it was ordinary. A plain building in the backyard turned out to be our "hotel." An elderly lady came out to meet us.

"I'm Francine Boudreaux," she told us. "I'm so pleased you could come. That's Kathy's place, you know. I've left everything pretty much like she had it. I'm sure she wouldn't mind you using it, since you're friends."

"Why, thank you," I said. "It's very good to meet you."

She smiled and handed me a key. "I put a few snacks in the refrigerator for you, so help yourselves. And after you unpack and freshen up, I hope you'll come to dinner. Maybe around six? I've invited a few of Kathy's old friends, and her sister too. It will be so good to hear about her!"

She looked like she meant it. I felt touched, almost upset about whatever had happened to make things go so wrong for all of them.

That's why Willis got in the first word when we got inside the guesthouse.

"Lacey, what in the world were you up to, the way you were talking to Eddie back there? I thought you were gonna quit all that sneaking around."

"I don't know what you mean," I said, checking the place out for traces of Kathy. I hoped Willis would back off if I didn't pay him any mind.

No such luck. "You know good and well what I mean." He put his finger to his chin in a silly pose that was supposed to look like me. "My goodness, isn't the weather nice? And what do you know about Kathy Woodbridge?"

"I didn't say that!"

"Close to it. Look, Lacey, either improve your interrogation technique, or give the man credit for enough intelligence to answer an honest question. Why don't you level with him?"

"Tell him Kathy hasn't told me anything? Tell him I'm just rubbernecking?"

"That's not leveling, honey." His voice became sweet again. "You're trying to help a kid who's in trouble. You don't have to pull the wool over anyone's eyes."

"Willis, do you think you can talk this one out with them better than I'm doing?"

"Frankly, yes."

"Then I'll let you do it."

Willis looked pleased—he'd won. I'd let him be in charge. It wouldn't take long for him to regret it.

🏵 25 🏵
April 1974, New Orleans
Kathy

THAT YEAR'S WINTER was a cold one, wet and windy. We hauled our puppets around under tarps, struggling against our heavy clothes and slickers. The Christmas performances of *The Snow Queen* had been white-and-silver enchantment—now we were working through the New Orleans history pieces, traveling from one school to another.

School is the same everywhere: smells of pine oil and chalk, and the shrill of teachers' whistles and electric bells. There's no bell to make spring come on time, though. Spring's lagging in tardy with a mouthful of lies, the way I used to do when I was a kid. I didn't even tell the principal the dog had eaten my homework—I said the fairies took it. The school psychologist really went to town with that one.

We were looking forward to opening *The Legend of Savitri* at the New Orleans Recreation Department Theater on the fourth of May. And that was the day Dad chose for his long-delayed visit.

We knew he was coming, of course, but there was nothing we could do about it. The *Savitri* production demanded every one of the puppeteers. Francine, the troupe's babysitter, was the only one to greet him. When we got home at eight, Francine let us into her living room, where Jamie was asleep in Dad's lap.

"Dad, how are you?" I whispered, wanting her to go on sleeping. "Thanks for helping with Jamie. Want me to take her off your hands?"

Dad stood, snuggling Jamie close. "Oh, no, I'll carry her over to your place. Back in a bit, Francine."

"Thanks, Francine," said Richard as we filed out, Dad still holding Jamie. He carried her to our house and laid her in her crib, pulling up the blankets and tucking her in.

"She talked to me for about an hour and showed me her toys. Quite a girl," Dad said with a goofy look on his face.

Jamie's "talk" was all baby noises, of course, at nine months, but she was very expressive. I could see she'd made a conquest. *I love you, Dad. It's so good to have you back.* I hugged him, suddenly and hard.

He smiled as we stepped apart. "I'll see you two in the morning. Don't want to keep Francine up." The door closed softly behind him.

"Kathy, you are something else. You can stay mad at someone until one second after they admire Jamie," said Richard.

"The whole problem was about Jamie in the first place."

"I'm glad you made up with him." Richard didn't sound all that enthusiastic.

We got ready for bed, and I turned out the light and slipped in beside him, overlain by a rectangle of sweet spring moonlight.

Jamie was playing on the white rocking horse I'd been given for my fourth birthday. But now it was Jamie who was four, riding it and singing nursery rhymes in a sweet high voice.

"I had a little nut tree.
Nothing would it bear

But a silver apple
And a golden pear."

Thu stood by, dressed in the habit of a Sister of Charity, weaving a Vietnamese song into Jamie's melody. Without warning, the horse turned into a real one, an enormous, muscular horse that leaped through a hole in the sky and disappeared. Thu nodded. "Tam biêt," she said, and went back to her song.
Cold fear drained through me. Where was Jamie? I heard shouting, and I knew Richard was coming with artillery. I tried to make Thu hide in a puppet theater, but she smiled and said, "I thought *he'd been a soldier."*

I woke to Richard shouting, thrashing, in the worst nightmare I'd seen him have yet. He was wound in a sheet, struggling to get free. He was so frenzied, I didn't dare touch him, but I fumbled across the room and turned on the light. Jamie woke and added her crying to the din. As I picked her up and soothed her, Richard sat up, blinking.

"Is she sick?" he asked after a few moments of unwinding the blanket and rubbing his face.

"No, you were yelling. You woke her up."

"Oh. Sorry."

Jamie had fallen asleep again, and I laid her in the crib. Richard straightened the covers and stretched out, and I turned off the light and lay down. *It won't help to nag about the nightmares. But they're getting worse.* I scrunched over and put my arm over him. We fell back asleep together.

Breakfast was ordinary—coffee and toast for us, in between spooning oatmeal and mashed banana into Jamie. A lot of Jamie's breakfast ended up on the floor, on her face, and on me, but she got enough of it. She didn't look upset by our bad night. I was, but it wasn't a good time to talk about it. Someone, probably Dad, was knocking at the door.

When I let him in, Jamie squealed with delight and held out her arms. He went right to her and lifted her high above his head. Banana and oatmeal smeared over him in several places, but he didn't wipe it off. I sponged myself off with a dishcloth, poured another cup of coffee, and set it on the table for him. I handed him the dishcloth too, but he ignored it. He set Jamie back in her high chair, and I hugged him. Richard started some more toast.

"I was wondering if Jamie needed anything. I mean, you have your furniture and so on, but what about clothes?" Dad asked.

"She's growing so fast, we don't even try for anything fancy," I told him. "Just diapers and T-shirts from the Sally Army."

"Do you have clothes for cold weather?"

"We won't need those until November, at the earliest." *Now we have something to talk about. He can be my father because I'm Jamie's mother.*

"Well, at least I want to get some good pictures of her. Is there a photographer anywhere close?"

"Francine would know."

"Why don't you give her a call? I only have today for shopping—all next week is medical appointments."

When I called Francine, she said her cousin was a photographer. His studio was in Gentilly.

"Why so far?" asked Dad. "It would be nice to patronize Francine's cousin, but there must be someone local."

He checked the phone book and found a photographer in Algiers, about a mile away. I called and made an appointment for noon.

"She needs a cute outfit for the picture." Dad was starting to take charge more than I liked.

"Dad, it's a waste of money. She'll grow out of it in two months."

"Baby pictures are important," he insisted.

We finished eating, chivvied along by Dad's impatience. There weren't any baby stores in the neighborhood, so Dad drove us over to New Orleans. We got to Maison Blanche as it was opening, and spent an hour in the children's department, looking at everything. Nothing was good enough to suit Dad. Richard stood away from us, ignoring the merchandise, even when Dad asked him what he thought. *He looks sulky. Is he embarrassed?*

Jamie was starting to whine and squirm by the time Dad picked out a white eyelet dress with a pink sash, and a pair of pink shoes. Then he dashed over to the toy department and bought her a Raggedy Ann. He was almost as keyed up as Jamie.

"We're going to be late for the photographer, Dad."

"Okay, let's go." He tried to hurry, but he couldn't seem to stop fingering fabrics, considering toys. Richard followed slowly, like someone who had nothing to do with us. I changed Jamie into the eyelet dress in the car.

We were about five minutes late for our appointment. As we came in, the receptionist gave us a startled look.

"I'm afraid there's some mistake," she muttered. She went into the back of the shop. We waited several minutes before another woman came out.

"When you didn't come at your time, we gave your appointment to someone else. Sorry," she said. Her face was blank.

"Can we arrange another time?" Dad asked. The woman looked coldly at him.

"I'm afraid we're booked up," she said.

Dad frowned. "We were only five minutes late! What's going on?"

"Sorry, can't help you."

Dad was breathing hard and his face was splotched-looking. *I can see what Sharon means about his health.* I shifted Jamie to one hip so I could take his arm.

"Let's go, Dad." We walked out.

On the sidewalk, Richard stood clenching and unclenching his hands. I wanted to yell at someone, to cry, to throw up. Instead, I pulled the scrap of paper with Francine's cousin's phone number on it from my jeans pocket. I marched to a phone booth on the corner and called him. If he was Francine's cousin, he was Creole. He wouldn't take one look at us and throw us out. He said we could come in forty-five minutes.

We scrambled back to the car for the long ride to Gentilly. We were late there too, but Francine's cousin was sweet to us and Jamie. He took pictures of her alone, and with Richard and me, and with Dad. He promised to mail them in a week.

"Can we go to a bookstore now?" asked Dad. "I want to get a baby album."

"I think Jamie's had it for now," I said. It was true. She was starting to whine, and if she didn't get a nap soon, a full-scale snit was in the works.

"Could Richard maybe take her on home? I do only have just the one day."

"Take her home in what?"

"Oh, we'll get a cab." *Why is he being so pushy? Is he covering up embarrassment about the photographer?* He flagged a cab and Richard got in with Jamie. He looked stiff and upset when he saw Dad pay the driver in advance.

Dad and I went to a bookstore downtown, one that turned out not to carry baby albums. But while he was there, Dad wanted to just about buy out the children's department.

"She won't be able to read for years," I objected, feeling embarrassed by his largesse.

"But you have to start reading to her. You should start right away, so she'll love books when she grows up." He was all teacher. He turned to a salesgirl. "We need some children's classics. *Winnie-the-Pooh, The Wind in the Willows, Peter Pan.*"

Half a dozen books later, I pulled him out of the shop. I got him about fifty feet along the sidewalk before he saw a stationery store.

"Maybe they have baby albums," he said.

They did. He picked one out, but he browsed along the aisle instead of going right to the cash register. He pulled a large book off a shelf, and I went to see what he'd found. It was another album, white with silver script on the front: Our Wedding. He put it back without comment and bought the baby book.

He was exhausted by the time we got to Gretna in the bridge traffic. *Is he sick? I don't like this.* I carried the packages in from the car, and he didn't try to help. Richard had undressed Jamie and laid the new outfit on the bed. Dad sat down in a chair with a thump. I hung up the dress and put the shoes away, sponged off the table, and put her in her high chair.

I arranged a snack plate of fruit and sweet rolls and started a pot of coffee. Richard cut up some fruit into tiny pieces for Jamie. He sat beside the high chair and fed her, making goofy faces to get her to laugh.

When the coffee was ready, I brought the pot to the table and poured out three cups. I set a plate at each place and put the snack plate in the middle. Richard took a sweet roll and sipped his coffee.

Dad sat up straighter in his chair and fiddled with the handle of his coffee cup. "I was wondering when you two were going to get married," he said.

Richard went as still as the loser in a game of freeze tag. After a moment, he shook his head. "Marriage isn't necessary if things are working, and it's one more problem when they aren't." His voice was cold and dismissive.

Dad adjusted the cup a millimeter. "Don't you think Jamie needs a father?"

"She has a father."

"What about when she starts school, though? Children can be cruel."

"I doubt it will be an issue. Lots of couples don't marry."

"I think most *parents* do. Even if it's a little late." He turned the cup a few more degrees. "What about you, Kathy? Do you believe marriage is passé too? I didn't think your mom and I had raised you to think that."

I couldn't slam out, the way I had when he told me not to move to New Orleans. I had nowhere to slam to, unless I went into the bathroom. *It was pretty nice to feel like Dad's daughter for a while. Didn't last long, did it?* I looked from one of them to the other.

"You're putting Kathy in a bad position," Richard objected.

"I don't think it's *me* who's putting her in a bad position," Dad snapped. "Kathy doesn't believe marriage is a thing of the past. When she was little, she always used to say, 'When I grow up and get married,' 'When I get married and have children.' Those expectations don't change, Richard. If Kathy isn't saying anything about them, it's because you've made her afraid to.

I think you're being unfair to my daughter." His face was flushed with anger and embarrassment.

Richard glanced at me. I couldn't lie, so I looked away.

"I'm sorry, Dr. Woodbridge," said Richard, "but this is none of your business."

"It's very much my business. You're taking advantage of my daughter, and I have an illegitimate granddaughter. I don't know how it could possibly be more my business."

He touched Jamie's head, and she said "Daaa." Richard motioned toward them, then pulled his hand back.

"Jamie isn't illegitimate. No baby is illegitimate."

"That may be the way your people look at it, but I'm afraid I don't agree."

Richard stood up, knocking his chair over with a crash. His nostrils were flaring in and out like a horse's, but he kept his voice low. "Dr. Woodbridge, Kathy and I have been together for nearly two years now. And you and your wife have been very liberal, very *tolerant*. Well, how do you think it feels to be *tolerated* for two years? Do you have any idea how I feel when you smile at me in your fakey, liberal way? It sticks out all over that you think you're such a great person to be smiling at a *black* man.

"But as soon as I'm not giving you what you want, the first thing out of your mouth is racism. I don't see any reason to see what the *second* thing is going to be. I might have to do an Uncle Tom act in your house, but this house happens to be mine. Please shut *my* door behind you as you *leave*."

All Dad's excitement had evaporated. Looking gray-faced and old, he stood up carefully and set his chair straight. He hesitated as if he were trying to remember something, then turned and walked toward the door without a word. Jamie whined and reached after him.

He paused a moment, but then he left without looking back. I heard the back door of Francine's house close with a little bang. A few minutes later, his car backed out of the driveway and was gone.

A few minutes later, Francine pounded at the door and charged in without waiting for an answer. She was in a full-scale Cajun fury, mad enough to spit nails.

"You kids got no manners," she said. "There wasn't no call to send Dr. Woodbridge off like that."

I tried to defend Richard. "He said maybe Richard's people thought it was okay to have a baby and not be married."

Francine glared at me, unconvinced. "Seems that's what *Richard* thinks."

"Maybe, but Dad didn't have any reason to make a racist remark like that." I couldn't understand why Francine was standing up for him. She was black too, more or less.

She folded her arms and looked us up and down. "You kids think you got racism? You got *nothin'* compared to how it was. Maybe your dad said something he shouldn't. Maybe he did. You ever put your foot in your mouth?

"Your generation's spoiled as hell. You never had it like it was. Me, when I was married, I couldn't even go to a restaurant with my husband. I could pass, and he couldn't. My kids weren't allowed to go to the school down the block."

"Francine," Richard broke in, "you chose to live a Jim Crow life. I'm choosing not to. I don't see any reason to discuss it."

"I didn't do any such thing, Richard. My husband and I were at some of those lunch counters in the sixties. We sat at the front of some buses. But we did what we could, and then we lived in the real world and got along as best we could, too. You think I sent you to my cousin for your pictures because he needed the *business*? I knew that place in Algiers was there, and I also knew they'd throw you out. Why're you such a fool?"

"I didn't spend my life being an Uncle Tom," Richard said. "I grew up in Europe."

"That where you learned all the empty talk? You give me the red ass, Richard. You run your mouth about 'Uncle Tom' this and 'Jim Crow' that, but what did you ever do to fight segregation? Nothin'. And you run your mouth about the war, but what did you do to stop *that*? Same nothin'. Easier to be a free rider than a freedom rider. Easier to be a baby killer than to buck the system, wasn't it, Richard?"

"Goddamn it, Francine!"

Francine turned to me. "What you think, your dad's such a racist he *wants* you to marry a black man? That's some racist, Kathy. Why don't you have more sense?"

"It wasn't me. It was Richard that got mad."

"And you sat there, didn't say nothin', you sat and watched, huh, Kathy? The way you do. Just let it happen. Your dad thought Richard was about to hit him. Why didn't you stop him, girl?"

"How could I?"

Francine folded her arms and slumped against the door. She looked tired and disgusted. "Honey, you better figure out how to speak your piece, 'cause no one else can speak it for you."

Richard took a jagged breath. "Francine, none of this is your business. Leave us alone, would you?"

"When my friends make fools of themselves, it *is* my business. You don't like what I say, *baissez mon cul.*"

Richard stepped back and looked Francine up and down with a snide grin. "Mark off a spot, Francine. There's quite a bit of territory there."

Francine gave him a hateful look and slammed out.

"What did that mean, Richard?" I asked.

"Don't worry about it." Richard bolted into the bathroom. Through the thin old door, I could hear him vomiting again and again.

When we went to rehearsal the next morning, Martin was awkward and fidgety, picking up puppets and putting them down again. Thu sat on the couch picking at the upholstery. She wouldn't look at us.

Finally, Martin blurted, "I wish you hadn't been so nasty to Francine yesterday."

"She was nasty to us," I said.

"Just the same, I wish you hadn't."

Richard turned on him. "Martin, everyone's telling us what to do, and we're getting tired of it. All we want is to be left alone."

After that, they *did* leave us alone. They said nothing to us but what was necessary for work. Eddie stopped knocking at the door with vegetables for us, and Francine was never pruning the roses or weeding when we walked across the yard.

I took Jamie to New Orleans one afternoon and found Eddie at his stand in the French Market. He pulled the old wooden stool over for me to sit on and took Jamie on his shoulder. It was almost like old times until I ruined it.

"You never come see us anymore," I said.

"It's tough, doll," he answered. "Richard's on some kind of tear, and nobody knows what's eating him. We still love you, but no one wants to deal with Richard till he simmers down.

What the hell's going on, anyway? You two not getting along or something?"

"He had a fight with my dad. And with Francine."

"Well, I heard about *that,* believe me. But Francine's not the kind to stay mad. She's all Cajun—blows up in a split second and it's all over in a day or so, tops. Up like a rocket, down like a stick. Looks to me, Richard's the one staying mad."

A truck pulled up to the curb, diesel exhaust and roar. We sat without talking till the engine cut off.

"Francine called him a baby killer," I said.

Eddie nodded. "On account of the war? I heard vets called that before. But he called her an Uncle Tom, didn't he? I'd say they're about even."

"Maybe so, but he doesn't see it that way. Dad gave him a lecture about Jamie and illegitimate babies, told him maybe it was fine with his people but it wasn't with us. It was kind of the last straw after the way he and Mom acted when Jamie was born."

"That was wrong, doll, what they did then, no question. But he's still her grandfather. Richard needs to cool it. I'm not saying it's easy, but if he can't forgive people for not being perfect, he's gonna be disappointed every time."

I can't forgive Dad, either. He told my secret, told that I wanted a husband, wanted to be a stupid old housewife. Said it right out loud in front of Richard. After that, I didn't care much when Richard kicked him out.

"He's been getting madder and madder about my parents and the race thing ever since Jamie was born," I said. "And he keeps on being messed up about the war. He says seeing Thu reminds him all the time. I don't know what to do."

"We don't know either, tell you the truth. We thought we'd stay away for a while, give Richard a chance to think it over.

Don't take it personal, doll, but that's all we can see to do for now. But if you need anything, let me know."

And that was all I could get out of him. He gave me a bag of fruit, which Richard wouldn't touch. I would never have dreamed, back when Richard was reading to me about forgiveness, that he had so much anger in him. He couldn't let go, and I was being pulled between him and everyone else. Eddie had said they still loved me, but I felt deserted.

Richard will probably leave me too before long. Everyone will. Maybe they should get a tour bus. The destination sign on the front would say, Leaving Kathy. Jamie's the only one who won't leave me. Maybe I should leave them first, just take Jamie and go.

Even Sharon only called once, and that was to tell me that Dad was back from his medical consultations at Ochsner Hospital.

"He has heart problems from his rheumatic fever," she said. "He's upset about you and Richard, too. Lousy timing, Sis." She left it at that, but I could see she was mad. *She and Sam would fit on the tour bus with the others. It's a big bus.*

The worst, though, was that Richard didn't talk to me or to Jamie either, and he never touched me. He didn't eat with us anymore, just took things from the refrigerator when he got hungry, which wasn't often. He had nightmares every night, and I was afraid to wake him up, afraid to say anything. I let him sweat them out. Eventually, he'd go back to sleep. Eventually, I would too.

Whatever feelings Richard had, he used them all in the puppet plays. He raged and pleaded, loved and wept, all through the carved mouths of hollow wooden dolls on the stage. He was brilliant. No one could keep up with him, even Thu. But he'd stopped acting at home, and I thought it might be for good. *I've always wondered what he feels about Jamie and me. Now I guess I know.*

Jamie was all I had left. While Richard sat in a corner, pretending to read, I'd take her on my lap and brush her soft hair. Then I'd tell her stories, quiet so he couldn't hear. About all the land around us and about the river, the animals and birds, and far-off places, too—wild horses in the desert and the windows of Rhyolite standing up narrow and empty. I told her everything I knew, because as long as I kept talking, she didn't cry. When tears ran down my face, Jamie traced them with her fingers and asked questions in her own language.

I wouldn't have thought people could live one week like that, but May went on and June came, and it almost began feeling normal. When things started to ease a little, I wasn't sure I cared anymore. *I don't think I can stand to be jerked back through one more cycle, one more trip around the daisy—he loves me, he loves me not.*

But one morning I came out of the shower and found Richard changing Jamie's diaper. After that, he ate with us sometimes, sometimes washed the dishes. One night he fixed dinner, like he had in the rooming house when he was getting over his Valentine's Day outburst. He still didn't talk, not one word.

We slept at the sides of the bed now, with a big space in the middle—the space where we'd tangled and loved and held each other to keep the bad things away. Neither one of us would touch the middle of the bed anymore.

I didn't know what to do, and there was no one to ask. I was startled when he finally did say something. It was the first week of June, getting hot fast. We didn't have rehearsal, and we were lolling around reading, trying to pretend the breeze from a fan was enough to keep the place cool.

"You want to get an ice cream?" Richard asked. It was like nothing had ever happened—well, not quite, since he still didn't touch me. But we put Jamie in the stroller and bought Popsicles at the market. Trying to lick them faster than they could melt, we meandered to the shade of a park.

There wasn't anyone else, so I drifted back into talking to Richard after that, doing things with him. It felt strange to pretend nothing had happened, but not as strange as living with someone who wouldn't even say, "Pass the sugar." We took Jamie for walks, went to the Quarter for ice cream on Sundays, and went to the grocery and the Laundromat together. On June 27, we went to the zoo.

We showed Jamie the farm animals in the petting zoo, and the ponies, the monkeys on Monkey Island. In a line of small cages, large animals drooped in the heat.

"Look at the polar bear!" I called to Richard. "Why is he green?" I asked. "I thought they were white."

"It's hot, and that dripping water is the only way he can cool off. The green is algae, from being wet."

"He looks miserable," I said.

"I think he is." We were hot too, so we crossed the road to the shady part of the park. We strolled around, and dashed up and down Monkey Hill, Jamie squealing as we swooped.

"Do you know where Monkey Hill came from?" I asked.

"Indian mound?"

"No, that's the story, but it's not true. They built it because New Orleans is so flat, they wanted to show the children of New Orleans what a hill is."

"You're kidding."

"Uh-uh. Fact."

It was almost cool there, in the shade of the live oaks, with their branches sweeping down to the ground and up again.

I felt better. *Richard might not love me, but maybe we could like each other?*

Or maybe we can love each other again? Maybe it will be all right. Everyone has fights, don't they?

Richard will change his mind about getting married. It will be a civil ceremony, not a church, nothing fancy. I'll wear a blue dress to match my eyes, the Motleys will be there, and my family, even Mom. We'll say, "Till death do us part," and then we'll kiss. Happy, a sunny day.

The June sun made us hot and thirsty. We got grape sno-balls at the refreshment stand. Jamie ate a lot of mine. She gobbled the syrupy ice and laughed, with grape running down her chin. We stayed to watch the zookeepers feed the seals, Jamie laughing even more to hear them bark. "Daw!" she yelled, and I knew she meant "doggie." I understood her.

A couple close to us stared. Just loud enough to carry, the woman asked, "Is that girl white?"

The man glanced our way. "Not anymore."

Richard drew his breath in with a hiss. I pulled him away from the seals, away from the white couple. Jamie started to cry, and I thought she could sense my fear and anger. She coughed and whined, and I saw her nose was running.

"Got a tissue?" I asked.

Richard rummaged through the pockets of his jeans and found one. "Is she getting a cold?"

I felt her forehead. "I don't know."

"Want to head home?"

"Maybe we'd better."

We went right back to the car. Jamie was sneezing and wriggling. I settled her as best I could. Richard drove us to Gretna.

I thought we'd have a loud night, but when I'd cleared Jamie's nose a couple of times, she settled down to sleep. I was used to Richard thrashing in bed, and he did, but no worse than usual.

I woke late the next morning in a quiet room. Richard was still asleep, half off the bed, tangled in the sheet. I thought how well Jamie had slept, and hoped that meant she wasn't getting sick after all. When I went to her crib, she was all twisted and jammed into the corner.

I turned her over to get her up and saw the bruises on her stomach and arms. I couldn't take it in. Even when I saw the dark stains on the sheet, I thought it was something to do with the grape sno-ball. And then I realized it wasn't. I screamed and ran to phone for help.

Francine came barreling out of her house as the fire truck pulled up, and it was hard to tell which one was screaming louder. An ambulance and police car arrived a few seconds later.

Richard and I ran out to tell the men where we lived, then we followed them to the house. One of the policemen turned and told us to wait in the yard. We hovered near the door, trying to see through the screen, scared to look.

When the door opened, two paramedics pushed past us with a stretcher. It was lumpy, with a sheet pulled up all the way. It took me a moment to realize Jamie was the lump. When I did, I ran down the drive after them, but they ignored me. They loaded the stretcher into the ambulance like movers loading a sofa, and drove away without using the siren. I stood at the end of the drive. People gathered and stared. Francine put her arm around me and steered me back toward the house. Her mouth was moving but I couldn't make out any words.

Richard stood at the door, where I'd left him. The policemen came out, and one of them said something to him, something I didn't hear. He and Richard went into the house.

The other policeman walked over to Francine and me. His starched blue uniform must have been pressed about one minute ago, and he looked like maybe he'd been wearing it when it was. He eyed us coldly. *He thinks we're trash.* I hung on to Francine's arm.

"You the mother?" he asked me.

"Yes."

His pale blue eyes flicked to Francine. "And you?"

"I'm her landlady," said Francine.

"I need to talk to this young lady alone."

Francine stood as tall as she could, which wasn't much taller than me. "You can't send me away. It's my own property."

"Police investigation, ma'am."

"I want your badge number."

He gave it to her and watched her in a bored way till she went inside. He pulled back one of the chairs at the patio table.

"Why don't we sit down right here, and you can tell me what happened." It wasn't a question. He was sitting down as he said it.

"Shouldn't we go inside with the others?" I asked. *I don't want to be alone with him.*

"No, we need to talk, just you and I." I saw Francine's kitchen curtain move. *She's watching.* If the policeman noticed, he didn't say. He took out a little notebook and a pen.

"Your baby's dead," he said.

He's mixed up. She was asking for her bottle just last night. She can't be dead. Not Jamie.

He waited, but I couldn't think of anything to say. *Not Jamie.*

He never took his eyes off my face. "She looked pretty roughed-up," he said. "How many times did he hit her?"

"He never hit her." I couldn't believe he'd said that.

His face was full of disgust. "That's not how it looks to me. There was blood all over the crib."

"He never hit her." *He isn't writing what I said. It doesn't count.*

"What about those bruises? He ever hit *you?*"

"*No.* He never hit anyone." I spoke louder, and the curtain moved again. But I knew Francine couldn't help.

"If you don't tell the truth, you could get charged along with him."

"He never hit Jamie. Or me. Ever, ever. That's the truth!"

"You can lie if you want to, but you can't change what happened."

Now that is the truth. I can't change what happened. I ought to feel something, but my feelings are wrapped in something padded. Like a movers' quilt.

Richard and his policeman came out into the yard. His policeman said something to me, but I didn't understand. My policeman stood up, and the three of them walked down the drive. I heard the car doors closing.

Francine came back as soon as they left. "My God, Kathy, what happened?"

I couldn't say anything—I sort of flapped my hand down the drive, where I'd had my last look at Jamie, not Jamie, a sheet pulled up all the way. A sheet-covered lump, like Sharon and me when we used to play ghost. *Jamie's a ghost.* I was shaking.

"What happened? Was she sick?" Francine insisted.

"A cold. Not real sick. I didn't think. . . ." I shivered in the morning heat.

"Where's Richard?" she asked.

I made myself pay attention to what Francine was saying. She was as small and far off as a puppet play. "The police."

"Oh, Jesus, honey. *Jesus.* Your folks know?"

"No, I have to call them now." I turned away to go back to the house.

She put a hand on my arm. I couldn't feel any warmth where she touched me. "Wait, Kathy," she said. "Come over to my place—you can use the phone in my guest room."

"Richard might call," I told her. "I have to be home."

I wanted to go back into the house. *Jamie will be in there, waking up, wondering what all the fuss is about. She couldn't have gone away. She isn't old enough to go anywhere on her own.*

"Soon as he does, come over, *cher.* I'll be waiting for you." She hugged me with a heliotrope smell.

"Sure, Francine." *Thank God she's going.*

The house was quiet and messy. *I better clean up. Strangers came in. . . . They must have thought we're hippies, same as Mom does.* I picked up the newspaper and Richard's pillow. *Jamie's new Raggedy Ann is on the floor. It's going to get dirty.* I propped it up in the corner of the crib. *Maybe I should tell it.*

"Jamie died," I said. "I have to make some calls." The doll watched me dial the phone.

Sharon wasn't home. I called my parents' number.

"Woodbridge." Dad's voice.

"Jamie's dead," I said. "She died in her sleep." *My voice is as flat as the lady's voice that says the time and weather.*

"*No.*" He sounded the way he did when I was little, when I did something bad.

"Jamie's dead."

"My God, what happened?"

"I don't know."

"Oh, God. Let me talk to Richard, honey."

"He's not here. He left with the police."

Dad's end of the phone went quiet.

"Dad?"

"Sorry. Kathy, oh God, Kathy, I don't know what to say. Your mother and I will be right there. We're leaving *now*." He hung up.

I put the phone down and sat on the bed, empty-handed. I didn't answer when Francine knocked, but she pushed the door open and came in anyway.

"You talk to your folks?"

"Dad's coming."

"I called Martin and Eddie. You can't be alone now, Kathy. Come over to my place."

"I can't. Richard might call."

Another knock, and Thu and Martin came in. "Where are Dom and Joss?" I asked. *You can't leave little kids alone. Something bad will happen to them if you do.*

Thu looked puzzled. "We left them with a neighbor." She put her arm around my shoulders. "You shouldn't stay here, Kathy. Come and stay with us."

"I can't." *They all say the same things.* The padded feeling was getting stronger, quilts between me and everyone else.

Eddie ran in. "My God, doll, what happened?"

I couldn't answer. I looked down at my knees and shook my head. Something strange had happened to words—they didn't work anymore. I was a foreigner who didn't speak the language. I let go and sank into the soft numbness. As hot as it was, I was

shivering, so I lay down and curled into a ball. Someone put a
blanket over me.

I heard something beyond the words bouncing around the
room. *Why, that's Jamie talking. That's funny, she isn't old enough to
really talk yet.* I listened harder, like tuning in to a faraway radio
station, and Jamie's voice wound on and on. I felt such relief,
listening to it. The language she was speaking was my language.
That was where I wanted to be, in that peace, listening to Jamie.
Someone jiggled my shoulder, but I wouldn't go back.

When I woke, the room was dim and quiet. I sat up and
looked around. Francine and Dad were sitting at the table.
Mom wasn't there. *Maybe she's lying down at Francine's.* As soon
as I thought it, I knew how idiotic it was to hope that. But I
couldn't help it.

"Richard called," said Francine.

"You should have woken me."

"We tried," she said. "You wouldn't wake up."

"What did he say?"

Francine glanced at Dad.

"Richard's been arrested," he said. "I offered to pay his bail,
but he wouldn't discuss it."

"Arrested? What for?"

"Second-degree murder."

"But he didn't do anything. Why did they arrest him?" I
tried to imagine Richard, what he looked like, what he might
be doing, but I didn't even come up with an outline, let alone
anything like Richard.

"He wasn't specific. Apparently there's some kind of evidence."
Dad stood up and switched on the light. He turned his head
and the glare caught his glasses. I couldn't see his eyes.

He was wearing his gardening jeans and a T-shirt he'd bought on a family trip. "Bullfrog Gold Mine" was marqueed across it. *The day he bought it, he put it on right away. The desert sun made the glitter blaze across his chest. Dad the superhero.*

Now the glitter was tarnished and flaking, and the shirt had an L-shaped rip. I wondered if I should get my sewing kit and fix it. I stared at it, planning stitches. I'd have to be careful at the corner, or it would pucker.

I jerked my mind back—Francine was standing up. "I have to go over to my place," she said. "I'll see you later." She shut the screen door carefully behind her, not letting it slap, the way we usually did.

"What else did Richard say?" I asked Dad.

"Just that he had to get off the phone. And he thinks it would make it worse if we visit."

"Worse?" I still felt groggy.

"I hate to say it, but he may be right about that. He said he'd call again when he gets a chance."

"Oh."

Dad sat beside me on the edge of the bed. "Look, honey, I know how awful this is for you. Would it make it easier if I take care of the arrangements?"

"What arrangements?"

"Well, the funeral. Things like that."

"I hadn't thought."

"No, no, I guess not. But we have some plots at Greenoaks—I don't know if I ever told you that. I'd like to bury her there—that's where your mom and I will be someday. Let me take care of it for you, please?" He sounded like he was going to cry.

"Well, if you can. I don't know what to do. Could you call Sharon? I tried earlier, but she wasn't home."

"Sam and Sharon are in Hawaii—medical convention. I put in a call to their hotel, but it sounded pretty chaotic. Anyway, I'm sure they'll call before long."

"Did Mom come with you?"

"No." This time, Dad didn't give an excuse.

I felt groggy again. "Would you mind if I took a nap now, Dad? I'm worn out."

"Why don't you settle down in Francine's guest room? That way, I can make some calls from here. I'm sure she'd be glad to put you up. Maybe I'll stay the night and we'll go back to Baton Rouge together in the morning." He sounded tired and old.

"Okay. Why don't *you* stay with her, though, like you did before?"

"I have an idea she'd like some company. You know, another woman, that sort of thing."

"I see." *He's right. I have to take care of Francine. She loved Jamie, and she must be terribly upset. Someone should stay with her, hug her and give her some comfort. Good thing Dad thought of it. . . . I'll get a few things together, go right over and help her.* I looked around my place. "It's sort of messy here, though. I meant to clean up, but I didn't have time. There's food in the refrigerator."

I got some pajamas out of the drawer, and my toothbrush, things like that. Dad walked me over to Francine's. He didn't say any more about Richard. Maybe he didn't know what he *could* say. Like me.

When Francine let us in, I hugged her. I didn't want her to be too sad.

"You take a rest now, *cher,*" she said. "*Fais dodo* for Francine." That was a good idea. She led me to her guest room, and I fell into the bed and went right to sleep.

The next morning, I woke up just long enough to take the packed suitcase Francine handed me, put it into Dad's car, and get in. I waved good-bye to her and scrunched against the car door. I slept all the way to Baton Rouge. When we got there, I headed straight for my old room and sat on the bed.

Maybe Mom will come in. Maybe she'll say she's sorry about Jamie.

I lay down, remembering to kick off my shoes so I wouldn't mess up the bedspread. The house was completely quiet—no sound of voices, no footsteps in the hallway.

Stupid, stupid. When do I quit hoping? Mom doesn't want to be with me. I'll never understand her. I'd give anything to be with Jamie. Wherever she is.

❧ 26 ❧
February 1975, New Orleans
Lacey

WILLIS WENT TO THE KITCHENETTE and looked in the refrigerator. I heaved our suitcase onto the bed and unpacked. Sorted our clothes and put his into the empty top drawer of the dresser. I opened the second to put in mine, but it was full of men's things, more or less crammed in. I opened the one beneath it.

"Lacey, for God's sake," Willis protested, looking up from opening a soda can. "You gonna ransack the place, now?"

"I'm not hurting anything, Willis." This third drawer was half-full of women's clothes. I held up a shirt. Just about Kathy's size, I thought. I closed that drawer and opened the bottom one.

It was full of little overalls, shirts, socks. Diapers. Baby things. I caught my breath and pulled out a little pink sweater to show Willis.

He wasn't paying attention—he was opening a kitchen cabinet to get a glass. But he got a surprise of his own. The shelves were filled with baby food—cereal, fruit in jars, even a nursing bottle. He stared as a rubber nipple rolled out and bounced on the counter. He blinked a couple of times. The nipple didn't go away.

I set my folded clothes on top of the dresser, making room by pushing aside a piggy bank. On an impulse, I grabbed the piggy and gave it a good shake.

"Lacey, what in hell are you doing?" Willis yelped.

I ignored him. Something was rustling in the piggy. The big rubber stopper in its stomach came out with a pop. I fished out a roll of dingy hundred-dollar bills. Ten of them.

"Lacey, don't!" He set his soda on the table and headed in my direction. I stuffed the money back in the piggy, then went to the closet and jerked the door open.

"Lacey!"

"Willis, there's a folded-up *baby crib* in here!" Behind it, I discovered a lovely dress, about a size two. Dusty and squashed, but almost unworn. White eyelet with limp pink ribbons. The tags swung from its pink padded hanger.

I pulled an album from the closet shelf. Willis, forgetting his scruples, craned his neck behind me as I opened it. Photographs. Professional photographs. One of a young child, a black child, wearing the beautiful little dress. Another of an older white man holding the child. Kathy holding the child. Kathy and a sullen-looking young black man. The child was nestled up to Kathy. Four pages of the album used, then nothing.

Willis sat heavily on the bed. "Oh, my God," was all he said.

I couldn't think of a word to add. If the house was the way Kathy left it, something had happened there. I wasn't sure I even wanted to know what. Richard was black. Kathy and Richard had a child. A child that didn't need her clothes anymore, didn't need her brand-new party dress. A child that didn't need her mother anymore. And Richard was in prison.

"Didn't need her mother. . . ." I'd been mouthing that one for a while, hadn't I? Running a little pity party for myself. Now I felt like the biggest fool in the world. I'd thought I had problems, when I was as well off as a woman could get—my daughter so smart and strong and healthy, my daughter who didn't need me because everything had gone the way it was supposed to.

Not quite the same as Kathy, was it? Kathy, with her four-page family album. I felt ashamed that I'd snooped through her private things, and I couldn't think of one thing I could do to help her.

As we showered and changed for the dinner, we fussed over details to use up the time. I put on makeup and removed all of it. Willis took the laces out of his shoes and threaded them back in. Six o'clock finally came.

Neither of us was in the mood to meet Kathy's friends. I dreaded having to make conversation.

We trailed silently across the patio to Francine's. I didn't have one idea what we could say when we got there. I was kicking myself for another reason—we were stuck. The only places in New Orleans where we could possibly get a room now would be hot-sheet motels.

Francine opened the door and led us into a room full of people. They all introduced themselves, and I was careful to keep them sorted out. Sharon and a redheaded man who turned out to be her husband, Sam. Eddie, of course. An Oriental woman whose name sounded like *Too.* Her husband, Martin, good-looking man with an Australian accent. He was in a wheelchair. They had a couple of little boys. Ten people, counting the kids. One good thing—I had maneuvered Willis into doing the talking.

❦ 27 ❦
July 1974, Baton Rouge
Kathy

WHEN I COULDN'T MAKE MYSELF sleep anymore, the sky was indigo and late summer stars were starting to show. I got up, a little shaky, and decided to see if I could find some orange juice in the kitchen. As I started down the hall, barefoot on the shag carpet, I heard Mom's voice from the dining room.

"Alan, I don't know why you wanted to bury her at Greenoaks. I refuse to spend eternity next to a colored child."

"She was our granddaughter, Virginia." Dad sounded shocked.

"*And* have the funeral at All Saints, for heaven's sake. At least it's closed-casket."

I stopped where I was. *I can't exactly go in and say hi after that.*

"Let's talk about something else." Sharon's voice.

So, they'd come home from Hawaii. *I wish I could see Sharon, but not if I have to go in there.*

"Well, maybe it's for the best after all," Mom went on, ignoring Sharon's protest. "Kathy can go back to school. No one has to know. She'll meet someone else."

I sucked in my breath hard before I remembered I didn't want them to hear me. To make sure it didn't happen again, I clapped my hand over my mouth.

"What about Richard?" asked Sam. He sounded gruff.

"He's been arrested, you know." Mom again.

"No, I didn't. Alan and I didn't have a chance to talk when he called. Why was he arrested?"

"I guess they think he did it. He *is* a little disturbed. Last time Alan went down there, Richard nearly hit him."

"Ginny, that's not so!" Dad said. "I felt nervous, but he didn't do anything."

A chair scraped. Something was set down with a sharp clink. "Why do they think he did it?" Sam asked.

"Alan says she was bruised and there was blood on the sheets. And she was all huddled into the corner of the crib." *Mom's voice sounds smug, almost happy.*

"That doesn't mean anything," Sam answered sharply. "Those are common features of infant deaths, including natural ones. What did the autopsy find?"

"There wasn't one," Dad said.

"There *wasn't an autopsy?* Didn't the parish do it? Didn't they *require* it?" Sam's voice was incredulous.

"No," Dad told him. "Orleans Parish requires them, but Jefferson doesn't. Kathy could have asked for one if she'd wanted it."

"You didn't *talk* to her about it?" Sam's tone was beyond incredulous, almost accusing.

"No, I didn't want to mention it. I mean, you being a doctor and all, it probably seems normal to you to slice someone up. I don't think Kathy could have stood the idea. She's not in good shape at all, Sam. She was crazy about Jamie."

"She loves Richard, too, and he's charged with a serious crime. He could go to prison for life. I can't believe you're burying the only evidence that could have cleared him." I'd never heard Sam so angry before.

"Maybe it wouldn't have cleared him," Mom suggested softly.

"Of course it would, honey." Dad sounded wobbly and old. "There was no need at all for an autopsy, Sam. I'm sure he didn't do it. He'll be all right."

I couldn't believe what I'd done. I'd thrown away Richard's only chance. I backed down the hallway to my room and closed the door without a sound.

I hid in there until the next morning, when I had to come out for the funeral. It was at Mom and Dad's church. Episcopal. No one knew Jamie had been baptized Catholic, and I didn't say. I figured that if there was a God, he couldn't care one way or the other.

Francine hadn't packed my jeans—they wouldn't have done for Jamie's funeral anyway, but the only dresses I had were my maternity clothes. Francine had picked the smallest one, but it flopped around my empty body and made me feel like crying. The Motleys were clothed as dark as nuns, all except Thu, who wore a white *ao dai*. She looked almost like a bride, and I saw Mom glaring. I wanted to tell Mom that white is the color of mourning in Vietnam, that she was wrong and ignorant. Anyway, if Thu wore white, what did Mom care?

My arms felt empty without Jamie.

It was a small service. None of my parents' friends were there, not even Aunt Ruth and Uncle Joseph. That's what Mom wanted—for no one to know. Mom sat at one end of the pew, and I hid behind the Motleys at the other. Sharon and Sam joined us, and Dad had the middle part all to himself, close to no one.

Father Davis kept his head down, as if he was trying not to notice anything. *Maybe he doesn't remember me.*

I still couldn't take in what was happening, still felt numb and padded. But Father Davis's words pummeled me—when he said,

"Though I walk through the valley of the shadow of death, I will fear no evil," they nearly got through. I had to make the padding around me even thicker. I hardly heard at all when he said, "The sun shall not smite thee by day, nor the moon by night." *You're not supposed to make a fuss at an Episcopal funeral.*

I didn't make a fuss.

At the cemetery, they had us leave before they lowered the little coffin. *I don't know why anyone would think that might help.*

When the service was over, I took Eddie aside.

"Let's go home, Eddie. I don't want to be here anymore."

"Your dad asked us all to lunch, doll."

"Please, Eddie? I want to go home." In Sharon's direction I mouthed, "I'll call you," and she nodded.

Eddie went and spoke to Mom for a minute, then came back and led me to his car. He didn't ask why I wanted to leave. I looked out my window, watched the city stutter off to its end as we drove out the Airline Highway. Finally, only weathered wood barns remained, standing silver-gray in patchy brown weeds. Undrained ditches lined the road—mosquito hawks and Jesus bugs darted and swooped along their still greenness. In the wind of the traffic, the paper peeling from the billboards waved hello, good-bye.

❧

I STAYED AT FRANCINE'S AGAIN when I got home. Sharon didn't wait for me to call her—she was on the phone right after breakfast the next morning.

"Are you okay?" she asked.

"Not really," I said. "How are things there?"

"Mom had a cow about you taking off yesterday," she said.

"Mom has so many cows, she could go into the cattle business."

"Do you care?"

"About her snit? No. What did Dad say?"

"Nothing. When we got home, he went out in the garden and started tying tomato vines. Mom kept yelling at him that he was ruining his suit, but he didn't come in. He didn't even answer."

I imagined Dad getting mud and manure and green tomato-vine stains on his white shirt.

"Kathy?"

"Yes?"

"Well, nothing. You didn't say anything, so I wondered if you were still there."

"Yes, I am. I am still. Definitely. Still. Here." It struck me as funny suddenly, that Sharon would wonder that. I started to giggle uncontrollably, then stopped with a little sob.

"Kathy, I don't like the way you sound. I'm taking off work and going down there. I'll be there as soon as I can get away."

"You don't need to do that."

"Yes, I do. I'm going. Right now, I need to talk to Francine, okay?"

"Okay." I got Francine. Then I went and lay down. I woke again to Francine shaking one of my shoulders.

"Richard's on the line," she said.

I wasn't sure if it was the same day as when I lay down. Maybe it was tomorrow. It didn't matter. I got out of bed and stumbled to the phone.

"Richard?"

"Hi, Kathy." He sounded cautious. I wondered if people listened in on jail phones. Probably they did.

"Hi," I managed.

"I've been calling and calling. Why are you at Francine's?"

"I don't know," I said. "What time is it?"

"Three in the afternoon, more or less. Why? Did you just wake up?"

"Sort of. When are you coming home?"

He drew a deep breath. "I don't know. The way it sounds, maybe in about ten years."

"But you didn't *do* anything!"

Or did you?

"I don't know," he repeated. "They say there's evidence. I don't want to talk about it, do you mind?"

Suddenly I was wide awake and burning with anger. "Yes, I do. I mind a lot. I just got back from Jamie's funeral, and now you say you might be getting a ten-year sentence, and you don't know what you've done. I want to talk about it."

The dial tone sounded in my ear. It didn't tell me anything I didn't already know. I went back to bed.

Sharon came the next day. I mostly slept for the next couple of weeks, but she took care of everything. She bought groceries and cooked, cleaned the house, and woke me up when the Motleys came to visit. At least one of them did come every day, usually bringing food. Thu took my laundry home and did it with hers. The last night of Sharon's visit, they had a potluck out on the patio table, and Sharon helped me take a shower and wash my hair. She fished out a pair of my jeans that hadn't fit since before Jamie. They did now.

Everyone hugged me. They all brought food, the dishes covered so bugs wouldn't get in. I had made a big pitcher of iced tea, and I started by pouring everyone a tall glass. Francine raided the mint by the back fence and rinsed it off to stick in the glasses.

We passed the dishes, a true Motley dinner of Creole, American, and Vietnamese food. Once again we sat around the table. Like a Motley family reunion, except that Richard was gone.

"How's Sam?" asked Eddie.

"He's fine," said Sharon. "I think we're going to get married sooner than we thought. We decided we don't want a big wedding."

"To Sam and Sharon—happiness and long life!" Eddie raised his tea glass, and the others did too.

"And then we really are moving down here. Any suggestions on neighborhoods?"

They debated Gretna, Algiers, and New Orleans. I was glad it all felt so normal, because I was tired of people treating me like I was sick. No one mentioned Richard, but the circle of chairs wasn't closed—the space between Martin and Francine was a little bigger than any of the others. *No one can decide whether he's one of us anymore.*

After dinner, Sharon and I wrapped up the last of the food and put it away. She tidied the refrigerator, throwing out some withered shallots and sponging the shelves. It was like all the other times we'd worked together in one of our kitchens, or in Mom's.

"Why'd you and Sam decide not to wait?" I asked.

Sharon went on arranging things in the refrigerator. "Sam and Mom aren't getting along these days. Dad either, for that matter."

I was confused. "Sam and Dad, or Mom and Dad?"

"Both. There was a real scene, the night before the funeral."

"I know."

"You *know*?" She looked up sharply.

"I was headed down the hallway when Mom made that crack about a closed-casket funeral."

"Oh, no. You *heard*?" Sharon closed the refrigerator with a thunk and sat beside me at the table.

"Yeah. Then all the stuff Sam said about the autopsy. It was all my fault we didn't have one."

Sharon's face was sad as she reached and touched my arm. "No, it wasn't," she said. "You didn't know."

I didn't know anything. "And now Richard's in jail."

She shook her head. "Sam thinks Dad should have said something. How could you have known there should have been an autopsy?"

"I should have known."

"Sam was really stunned by what Mom said. Did you know she felt that way?"

"She wasn't ever that direct before," I said. "But I knew all along. Look how she never came to see Jamie. Look at Uncle Joseph. I guess they were more alike than we realized."

"Anyway," said Sharon, "Sam's too upset with them for us to go through a big family wedding. And Dad feels guilty as hell about Richard, and I think he's trying to feel better by lashing out at Mom about being a racist. Not that that's unfair." She rubbed her eyes with the heels of her hands. "I'm sorry you heard what she said."

"It doesn't matter. She had a million ways of letting me know."

"All those headaches," Sharon agreed. "Whenever she had to deal with Richard or Jamie, it was headache time again."

"Why didn't we pick it up from her?"

"The racism? Dad, probably. He has all those ideals, and she never dared to say stuff like that in front of him. Not until that night, anyway."

I shrugged. "He didn't live up to the ideals in the end, though, did he?" *Dad's trying to protect me, and he's willing to sacrifice Richard to do it. Does the color of Richard's skin make it any easier for him?*

Sharon left the next morning. When I went back to work, I found that Thu and Martin had hired a couple of students to rehearse for the coming Christmas production. I was surprised I still had a job, but they introduced me to the new people as if nothing had changed.

Thu brought the teacups, and we sat down to discuss the new production. The company was learning a script about two children who go on a magical journey one Christmas Eve.

"I'd like you to specialize in scenery and effects now," Martin said. "And helping Thu make puppets. We're thinking of expanding to two troupes—that's why we're training apprentices like Dave and Nancy here."

He nodded in the students' direction. "And we need a permanent stage manager, so I'm hoping you'll take that on." He didn't mention Richard. *He's keeping things flexible so he can hire Richard back or do without him, depending on what happens.*

Depending on what happens. . . . Everything depended now on what happened to Richard. But every time I talked to him, he sounded fainter, less like anyone I knew. He had a lawyer, someone from the public defender's office. The lawyer had made a motion to drop the charges, but it had been denied. It looked like Richard was going to trial.

When he phoned to tell me that, I felt my heart squeezed like a sponge. "Do you think you'll get a fair trial?" *A black man. A white woman. Baby dies. Murder. . . . Good lord, a Jefferson Parish jury. No autopsy. All my fault.*

"I don't know." His voice was empty. He didn't sound like he gave a damn.

I knew he'd hang up on me again if I didn't change the subject. "What's your lawyer like?" I asked.

"Well, I'm not sure he's that interested, but maybe we'll work something out."

Why does he sound so guilty whenever he talks about it?

Why can't I ask him straight out?

Well, that would sound fine, wouldn't it? What would I say? "Gee, Richard, I've been wondering—did you kill Jamie?" *Great. That would be great.*

All my fault.

"I have to go, Richard." *I can't take any more of this. I can't think about it anymore.*

But I couldn't think about anything else. I saw picture after picture of my Richard—Richard who couldn't be guilty. Richard, sitting on the bed in his Chimes Street apartment, back propped against the wall, reading about forgiveness.

I was sure he hadn't hurt Jamie—until the little whisper started in my head. *He was always strange. Even when I first met him, he wasn't on speaking terms with his family. Richard crawling out from under the Thanksgiving table. Jumping out of his chair the day of the quarrel, scaring Dad.*

He never hurt anyone. He had problems and we quarreled, but he never raised his hand. Not once.

He didn't want Jamie, remember? "You don't have to keep it." *Not the first time he killed anyone, either.* "I sure aimed a howitzer at places where people lived and fired it. What do you think happened at the other end, Kathy?" *Baby killer, that's what they call them.*

No. Not Richard. I built a wall against the voice with pictures of Richard changing Jamie, feeding Jamie, telling her stories. Richard, walking with me and Jamie, glittering with puppet snow. Richard, the last day at the zoo, digging in the pockets of his jeans for a tissue so she could blow her nose.

The whisper came through the wall. *Richard's an actor. You heard him that night he didn't know you were listening—"I'm trapped. I can't get out." That's what he really felt all along.*

I made myself remember Richard setting his box of puppets on the floor, wrapping me in his arms and his love. Richard, the idealist, wanting to help other veterans. Richard and the puppets, working for peace.

Is that what you call peace? Days of cold silence? Screaming nightmares? Even if he didn't do it on purpose, he could have sleepwalked—could have killed her in some crazy dream.

No. He never sleepwalked.

Maybe he smothered her. Maybe she was keeping him awake and he just couldn't stand it. She was getting sick—like the time he'd gone to sleep in the Volkswagen.

No, not like that time. There was a big difference. This time, she wasn't crying. I would have heard if she was.

Maybe she wasn't keeping him awake. He still might have sleepwalked. He was strong enough—he could kill a baby easily.

Not without her making a fuss. I would have woken up. There was no way I wouldn't have woken up. I always had, as soon as she cried.

The whisper was gone, and I knew I'd found the answer. Richard couldn't have done it. But no one was going to ask *me.* I had to tell them anyway. I called the lawyer.

"Public defender's office," said a nasal female voice with an Irish Channel accent.

"Hello? Can I speak to Michael Heard?"

"May I ask who's calling?"

"My name is Kathy Woodbridge. I'm calling about Richard Johnson."

"I'll see if Mr. Heard is available."

I waited a long time. "He's in a meeting. May I take a message?" Bored, indifferent tone. I heard gum pop.

I left my phone number. The lawyer didn't call me back. Over the next week, I tried over and over, hoping that someone else would answer the phone. But it was always the same girl. She had enough phone messages from me to paper the office, if she was writing them down at all.

I had to talk to someone. I combed my hair and trailed up the street to Martin's house. He and the boys were gone, but Thu let me in with a smile and put the teakettle on.

"Richard won't say anything about what happened," I said when we'd both settled on the couch. "I don't know what to think."

"You think he did something?" Thu asked, her voice shocked.

"I did. I mean, I wondered. Because he never said he didn't. But I thought about it, and he couldn't have. There's no way I could have slept through something like that."

"But why isn't he saying that to the police?"

"I'm not sure he's not. But he sounds more like he's guilty every time he talks about it. He can't be, but he won't say he's not. All he says is that he doesn't know. And back then . . . when it happened . . . I should have asked for an autopsy. Then they would have had to let Richard go."

"And now no one will ever know." Thu sounded bleak.

"That's about it." We watched the steam rise off the tea. "Except, the longer he stays in jail, the more he's giving in," I added.

"Kathy," said Thu after a moment, "I want to tell you some-thing I never told anyone. Promise me you'll never tell. Not even Martin."

I nodded. *What could she say to me that she hadn't said to Martin?*

"When we were hiding under the stage during the siege, well, Martin wasn't conscious. I'd creep out to . . . go to the bathroom, but . . . I'm sure you know what I mean . . . he couldn't. I tried to keep him clean, but there was a smell. Even in the cold weather, you could tell people were in the building somewhere."

Thu bit her lower lip and looked away. "So one morning, when I was out of our hiding place, I took my own . . . excrement . . . and I wrote VC slogans all over the walls with it. That way, the soldiers wouldn't look any farther, if you see what I mean."

Thu was red-faced. I wondered why she was saying this. And then I realized. *She's telling me to do anything I can to defend the person I love. Like she did. Like Savitri did.*

I had to get Richard out of jail. He couldn't have hurt Jamie, but the longer he stayed there, the more they were all convinc-ing him he had. He had to get free and think, figure out what happened. And I had to tell Richard I knew he was innocent.

Even if he didn't want Dad to bail him out, I could pay his bail with my own money. *What money?—I don't have a thousand dollars. But if I sell the Volkswagen, I can get it. He can't be mad if it's not Dad's money. Why didn't I think of it weeks ago?*

I set my teacup down with a crash. "Thank you, Thu. I have to go. Right now. I'm sorry. I'll be back. Thank you for telling me, and I'll never say anything to anyone."

Selling the car took longer than I expected, but I came home in a taxi with enough money for Richard's bail. I gloated over that money. I could help Richard. The autopsy wouldn't matter.

When he called that night, I was happy, impatient to tell him the news.

"Hi, love," he began. He sounded lighter, almost relieved. It had been a long time since he called me that, too. Did he know somehow that I was going to get him out?

He kept speaking, but it took me a minute to realize what he was saying. "*What did you say?*"

"I worked out a plea bargain," he repeated. "They reduced the charge to involuntary manslaughter. I pled guilty to that. My lawyer says he thinks I'll get off with five years."

The money for Richard's bail was in my purse, but it might as well have been blowing down the street. I realized the phone was beeping, that Richard had hung up as I stood there mute. I called Sharon.

Before I could tell her, she cut in. "Kathy, I was just trying to call you. Please get up here as soon as you can. Dad's had a heart attack. He's in the hospital. *Please,* Kathy."

I stuffed the money into my piggy bank. Then I packed a few things in a suitcase as fast as I could. I was almost to the curb when I remembered the car was gone.

❧ 28 ❧
February 1975, New Orleans
Lacey

AFTER THE *HELLOS* and *pleased to meet yous* were said, there was a babble of questions about Kathy. I looked Willis's way. He wanted to handle it his way, now let him handle it.

I was dumbfounded by the performance he put on. He told them enough of what they already knew to make them think Kathy had taken us into her confidence, that we had some right to speak for her. He wove the most seamless web of honesty and lying I'd ever heard. In all the years I'd been married to him, he'd never done anything like this.

At least, he hadn't as far as I knew. That was a thought.

"Kathy's doing all right, but not great," he said. "She came to work with my wife back in December, and Lacey got concerned about her. It was obvious she was in some kind of trouble. Lacey's the kind to take in stray kittens anyway, so she decided to help if she could.

"So, she called Sharon back in December," Willis went on, not mentioning that I'd lied about what I wanted—and Sharon, still smiling, didn't say anything about it, either. "After Lacey learned that Kathy's dad had passed away in the fall, she wouldn't have wondered why Kathy was unhappy but would've just tried to comfort her. Except it seemed peculiar that Kathy would run away from her sister's house in Baton Rouge right after their dad's funeral.

"Kathy's résumé had disappeared, and Lacey was sure Kathy had pulled it to keep the company from checking her references. And then Lacey saw the address from an envelope Kathy received"—once again, he was telling the precise truth, but lying in his teeth in the implication—"the address of a convict in Angola state prison."

They all looked up sharply, like a bunch of terriers when a cat runs by. Willis didn't turn a hair. He kept on, smooth as a politician.

"We had no idea what Lacey should do," he went on. "She didn't want to take it up with the management of her company. She was afraid Kathy would lose her job. But Lacey has her responsibilities, too. She had to look into it. By accident, we found out about Richard and the baby."

He skipped over the fact that this discovery was exactly half an hour old. "But we're not real clear on what happened, and we didn't want to upset Kathy by asking too much."

Good lord! And he'd said *I* was devious! I shut my mouth hard to keep my jaw from dropping.

I jerked my attention back to the group. Eddie was talking. "What do you know about Jamie?" he asked Willis.

"Only that Kathy had a little girl. What happened?"

I stole another look at Willis, wondering if there was an Olympic event for skating on thin ice. If so, he was a shoo-in. But no one seemed to mind him asking.

"She died," Sharon said. "We never found out exactly how."

"Kathy didn't tell you?" I asked.

Sharon shook her head. "She doesn't know. Richard got arrested, and he plea-bargained guilty to involuntary manslaughter. And he never did say why."

"Didn't she ask the police about it?" I asked. I couldn't believe she wouldn't at least do that.

"She didn't have any rights, since she and Richard weren't married," said Sharon.

"Did Richard do something to the baby?" Willis asked.

"That's the question, isn't it?" said Eddie. "We wish we knew. But there wasn't an autopsy, there wasn't a trial, and Richard won't say anything. We all gave up on him."

Sam spoke up unexpectedly from the corner. "*I* didn't."

Part 5

29
April 1975, San Pedro
Kathy

"Hey, Kathy, want to take our lunches to the park?" Lacey called to me from the office kitchen, outshouting a mixer truck in the driveway.

"It's raining." I didn't even check. It had to be raining. It had rained every day for weeks.

"No, it isn't." The truck pulled away, but her voice was still set at yelling pitch. She came to my desk and repeated her words in a normal tone—a sort of corrected replay. "It isn't. It's gorgeous outside."

"Lacey, it has rained every day since you got back from New Orleans. I think you brought the weather with you in your suitcase. We ought to be building an ark, not a bunch of buildings."

"Huh. A concrete ark. . . . Sounds like a Giannini project, all right. Grab your lunch, girl. The sun's out."

I did. The truth is, I was so stir-crazy from the wet weather, I might have gone on a picnic even if it *had* been raining. We picked our way through the puddles to Lacey's car, and she drove to a park with a panoramic view of the harbor, with its all-green suspension bridge standing up against the water and sky.

She spread the comics section of a newspaper on the damp concrete picnic table and split the sports section for us to spread on the benches.

"I think our company must have built this one," she said, wiggling a crumbly-looking piece at the table edge. She set her lunch down and gave it a doubtful look. "Bet you a nickel we get ants."

"No bet—you'd win for sure," I said. I looked around. "Nice view. The bridge is pretty."

What I really felt was something close to panic at being on a hilltop, so much in the open. The sky was too big. I had a dizzy realization that I was standing on the *side* of the earth, that I could fall into the sky.

"The Vincent Thomas?" said Lacey, looking over her shoulder at the bridge. "It's kind of stubby. Not like the Golden Gate. You ever see the Golden Gate?"

"I did once. My family drove out West once on vacation."

The openness of the hillside reminded me of Dad and Jamie underground. And Richard locked up in a cell. I took a deep breath, pushing against the tightness in my chest.

Lacey sorted through the rest of the newspaper and looked at the headlines. She showed me the front page. Pictures of helicopters and people scrambling to get on them. "I see the war is finally over."

I wondered if Thu had any family over there. And I wondered about Richard. *Will he care? Did he ever care about anything? Or is he still just an artilleryman, destroying things too far away to see?*

Lacey squashed an ant. "I knew it."

"Eat fast," I suggested. I folded the plastic wrap from my sandwich, then unfolded it again. "Lacey . . . ."

"Um-hmm?" She was still looking at the paper.

"What would you do if someone wanted to talk to you and you didn't want to talk to them?"

"Depends on the circumstances." She looked up, interested and sympathetic.

I floundered on, trying to remember what I'd told her, truth and lies. "There was this guy, and he did something bad . . . or I thought he might have. . . ."

"You're not sure?"

"Well, I can't decide. But now my sister wrote me and said I should talk to him. She says it's not the way it looked."

"But you don't want to?"

"I don't know what I want."

I didn't say any more about it, and Lacey didn't push me. Out in the harbor, a cruise ship was inching toward the ocean. I wondered what it would feel like to be the kind of person who went on cruises.

We drove back to the office to make concrete picnic tables or something else equally uninteresting. As the days went by, and then weeks, I didn't get in touch with Richard. I just couldn't take any more.

It was all I could do to keep going at all. I only did things I had to, like go to work and buy food. I did visit the library, but that felt necessary.

Other than that, I more or less hid in the apartment. It was bare, and I made no effort to fix it up. I owned only the things I had to—a single mattress and some kitchenware. And work clothes, all from the Salvation Army. *As far as I'm concerned, they still belong to their former owners. They're like a crowd of unwanted guests crammed behind the closet door. For all I know, they talk to each other in there. I'm not listening.*

Every weekend, I spent most of my time sitting on the mattress, my back propped against the wall, reading mysteries. I never tried to guess "whodunit," because I didn't care. More and more, I couldn't even look at the words. I'd open a book and stare at a page. Or I'd read the same paragraph over and over without getting the meaning.

The time when I could push Richard and Jamie out of my mind for even a little while was past. I hadn't written to Richard, because I was waiting for him to get out of prison. I knew what I'd do then. I'd go wherever he was and ask him to his face if he'd done anything to Jamie. It wasn't a question I could ask in a letter. Or on a prison telephone line. So, I had to wait and imagine.

"Richard, what did you do that night?"

"Nothing. I didn't do anything."

"Then why did you plead guilty?"

"It was a white man's court. I couldn't expect any justice."

"Lots of white *people were trying to help you. Why wouldn't you let my father help, or Sam, or me? Why wouldn't you let your friends visit? Why wouldn't you let me pay your bail? I sold my car to pay your bail."*

"I should never have been arrested. I was innocent."

"Then why did you say under oath you were guilty?"

I went through this discussion over and over. When I got to the last question, Richard always disappeared. The day I could ask him in person, he'd have to face me and answer me.

No, I wouldn't write to him. I didn't write to the Motleys, either. I couldn't, not until I talked to Richard. Maybe they thought Richard had hurt Jamie, that he'd done it all along, that I knew. When he pled guilty, he pled guilty for me too.

And maybe I *was* guilty. I felt like it was my fault. Maybe I didn't take good enough care of Jamie, didn't feed her right or keep her warm or something. Maybe I should have noticed she was sick earlier, that day at the zoo.

"Was your little pickaninny worth killing your father for?" Mom's voice. *"Kathy, it was all your fault. You were a bad mother."*

"No, I wasn't."

"I refuse to spend eternity next to a colored child."

"That's a horrible thing to say. And I wasn't a bad mother."

"At least it was a closed-casket funeral."

"You were the bad mother. Not me. I loved Jamie. You never loved me."

"You've always been so difficult."

I pushed her voice away, but I knew she'd come back. Maybe I *was* losing my mind. And I had four and a half years to go.

San Pedro had no seasons, so I didn't notice the time passing. One Saturday, I realized it was June 28, the day Jamie had died. I wanted to get away, but I had no place to go. I decided to at least get out of the apartment.

The sidewalk was bumpy, with weeds coming up through cracks in the cement. Phone poles were staple-studded, covered with vertical litter about last month's rock band performances. As I went south, the stores got seedier, then gave way to rooming houses. Peeling concrete steps were bleachers for men with bottle-shaped paper bags. I strode right past them. I wasn't afraid like I had been when I first came to San Pedro.

I had never walked more than a block or two this way on Pacific Avenue. The ocean was in front of me somewhere, I knew. I expected the street to end at a beach, but instead there was a shaky fence and a tumbledown cliff, with a long view of water and rocks beyond. I slipped though the fence.

The slope was terraced, not as steep as I'd expected. On the flat part of each terrace was a strip of asphalt, all that was left of a neighborhood street, complete with curbs and palm trees along the crumpled parkway. Spaced at city-lot intervals were concrete foundations, open to the sky now. I scrambled down onto the first terrace and actually looked both ways before crossing the street. Two feral cats bolted into the underbrush.

I sat on a flight of concrete steps that went nowhere, watching the surf. Watched and listened: first the thump when a wave hit, then a hiss as it was sucked back through the rocks, along with a rattle of sea stones like a load of bricks falling off the back of a truck.

I'm worn out, thinking about Jamie. Wondering why. What I did wrong. Whether it had to happen and why it had to.

I looked up, out to sea. The larger waves broke far out, smaller ones came closer. *If I swim out past the surf, I'll never make it back. They'll think it was an accident.* I picked my way down the steps, then down the slope toward the ocean.

I didn't get that far. My foot skidded on a stone and I fell. I slid almost ten feet, and came to rest against a tall, feathery plant with licorice-smelling leaves.

My ankle hurt like hell, and I started crying from the pain and then kept on crying about everything that had happened, going back to the day I first met Richard.

The good things hurt worse than the bad, because they've all turned into nothing—Richard's love, Jamie's sweetness, even Dad's change of heart. I can't face my friends now, my family's gone, and my stupid little dreams about a husband and a baby are like the splinters of a kicked-apart dollhouse.

I was almost retching by the time I ran out of tears. I looked around to see if anyone had heard me.

There was no one in sight. In the mist over the ocean, I could see a faint blue island. Beyond it somewhere would be Vietnam. Everything that had driven Richard was there.

Most of Thu's life, too—her city, invaded and bombed, her friends and family dead, for all she knew. The theater, where she'd hidden, where she'd saved Martin. She'd lost almost everything and survived anyway. Now she had Dom and Joss, her artwork, her friends, her faith, Martin, and the puppets. I'd never asked her how she did it, but now I remembered she'd told me: *"Like a dancer on a tightrope, don't look down."* *"We did all we could. Everything beyond that is fate."* I would have to borrow her stubbornness awhile, since I had nothing of my own to go on with. I stood up. I was exhausted, feeling bruised in the middle, almost hung over from crying. I needed to get home.

A motion in the bushes startled me, but it was only a stocky ginger tomcat. He looked like Mew, only grown up. He strolled out into the sunlight and stood at my feet.

"Kitty?" I said tentatively, feeling foolish. He came to me, and I sat beside him, stroking his head. When I finally started back, he followed as I limped up the slope, scrambling in the steep places. At the fence, I bent and picked him up. He stayed in my arms all the way home, looking around and acting as if trusting me wasn't stupid at all.

I left him at the apartment and limped to a store to get him food and other things. When I got back, he rubbed against my legs and meowed. After he ate, he sat on the bed with me and purred. I petted him and he curled up next to me. *What's your name, kitty? Henry, that's his name. I'll call him Henry.* After a while, we drifted toward sleep. *He's not afraid he'll die in the night because I don't know how to take care of him.*

I went to work on Monday, but I wasn't good for much. I was still limping and I felt sick. Lacey took one look at me and gave me a bunch of filing I could do sitting in the back room.

She didn't check to see whether I was getting very far with it, either. I appreciated her being so understanding.

Still, when noon came, I tried to give her the slip. But she caught me taking my lunch out the back door.

"Want to go for a picnic?" she asked.

"No, I have to . . . . I mean, I guess not." I couldn't even think of a decent excuse. Another heart-to-heart was the last thing I wanted.

"Something wrong?" She looked at me with searching concern.

"No. I mean, I don't know. No."

"You okay?"

"I don't feel too good. But I'm not sick or anything, just tired."

"Why don't you sit in the lunchroom, then? Better than back there in the yard with the trucks. I have to go out, so you'll be on your own unless the phone rings. I brought in some strawberries, too. Willis and I went to Oxnard last weekend, and we got a flat of them. Help yourself, 'cause they won't last."

Perfect. I had no idea where she was going, and I didn't care. I sat and nibbled at my lunch without much appetite. I wasn't thinking of Mom much anymore, or Richard either. Thu, if anyone. Martin, becoming a father *after* the shot had crippled him. And Sam, warning Richard not to get so sidetracked on the bad things that he couldn't see the good.

I ate a bowl of Lacey's strawberries. I cried a little at the idea that I couldn't give one to Jamie. She would have liked them. They were sweet and juicy.

For the rest of the day at work, I faked it, and I went to bed as soon as I got home. I ached all over. I was half asleep when someone knocked on the apartment door. I tried to ignore it, but the knocking kept on.

I got up and opened the door to Marilu Collins. She waved an envelope. "Brought your mail up."

She was wearing a long batik robe and gold hoop earrings big enough for a gerbil to jump through. She handed me my letter and tossed her hair back, freeing it from snarls in a necklace of heavy coins. Henry poked his head out the door.

"You *are* supposed to get permission for pets," she said, so mildly I could tell she wasn't going to make me get rid of him.

"I'm sorry. I thought it would be all right because you have one."

"Well, yeah. I mean, it is. But *one* cat—I mean it, Kathy. No more. Don't turn into a cat lady on me."

"Okay." I started to close the door.

"Wait a sec, I came to tell you something. I'm starting to fix up the other apartment. I'm using casuals, and they'll be around all day while you're at work. So, lock your door. I mean, they're probably all right, they won't make any problems, but lock it anyway."

She glanced at Henry, who was surveying her as if *he* were the building owner, not her. She laughed. "Where'd you find him?"

"At the end of the street in that place with all the ruins."

"Oh, the Sunken City. You're not supposed to go down there."

"I slipped through the fence."

"Wouldn't do it again, if I were you. I mean, the ground's still sliding, and tough people hang out down there, too."

"There wasn't anyone there at all."

"Just the same, be careful, okay?"

"Okay." That time I managed to close the door. I looked at my letter. It was from Sam. I opened it.

Hi, Kathy,

Haven't heard from you in a while, and I wanted to ask how you're doing—really ask, not just some quick "how's it going" on the phone. You have a lot of hurts to get over, and I don't want to crowd you. You'd think this would be easier for me because I deal with some tough things in my practice. But you're my family, and it's different.

I've been thinking about Jamie. I've always suspected it was a case of crib death, even though I didn't see her. We still don't know much about why some babies don't make it. But it's well known that premature babies of young mothers are at high risk, no matter how well they're cared for. I'm convinced that Jamie's death wasn't anyone's fault, not yours and not Richard's either. I wanted to say that to the court, but I never got a chance because Richard decided to plea-bargain. I can't figure out why he did that.

I've kept in touch with him, even though at first he didn't want to see anyone. He's in Jackson now—maybe you didn't know that. That's the prison for people who need psychiatric help. His being there isn't necessarily bad—a few doctors there do know what they're doing.

Now that he's in treatment, he may decide to discuss it with you. If that happens, I'd seriously advise you to at least hear what he has to say.

I only have one other request—if you need help, get it. If there's no one close you can talk to, let me know. I'll find someone for you. I've seen what mothers go through when they lose a child.

Sharon and I both wish you'd come back to New Orleans, and every time I see Thu and Martin, they say they want you back. They've never gotten another good scene painter—they just shelved a bunch of stuff when you left. They'll eventually have to replace you, of course, but they haven't yet.

Eddie says to tell you he misses you too. Whatever you need, though. We all love you.

Sam

❧ 30 ❧
July 1975, San Pedro
Lacey

SAM CALLED TO TELL ME he'd written to Kathy about Richard finally getting some treatment. So, I wasn't surprised when Kathy's mood went up and down like a roller coaster over the next few weeks. I spent a fair amount of time dreaming up mindless tasks for her so no one would catch on that she wasn't pulling her weight. I did George's work fast and put it on Kathy's desk so she could be the one to take it to him. Most of the time he was gone anyway—the dry season was back, and concrete construction was in full swing.

I tried to help her without her resenting it, but she was touchy as hell. And I had to keep remembering that, as far as Kathy knew, I had no idea what was going on. I'd tell her someday, of course, but this was not the time.

Willis, watching me get dressed one morning, gestured toward my new shoes.

"Sure you want to wear those to work?"

"Why not?"

"Might mess 'em up, walking on all those eggshells."

I flapped my hand at him. "You're just as worried about Kathy as I am, ever since we went to New Orleans."

"That's so. That trip sure wasn't any second honeymoon. Can we try again next Mardi Gras?"

I buckled my watchband and stepped to the mirror to put on my earrings. "You better get reservations right now, if you're planning that. Otherwise, we'll be at Francine's again."

"I *have* reservations."

I looked into the mirror to see Willis standing behind me with a silly grin on his face. I figured he was making a pun so I flapped my hand again. "You had *that* kind of reservations all along."

"No, I mean real ones. At the Monteleone. For Mardi Gras week."

Every other time we'd gone, we'd stayed at some second-rate motel. "The whole week at the Monteleone? We better start saving for that now!" I put on lipstick and checked the effect. Too red. I rubbed it off and tried taupe.

"That's why I don't want you to mess up your new shoes." Willis was back to kidding.

"I never even said I'd go, Willis."

"You'll have all this business with Kathy worked out by then, and you won't have started college yet."

"Who said I was going to college?"

"You've gotten a taste of working with other people's problems. I'd like to see anyone stop you now."

I turned from the mirror. "I think I'm Mardi Gras'd out, to tell you the truth. Why don't you go by yourself this time?"

"Uh-uh." Willis shook his head. "Sweetheart, this year was our silver wedding anniversary. But it's been a tough year for both of us. We need that second honeymoon. Twenty-five years ago you said you were gonna love, honor, and obey me. You're good at the first two, and I never expected the third. Never even wanted it. But I sure want one week of your time, all to myself." He went down on one knee like he was asking me to marry him again. "Can I have it, honey, please?"

"Well, since you put it that way, of course you can." I pulled him up and into an embrace that turned into a preview of that second honeymoon. Twenty-five years, and Willis was still my love.

❧ 31 ❧
July 1975, San Pedro
Kathy

MARILU'S CONTRACTOR STARTED at the break of dawn. I woke to hammering and the banshee wail of an electric saw. Henry was careening around the place like a sideways yo-yo.

I fed Henry and tried to comfort him, but he was trembling all over. I took him on my lap and petted him to calm him down, but he tensed every time the saw screeched. I rubbed around the corners of his mouth where he liked it most, and started to sing to him.

> "I had a little nut tree.
> Nothing would it bear . . . ."

And then I lost it, almost as bad as that day at the Sunken City. I sobbed and wailed. Henry ran and hid, even more frightened than before.

I stayed home from work that day. Wasn't as if I was much use there anyway. I dragged myself in almost every morning and tried, but I wasn't worth even the little they were paying me. I was starting to wonder why Lacey didn't get them to fire me.

I knew she covered for me a lot. Mr. Giannini and George were gone most of the time, supervising projects. They didn't notice us, as long as the work got done. And it did. Lacey saw to that. Lacey worked double—her assignments and most of mine, too. I felt guilty whenever I thought about it. That didn't improve my mood, either.

The construction in the other apartment only went on a couple of days. I waited for Marilu to put out her rental sign, but she didn't. I went into the shop one day to ask about it.

"Tell you the future . . . . Oh, it's you. What's up?"

The change of tone from portentous to commonplace made me smile. "You can tell me if my future is bringing me a new neighbor. What's happening with the other apartment?"

"My nephew's moving into it on the first of August."

That explained why she'd gotten around to renovating it. I wasn't happy to have kin of Marilu's next door. I hoped he wouldn't be a warlock or something.

July passed, and Jamie's birthday. I went to work that day and tried to do a good job. I didn't get all the way to normal, but it was a lot better than if I'd given in to the memories. The old whisper started in my mind again. *What if . . . . What did he do? . . .*

I told the whisper to shut up. It did, at least for a while. I went home with a feeling that I'd won something real.

৵

The first Saturday in August began with a flurry of boxes as Marilu's nephew moved in. I tried to stay out of sight, not sure I wanted to give him a chance to be a nuisance. *He's probably weird.* When someone knocked on my door about six in the evening, I thought about not answering.

I decided to get it over with and opened the door to a guy about my age, very straight looking. He was blonde and freckled, only a few inches taller than me. Glasses, short hair, khakis, polo shirt.

"Hi," he said, as soon as I opened the door. "I just moved in. My name's Daniel."

"Hi, Daniel. Pleased to meet you. Marilu told me you were moving in." I hoped that was all he expected.

"She probably said to look out for a tall, dark stranger."

"Well, you *are* a *stranger*."

"That would be about Aunt Marilu's usual batting average." I laughed. "Don't you believe in psychics?"

"Some psychics, maybe. . . ." The thought *Just not Marilu* hung in the air, but neither of us came right out with it.

"Would you like to come in?"

"Sure, just for a minute. Or else . . . . I need to go get a pizza or something. I'm not unpacked yet. Would you join me?"

"There's no place close, and I don't have a car."

"Isn't it handy that I do?" he asked, wide-eyed. I laughed again and went inside to get my purse.

At my favorite pizza place, we ordered at the counter, got sodas, and sat at a corner table.

It's weird to sit across from a guy who isn't Richard. It's not a date. It's not. Just a couple of neighbors having a pizza. I made polite conversation while we waited for our order.

"So, Marilu's your aunt?"

"My father's sister, and believe me, she's the black sheep. Well, not a black sheep exactly, just the family oddball. No one knows what to think of the psychic stuff."

"She seems to make a living at it."

"True enough."

"What brought you to San Pedro, Daniel?"

"Cheap housing while I go to school at Cal State Long Beach. I like San Pedro, too. It has a lot of character—more than most of the beach towns."

"It has a lot of *characters,* too. Pacific Avenue is pretty down and dirty."

"It looks that way. But you know, *Pacific Avenue* does mean *the way of peace.*"

"You could have fooled me. It reminds me of the joke about the little kid whose mother found him digging in a manure pile. She asked him what he was doing, and he said, 'There must be a pony in here somewhere.'"

Daniel laughed. "That's the way of peace for you. Root through the crap, dreaming of ponies."

The waiter came with the pizza. As we each took a slice, I asked Daniel, "What's your major?" I would have bet any money he'd say political science.

"Marine biology."

Guess I wasn't any more accurate than Marilu. "What do you do with that?"

"My big interest is coral reefs. Probably most of the jobs today are in marine ecology. Or I could go in the other direction and work in fisheries management or push the oil companies' agendas."

I gave him a startled look.

"Oh, I'm not doing *that,*" he added quickly. "I'm also not taking some damned desk job writing about the ocean for a government agency. I want to be in the water, not pushing paper in some Sacramento high-rise."

"Why would you? Work in a high-rise, I mean?"

"I dunno. People do. Money, I guess. They start off studying oceanography because they love the ocean, and then they take a desk job because it pays better."

"So, why *wouldn't* you?"

"I gather you've never tried diving."

"No, I can't even swim much." *I hate the ocean. It reminds me of that day—the anniversary of Jamie's death, when I was going to swim out and drown. I haven't gone near the water since, not one time. Whenever I hear foghorns at night now, I pretend they're trains.*

Daniel had a faraway look in his eyes. "There's almost no words for how beautiful it can be when the visibility's good. It's magical. You want to go deeper and deeper, to stay down forever. The heck of it is, the deeper you go, the faster the air gives out."

"I guess I just don't get it." *I wasn't especially interested, either, but I made myself sound pleasant, at least.*

He shrugged. "Astronauts are at a loss for words when they come back to the world too. The funny thing is, anyone could dive, but almost no one does." He laughed lightly. "I should shut up about it. If everyone found out what it's like, I'd have to stand in line."

"Don't worry—I won't be part of the crowd." He looked up at me, surprised. "But I'm glad you love what you do. It *does* sound beautiful."

"What do *you* do?"

"I'm a secretary for a construction company."

Not much to talk about there. He loves his work. I used to love the puppets. I miss Martin and Thu and the Motleys. And they want me back. . . . Why don't I go? Why?

❧

DANIEL AND I saw each other occasionally on the stairs, but I didn't spend time with him again until the last weekend in August. Late in the afternoon, he knocked on my door.

"Can I come in?" He seemed full of excitement.

I opened the door wider and stepped back. He might as well see for himself that I didn't have a couch or anything else to make guests feel welcome. But he didn't seem to care.

"Want to look at the nova tonight?" he asked.

"What's that?"

"It's a star that suddenly gets brighter. This may be the best one since 1942!" He was almost wiggling with delight, like a puppy with a new toy.

"Isn't it the ocean you're interested in?"

"Gotta do something at night." He laughed. "The sky's almost as good as the ocean. It *is* an ocean, really. Just one I can't dive in."

"Do you have a telescope?"

"Not yet. I want one someday, though. But this nova's so bright we won't need one. Aunt Marilu gave me the key to the roof stair. It's flat up there—perfect for looking at the sky. You ever been up?"

"No, I haven't. Is Marilu going to see it too?" No way I was going if Marilu was. She'd talk my ear off about astrology or something.

"Uh-uh. Don't get me wrong—Aunt Marilu's a sweetie. But when it comes to anything scientific, she drives me nuts. You know what she said when I told her I was studying oceanography? She asked me if I was gonna talk with the dolphins." He rolled his eyes. "Didn't occur to her that they might not want to talk with *me*."

When it got dark, I knocked on Daniel's door. He came out and handed me a wadded-up blanket. Then he unlocked the third door, and I followed him up the dusty stairs. At the top, he unlocked a trap door, and we stepped out onto the roof.

Gravel was underfoot, and pipes stuck up here and there. I helped him spread the blanket on a clear spot, and we sat on it, looking up.

"Over there! That's it!" He pointed to one of the brightest stars.

It didn't look much different from the other ones to me. "Isn't that the evening star?"

"No, that one's over there."

We sat on the blanket and looked for a while at the sky. And at each other.

"Kathy?"

"Mmm-hmm?"

"Are you dating anybody? I mean, I don't want to seem pushy or anything, I just wondered."

I wished he'd wonder about the stars or the ocean or something. I moved farther away from him. "No, but . . . ."

"Are you getting over someone?"

"You could say that." *I'm getting over a couple of people. I don't want to talk about this. Leave me alone.* I stood up and tripped on a fold of the blanket.

Daniel shot out a hand to steady me. He hadn't touched me before. *His fingers are almost hot, like Richard's.*

"Maybe we could just go out sometime?" he asked. "I'd like to get to know you."

"Maybe," I said. "I didn't bring a sweater or anything. I'm cold. Let's go in now."

The next night, I saw him in the hall, going up to the roof again to look at his nova. I smiled and waved, and closed my door. *I'm not giving him a chance to ask me again.*

But that night I dreamed that Daniel and I went up to the roof to make love. When he reached out his hand to touch me,

I turned into a shower of stars, falling around the Snow Queen in the puppet theater.

On Wednesday, I got a letter from Richard. I brought it up to my apartment when I came home in the afternoon, but I just laid it on the table, still sealed. Wherever I looked, it jumped right into my field of vision. I tried not to think about it while I fixed dinner. When I'd sat down to eat, I opened it.

Dear Kathy,

I haven't heard from you in a long time. I'd decided to leave you alone and let you get on with your life. You had a hard time, and most of it was my fault. But Sam asked me to write one more time.

There's one thing I have to tell you about. And then you can be the one to decide what we should do. If you don't want to even talk to me, I'll leave you alone, I promise.

I got moved from Angola to Jackson about six months ago. Jackson is a prison, but it's a hospital, too. I got into a program here for veterans with problems. They've been concentrating on helping me make some memories conscious so I at least know what happened.

The reason I'm telling you is that it has to do with the night Jamie died. I'm sure you remember my nightmares. I don't know if I ever said anything understandable in my sleep, but the dreams were usually about being trapped.

I'll tell you what it goes back to:

One night during the war, we came under fire, and a buddy and I got separated from our unit. We hid in an old building. It was deserted—dark and damp, with boarded-up windows. Some wooden crates were stacked against the back wall, and I sheltered by them. They probably saved my life.

The building didn't get a direct hit, but a round came close enough that the roof collapsed. I was trapped in the wreckage, and so was Ben, my buddy. He was badly injured. I couldn't move to help him, and I spent most of the night listening to him as he groaned and gasped and finally died.

In the morning, they pulled us out of the ruins, but of course it was too late for Ben. I had a broken arm and some other injuries. It was about the end of my tour of duty anyway. They sent me home, and that was the last I saw of the army.

I didn't remember that night, not in detail. It was too awful. But I've had the horrors about it ever since. It doesn't take much to make me feel trapped.

Oh, God, that's what he meant that night when I came back from Tex's class, when he was screaming he was trapped. But why did he have to be so secretive? Why didn't he tell me about the war? How was I to know?

Of course, claustrophobia is a bad problem to have in prison. I got so out of it for a while that they couldn't put up with me in Angola any more, and that's how I got sent to Jackson.

I remembered something else in treatment. It's about the night Jamie died. I woke up and heard her gasping for breath. If I'd known how to save her, maybe I could have, but I didn't even know it was her. It was dark and hot—humid like nights in Vietnam. I was back there, trapped in that goddamned building, hearing Ben gasp for breath.

I wish like hell I'd known what was going on. Sam says that premature babies often have breathing problems and that crib deaths are more common with them. I wish I could take comfort in statistics, but I can't. I still cry sometimes, remembering her.

It means a lot to me for you to know I didn't hurt Jamie. I pled guilty because I felt guilty—about Vietnam and Ben and about Jamie too, and because I was confused and scared at the time. I wish I hadn't.

I wish he hadn't too. I wish he'd trusted me enough to let me in on what was going on. I gave up plenty for Richard—got terrorized by Green Coat, got put down every time I had to deal with strangers. I even lost most of my family. I'm sick and tired of being a one-woman Civil Rights Movement. Dad was right—it's too soon for this kind of relationship to have a chance.

I'm probably going to get either parole or an outright pardon before long, because I have a real lawyer now and he's working on it. When I get out, I'm going back to work for Martin and Thu. And I'm staying in treatment until I get a handle on my problems. Maybe you want to stay in California, and

maybe if you do come back, you won't want to see
me. I won't blame you, if that's how you feel.

But I wish you'd try to forgive me and let me
know if we could at least talk. I've changed a lot, and
it's my dream to get back together with you someday
and show you how much I still love you.

Richard

By the time I was through reading, I was sobbing. I didn't
bother going to bed—I was sure I wouldn't sleep anyway. Toward
morning, I fell asleep sitting up. I woke with hardly enough time
to get to work. I had stewed about it for most of the night, but
I had made my decision.

*I won't even answer him. I won't go back to New Orleans, if
that's what he's doing. I need a better job, and I'll start looking for
one soon—here in California. Maybe I can do scenery or costumes
for a TV or movie studio. I'll get to know Daniel and live the way
everyone else does. I've had enough of trying to be a hero. I'm not
cut out for it.*

I went to work, but I felt hollow and headachy from not
sleeping. Almost as soon as I got there, I dropped the coffeepot
and cut my hand on the broken glass as I tried to pick up a
shard. Lacey brought me the first aid kit and cleaned up the
rest herself.

She set me to boxing up files of some finished projects to
take to storage. It was dusty work, but at least I didn't have to
talk to anyone. I spent the morning daydreaming.

*I work for a movie studio and make lots of money. I live in
a nice apartment in Hollywood. On Saturday night, I put on a
dress—not one I bought from the Sally Army, a brand new one.*

It's Wedgwood blue to match my eyes. I put on makeup and stockings and diamond earrings. I know Daniel thinks I'm pretty when he comes over to take me to dinner.

At lunchtime, Lacey stuck her head into the file room and told me she had a picnic lunch. I figured she wanted to ask what was wrong with me these days, and I almost refused to go. But then I changed my mind. I'd have to give her some kind of reason sooner or later.

I was right about what she wanted. "What's going on, Kathy?" she asked, unwrapping a couple of burgers. "You look like the wrath of God."

"I didn't sleep well."

"Any particular reason?"

"I got a letter from someone I used to know. It was a little upsetting." My voice was dismissive.

"From Richard?" she asked.

I was sure I hadn't heard her right. "Excuse me?"

"I said, did you get a letter from Richard Johnson?"

I thought I was going to faint. "How do you know about Richard?" I asked, my voice cracking.

"Give me a break, Kathy. You came into Giannini's last December looking like you were in bad trouble. I cared enough to find out what kind of trouble it was."

I felt a hot flush of anger. "What else do you know?" I asked.

"Your friends in Gretna told me the whole story when I was back there in February. You and Richard, Jamie, your dad, and how your mother treated you."

"My friends in Gretna!" I could not believe what I was hearing. Lacey had looked up the Motleys, everyone I knew. "How did you find them?" I asked. This I had to hear.

"Eddie phoned me. And before you ask how, your sister gave him my phone number."

I was dizzy with anger. I wanted to smack her so bad, my hand tingled. "Lacey, I don't believe this. You went to my *sister*? How did you get *her* phone number? And how could you sneak and pry like that, and lie to me?"

"*You* lied to *me*. From the first day." She still wasn't raising her voice. "You stole your résumé out of George's office, and you lied about where you were from. You told me you were from Illinois. You have a southern accent, and you're from Illinois?"

I jumped off the bench, scattering napkins. "Yes, I am! I was born in Evanston. *I* don't lie. *I* don't sneak. And I don't believe this. *How in hell did you get my sister's phone number?*" I didn't care if she got me fired—I was quitting anyway.

"I must have gotten it from your employment application, wouldn't you say? Since you don't sneak, I mean."

I felt like I'd been hit in the stomach. All my fury went out of me like a bubble popping. There was nothing I could say. I had no right to call anyone else a sneak. I dropped back onto the bench. I was shaking with a tired, let-down feeling left over from the anger.

"I thought you were my friend, Lacey," I said. My voice was hoarse as an old beggar's.

"If I wasn't, I wouldn't have done all your work for you the past two months. You needed someone to help you, and I decided to try. I hope someone would do the same for my daughter."

I didn't know how to answer that.

"What did Richard say?" she asked again, still pleasant and patient.

"He's going to get out of prison." There wasn't any reason not to tell her, since she knew everything else. "He never did anything to Jamie. They're going to let him out."

"How's he holding up? That was some awful experience he had, going to prison when he hadn't done anything."

"I don't know how he's doing—he said he was getting help. He asked me to come back."

"So, you're going?"

"No, I'm not. There's a guy here asking me out, and he's nice. I'm staying here."

It was her turn to be astonished. "Who is he? You never said anything about anyone."

"I just met him. He's Marilu's nephew. He moved into the apartment next door, and we went looking at the stars. He's studying to be an oceanographer. I want to go out with him."

"Did you tell Richard all this?"

"No, I'm not going to answer his letter." I concentrated on shredding the burger wrapper in my lap.

"Why not?"

"I've had enough. I want to live like other women do, get married and have kids. Not worry about some guy acting crazy, or whether my family likes him. Or whether we can find a place to live, or go to a photographer's, or even walk around together without getting insulted." It was all pouring out. I realized it was pretty incoherent. I wadded the paper into a ball and threw it toward the trash barrel. I missed by a mile.

Lacey got up and retrieved the paper. She dropped it into the can and came back to our table. "Tell me something, Kathy," she said. "What was the problem between you and your mother?"

"She's a real witch. And she never cared about me. Just her middle-class white friends and her middle-class white life."

"What was her objection to Richard?"

"She said he was disturbed and no one would accept us. And that we lived like hippies."

"Is that different from what you just said yourself? Is your mother the person in your family you want to be like?" Her voice was polite, just asking, calm as if she were asking if I wanted ketchup on my French fries.

"That's not fair!" I snapped. *There must be some difference. Except there's not.* Tears spilled down my face, and I didn't even try to wipe them away.

She reached out and touched my arm.

I looked at her hand. *The brown back of it and the white palm like Richard's. Like Jamie's little hands.* I started crying then for Richard and for Jamie, for everything I'd had that last day at the zoo. *I didn't even get to say good-bye. But there's no use pretending I can get any of it back.*

"I don't want to start up with him again," I finally said. "It's too hard."

"So, just letting him know you got the letter and have some sympathy for him is starting up again? Look, Kathy, he's getting treatment for his problems. He didn't do anything to your daughter. Why don't you at least let him know you're not holding a grudge?"

"I'm afraid it might not stop there."

"Listen to me, Kathy Woodbridge. You wouldn't be afraid of getting involved with Richard if you didn't still love him. You know as well as I do, that's where you belong."

Richard's hands, his eyes, the way he laughed—clear as a photo in an album. Richard shaking glitter from his clothes. Working a marionette. Reading a book. Holding Jamie. Don't think about it anymore. Slam the album shut.

"No, Lacey," I said. "I am not going back to Richard."

"You love this other guy?"

I tried to say I did, but I couldn't. *When Martin was shot, Thu didn't run away and find another husband. Maybe a hero is just someone who does what they can, someone who doesn't run away. The way I've run away, every single time. Like I want to do now, run to this dream about Daniel. And when this fantasy wears out, another one, probably. What will I do when they're all worn out?*

"Don't love him, huh?" she said. "But this other guy would be a lot easier, wouldn't he? No one giving you hell for being with a black man. No more thinking twice about holding hands in public, or having waiters in restaurants seat you back by the kitchen. Hey, Kathy, you could even join the country club.

"You'd just know for the rest of your nice white life that you'd thrown away the man you loved when he needed you most. What kind of future can you build on that, Kathy? And how will it feel to lie in another man's arms, wondering what happened to Richard?"

❧ 32 ❧
September 1975, San Pedro
Lacey

MR. GIANNINI WAS PUT OUT that Kathy was leaving at such short notice, but I told him it was a family emergency. I felt it was fitting to round things out with one last misrepresentation.

I helped Kathy pack the stuff she wanted to take—it all fit in a suitcase, if you don't count the cat. Willis hauled the rest to the Salvation Army. We drove her to the airport on the evening of September the seventh. She sat in the backseat with her cat carrier. I didn't see Henry, but he howled so much, I had no doubt he was there.

Kathy leaned forward and stuck her head between the front seats. "Lacey?"

"Mmm-hmm?"

"How *did* you find out about Richard?"

"You didn't do a good job of covering up, you know."

She pulled back a little. "What do you mean?"

I turned to face her as much as the seat belt allowed. "Oh, Kathy," I said, "stay away from a life of crime—you're no good at hiding things. First you pick an apartment building with a landlady on the premises. You're the only tenant, so she has no one else to think about. To top it off, she's a psychic."

"Does Marilu really know anything?"

"Occult, you mean? Probably not. But psychics are good at reading people. And for all she knew, you'd be in the shop, buying advice from her. So, she kept her eye on you. I don't think she'd have gone so far as to open your mail, but she looked at the envelopes and remembered the return addresses. You even gave her a check with your Gretna address on it, for goodness sake."

I was afraid she'd be angry, but she laughed. "Knows all, sees all, tells all, you mean?"

"Can't say you weren't warned."

"How did you get my sister's phone number?"

"Marilu gave me her name and told me she lived in Baton Rouge. I looked in the phone book. The library has directories from all over the country."

"But how could I have known you'd go to Marilu? Why would anyone have thought you'd go all the way to *Gretna*? How many people would have done that?"

"I know. I had some problems of my own, Kathy. My daughter went off to college—I just felt so useless for a while, there. And I apologize—in a way. But Kathy, do you wish I *had* minded my own business? I'll let you be the one to decide. If you say so, the next time someone needs help, I'll just walk on by."

She didn't say I should have kept my nose out of her affairs. So, I guess that was my answer. For a while, she didn't say anything.

"You okay now?" she finally asked. "I mean, about your daughter and all?"

"I'm okay. I'm applying to go back to college myself."

"I'm glad. That office is a crummy place to work."

Willis pulled into an airport parking garage and found a spot. He hauled her suitcase and cat carrier out of the car. We took the cat to the counter where we had to ship him, and went to sit with Kathy at the gate.

"By the way," I told her, "Francine has your thousand dollars for you when you get back. I can't believe you ran off and left that in a piggy bank. And then turned up in San Pedro desperate enough to take a job at Giannini's."

"What are you going to study when you go to school?" she asked me.

"Sociology or social work. I like helping people."

Kathy nodded. "I guess it's that or the FBI."

She sounded like Angela. I shot her a look to see if she meant it seriously, but she grinned back at me. Wasn't much I could say—she was entitled. Willis gazed at the people walking by in the concourse, perfect innocence in every line of his face. Kathy had no idea he'd been as nosy as me. Men always get away with more than women do.

There was still one thing *I* wanted to know. "Kathy, how did you snitch your résumé from George?"

"When I worked for Martin, I did scenery and special effects. A lot of it is almost like magic tricks, making things appear and disappear. And George is hardly the world's smartest audience."

"But what would you have done if you hadn't had a chance to take it?"

"Actually, it was all made up. Snitching it was just an impulse."

"Sneaky, sneaky," I said fondly.

When it was time for Kathy to board, I gave her a big hug and a kiss, like I always gave Angela when she went away. Willis stood around, looking embarrassed and out of place.

"Don't give us the tears, now, Kathy," he said. "We'll see you in February."

Kathy hugged him, too. His sheepish look made me wish I had my camera.

On the way home, I drove. We listened to soft music on the radio, not saying much. At the end of the freeway, I turned off onto Pacific Avenue. I noticed an Apartment for Rent sign in the front window of The Mystic Eye.

"I have to put an ad in the paper for another secretary when I get to work in the morning," I told Willis.

"Make that two secretaries," Willis said.

"Well, Willis, I can't just quit."

"Why not? Why'd you take that job in the first place?"

"You know why. To save for Angela's college. And so she'd get to have pretty clothes and stuff while she was in high school."

"And now she has her scholarship and her job. You know, there are good points about not being needed so much. Like being able do a little for yourself for a change. Think about it."

The light at Ninth Street turned red just before we reached it. I turned to Willis.

"You know what Angela said to me? She said 'Mama, I appreciate all you've done for me. But I've passed the point when you need to change my diaper. What would you think if I called you in here to put my underwear on me? Let's move on, okay?'"

Willis howled with laughter. "That Angie is something else."

He reached over and squeezed my hand quickly before the light changed. "You too, you know that, honey? I'm proud of what a good mother you were for Angela, and for the way you helped Kathy, too."

"Now they're both on their own," I said, a little sadly. The empty feeling flitted through me—not the heavy thing it was when Angela went away, almost transparent this time, almost just a memory.

"I can hardly wait to see what you'll do next," said Willis. "Don't waste any more time on Giannini. Make the ad for two secretaries, okay?"

I put on the blinker, checked Pacific Avenue in the rearview mirror, and made the last turn for home.

❧ 33 ❧
September 1975, Over New Orleans
Kathy

THE PLANE CIRCLED above Lake Pontchartrain. From my window seat, I looked out over the lights along the river and across the bridge, marking my path home. I'd never flown into New Orleans before, and I would have taken a Greyhound this time, but Lacey had insisted on buying me this ticket. I loved coming back like a princess on a flying carpet. It made me feel how much had changed.

When I'd called and told Richard what I'd decided, he said he didn't think it would be long before he was released. But he wouldn't go right back to Gretna. He was going to Texas first, to spend some time with his parents.

"Your *parents?*" I'd nearly dropped the phone. "How did you make up with *them?*"

"I let Sam tell them the whole story. It was my dad who got the lawyer."

"Are they going to be weird about us, the way my parents were?"

There was a pause at the other end of the line. "Does that mean you're coming back to me?"

I thought it did, but I wasn't sure. I was coming into New Orleans as I'd come into San Pedro, not knowing the future—but I wasn't afraid of it anymore. And I wasn't in a hurry about it either—not to marry, certainly not to have another child. Maybe someday. Maybe with Richard. I didn't know, and didn't need to know.

Maybe one day I'd even be friends with Mom again. Maybe she'd change her mind about things. Remembering Dad, she might learn from who he'd been. I wanted to be ready if she did.

The dark lake below us was crossed by the Causeway's twin lines of light. Over in Gretna, the Motley family would all be asleep. But I imagined them the way I knew them best. *Eddie at his stand, with the smell of fall tomatoes filling a hot afternoon. Francine in the kitchen, cooking some wonderful Creole dish, shallots and shrimp on the cutting board beside her. Dom and Joss admiring their phoenix kite, longing to be old enough to fly it by themselves. Sam and Sharon walking hand in hand in the Quarter.*

I even saw Dad and Jamie as I'd imagined them the day Richard and I walked in our glitter-spangled clothes. *Dad, younger than when I saw him last, Jamie older, maybe about nine. Dad, holding Jamie's hand, bends down to listen to what she's saying.*

The Dylan Thomas poem I thought of that day: "They shall have stars at elbow and foot . . . and death shall have no dominion." Jamie's face is turned up toward Dad as they walk away. But they stop and look back when they reach the corner, smile and wave, a little girl and her grandfather going on an adventure.

I almost waved too, sitting there on the plane. *Xin chào, Dad. Xin chào, Jamie. And tam biêt.*

Xin chào, Martin and Thu, working on the new puppet play. Maeterlinck's The Blue Bird, *about two children who go on a magical quest one Christmas Eve, seeking the joy that has always eluded them. They only find it when they return home, where it was waiting for them all along.*

Dark blue for the backdrop, with little stars like sweet-olive blossoms. The bird can be a lighter blue, greener, almost turquoise. I'll need designs for the other puppets, too—the children and the fairy, the dog and the cat, all the odd characters they meet on their journey.

I wish I had my pencils, and time to make one quick sketch. But it doesn't matter—I won't forget.

ANNE L. WATSON is a retired historic preservation architecture consultant and now pursues a variety of interests, including photography, soapmaking, and puppetry. She is the author of several other books, including the epistolary novel *Skeeter: A Cat Tale*. Anne has lived at various times in New Orleans, Baton Rouge, and San Pedro, California, the settings of *Pacific Avenue*. She currently lives in Olympia, Washington, with her husband and fellow author, Aaron Shepard. Please visit her at **www.annelwatson.com**.

Printed in the United States
100970LV00001B/162/A